The
Book of
VICES

EDITED BY

Robert J. Hutchinson

RIVERHEAD BOOKS

New York

1995

The
Book of
VICES

A Collection of Classic
Immoral Tales

To my children,
Robert John and James Timothy,
and to my wife,
Glenn Ellen,
the source of all my happiness
(and many of my vices)

RIVERHEAD BOOKS
a division of G. P. Putnam's Sons
Publishers Since 1838
200 Madison Avenue
New York, NY 10016

Library of Congress Cataloging-in-Publication Data

The book of vices : a collection of classic immoral tales / edited,
by Robert J. Hutchinson.

p.   cm.
Includes index.
ISBN 1-57322-006-X
1. Deadly sins—Literary collections. I. Hutchinson, Robert J.
PN6071.D33B66   1995   94-41450 CIP
808.8'0353—dc20

Printed in the United States of America
1   3   5   7   9   10   8   6   4   2

Book design by Chris Welch
Illustrations courtesy of Dover Publications, Inc.

This book is printed on acid-free paper. ∞

Contents

• • •

I prefer an accommodating vice to an obstinate virtue.

—*Jean-Baptiste Molière*

The vices help make virtues just as poisons help make medicines. Diluted and blended correctly, they are quite useful against the evils of life.

—*François de La Rochefoucauld*

Introduction

• • •

Half the vices which the world condemns most loudly have seeds of good in them and require moderate use rather than total abstinence.

—*Samuel Butler*

It is a truism in psychiatry that people are often the most obsessed with a trait when they are, in fact, veritable exemplars of the opposite. People obsessed with honesty, for example, often turn out to be pathological liars.

Whatever trait we congratulate ourselves on most is undoubtedly what we most lack.

The man who brags about his wealth is almost certainly tottering on the brink of financial disaster, and the woman who is most convinced of her beauty no doubt spends many long hours in front of the mirror, desperate to tidy things up.

When an age such as our own, therefore, spends so much time celebrating vice—noisily proclaiming its utter depravity and dissolution—you can be sure that it is, in fact, afflicted with the worst kind of moral fastidiousness.

Pedagogues, pedants, and preachers now noisily exhort us to new heights of virtue when, in fact, the problem with modern society is that it has *too much* virtue, not too little. The British writer G. K. Chesterton saw this problem clearly in the early part of this century. In his classic work *Orthodoxy,* Chesterton wrote:

1

The modern world is not evil; in some ways the modern world is far too good. It is full of wild and wasted virtues. When a religious scheme is shattered . . . it is not merely the vices that are let loose. The vices are, indeed, let loose, and they wander and do damage. But the virtues are let loose also; and the virtues wander more wildly, and the virtues do more terrible damage. The modern world is full of the old Christian virtues gone mad.

Indeed.

But our problem is far worse. Not only have the old virtues been let loose and are wandering and doing damage, but there are powerful forces in the modern world doing their level best not merely to shame the vices into silence—as you would an obstreperous uncle—but to actually lock them up or exile them to barren islands off the coast of Cuba.

The Puritan impulse that has let loose upon an unsuspecting world untold legions of baby-faced lawyers now seeks to eradicate vice through a campaign of legal unpleasantness that, in an earlier era, would have resulted in open rebellion.

The grim partisans of virtue, on both the political left and right, have decreed that we can no longer smoke, drink, spit, belch, overeat, leer, swear, prevaricate, skinny-dip, brag, put on airs, loaf, carouse, lie, or tell crude jokes.

Many universities today, which in ages past were hotbeds of adolescent lust, have produced elaborate codes of sexual conduct that require beleaguered undergraduates to request permission, verbally or in writing, as they proceed with each step of seduction, from a kiss to unfastening a top button of a shirt. The health police have decreed that anything worth eating, from movie popcorn to charred steaks, be declared in open violation of health and safety codes and banned outright from all places of public association. And the lawyers who now rule the land seek to make it a capital crime for anyone to produce any statement, *objet d'art,* poem, political commentary, thought, or opinion that someone, somewhere, for some reason, might find "offensive."

It is the basic contention of this book, therefore, that what humanity desperately needs today, at the turn of the millennium, are some good old-fashioned *vices.*

We suffer from a sickening overabundance of virtue.

Aristotle himself said that an excess of virtue is, in fact, a form of vice. What he championed was the golden mean: neither asceticism nor self-indulgence, but moderation.

This was also the code of the great Epicurus, the Greek philosopher who taught that just because too much of a good thing might give you indigestion that is no reason for skipping lunch.

The ancients saw clearly that the human soul is a delicate ecosystem in which the appetites must be balanced as carefully as a recipe for lamb stew. Too much of any one ingredient, even a good ingredient such as salt or pepper, will spoil the entire dish.

INDEED, IF SOCIETY eradicates the vices, what will it use to overcome the virtues when, left unpruned in the garden of the soul, they grow out of control and begin to strangle the flowers of the human spirit?

Like all good things, virtues can, like white blood cells in the human body, metastasize. When they do, prudent people begin seeking antidotes that, while not eradicating the virtues altogether—which would be as foolhardy as eradicating all of the white blood cells from the body—simply . . . *control their growth.*

These tonics for the soul are what we call the vices.

As La Rochefoucauld said, the vices, if diluted and blended

3

properly, can act as medicines for the soul, neutralizing the effects of overabundant virtues. The French epigrammatist was not saying, of course, that vices are necessarily good in and of themselves or that they should be taken straight. Indeed, like the poisons that are used in making medicine—modern antibiotics are, of course, essentially poisons that, it is hoped, will kill bacteria before the antibiotics kill the patient—vices are destructive in and of themselves. If used by healthy people, vices, like medicines, will make them sick.

But here is the essential point: What may be harmful to a healthy person is actually beneficial to someone who is sick, either of the spirit or the body. Under certain conditions, therefore, vices can have salutary effects.

In the classical tradition, seven of these deadly poisons of the soul were catalogued. If diluted and blended, they were believed to be useful antidotes for certain diseases of the spirit. Their Latin names, and their English equivalents, are as follows:

- *Luxuria* (Lust)
- *Avaritia* (Avarice)
- *Acedia* (Sloth)
- *Gula* (Gluttony)
- *Superbia* (Pride)
- *Invidia* (Envy)
- *Ira* (Anger)

All of these potent purgatives would come in handy today.

Those afflicted with a bad case of self-discipline—who, for instance, rise at five A.M. in order to jog ten miles, never miss a bill payment, and organize their closets as though they were preparing for a Marine Corps inspection—could use a good dose of sloth. Many married couples today, burdened by the demands of their work and home lives, should receive regular injections of lust to eliminate the virulent strains of chastity coursing through their veins.

In the face of the endless depredations and mindless imbecilities of national governments, every citizen should be inoculated with a powerful vaccine of rage. Everyone in the industrialized world would benefit from throwing open their windows, sticking their heads out, and—as did the Peter Finch character in the movie *Network*—screaming, "We're mad as hell, and we're not going to take it anymore!"

Half of the social problems now plaguing Western nations—from drug abuse to teenage pregnancy—could be remedied with potent injections of pride followed up with a daily radiation treatment of envy.

I personally wish that some of my friends would have a little more avarice, so they would buy a forty-two-foot Bertram yacht from which I could fish for yellowtail off of Catalina. It's always easier to have friends who own a boat or a Maui condo than maintaining one yourself. Avarice is a wonderful vice for one's friends and relatives to have, although it is expensive to possess oneself.

Even gluttony is, in my opinion, a healthful vice. No one can convince me that the pencil-necked joggers you see hobbling along our city streets are, in any meaningful sense of the word, either happy or healthy. The fellowship of gluttons will triumph in the end: There are already news reports that a daily glass of Merlot eliminates heart disease. Woody Allen may well prove prophetic. In his 1973 film *Sleeper,* he predicted that scientists of the future would prove that what kept twentieth-century people alive were the steak and ice cream they ate, and that, in fact, they nearly killed themselves by eating such toxic substances as oat bran.

· · ·

THE PROBLEM WITH the vices, however, is that we have lost the knowledge of how to cultivate them properly.

Because, as Aristotle taught, vice is essentially a habit, success in vice requires explicit instruction as well as ongoing exhortation and training. Yet today's public leaders, celebrities, and film stars no longer provide a clear and unambiguous example of vice as they once did. There are no longer such towering figures as Benjamin Franklin, who wrote his famous "Letter on Selecting a Mistress," to provide practical tips in the ways of viceful living. Where are the great degenerate stars of the past, such as Mae West, who is credited with the epigram that "too much of a good thing . . . can be wonderful"? Young people must, in effect, discover vice on their own, stumbling awkwardly and making numerous embarrassing and needless mistakes.

Frequently, in their innocence, young college students believe they are living a wild and debauched existence when, in fact, they are living monuments to virtue and self-restraint. Nor are they alone in their delusion. As the social critic H. L. Mencken pointed out in his marvelous essay, "The Libertine," the average man doesn't have enough money, or enough guts, to be genuinely corrupt, but that doesn't prevent him from admitting "by winks and blushes that he is a bad one." Unfortunately, said Mencken, "at the bottom of all that tawdry pretense there is usually nothing more material than a scraping of shins under the table." Confronted by a truly depraved and willing woman, for example, the average married man, basically a decent and impoverished fellow, will slink off in nervous trepidation.

Once again, the clear-thinking Chesterton recognized this same phenomenon of mistaken identity in the case of virtue. In 1905 in *The Illustrated London News,* he pointed out that it is frequently possible for someone to be without a vice not because he or she possesses the requisite virtue but because of an absence of even the *capacity* to commit a sin. In a way, Chesterton was making, in a Christian context, the same point Nietzsche did earlier: that vice and virtue are not nearly as simple as they appear on the surface, and that, to truly understand the inner motivations of the human soul, you must probe much deeper than the mere outward surfaces of actions and words. Human beings have a singular talent for elevating their basest impulses into lofty virtues; and the most craven acts of self-interest are almost always cloaked in the silken robes of noble intentions.

In other words, it is one thing to turn the other cheek in order not to return evil for evil; it is quite another to do so because you . . . *have no choice.* One is an act of virtue; the other is an act of cowardice. This is how Chesterton put it:

> Some priggish little clerk will say, "I have reason to congratulate myself that I am a civilised person, and not so bloodthirsty as the Mad Mullah." Somebody ought to say to him, "A really good man would be less bloodthirsty than the Mullah. But you are less bloodthirsty, not because you are more of a good man, but because you are a great deal less of a man. You are not bloodthirsty, not because you would spare your enemy, but because you would run away from him."

There are a number of reasons why this book is needed.

First of all, unlike in books purporting to teach morality, you will actually want to read the stories in this book. If you hand an eighteen-year-old college kid a collection of uplifting stories celebrating the virtues, he will delve into it with all the haste and enthusiasm he will show toward his calculus textbook. If, however, you hand this same eighteen-year-old *this* book, and explain that it is filled with stories of lust and general depravity, you can be sure that he will at least thumb through it, looking for the good parts. Such a student will therefore be exposed, at least indirectly, to the basic *concepts* of vice and virtue—which may well be a revelation all its own.

Secondly, stories and poems celebrating vice give young people certain fixed reference points. As they read the twenty-five-year-old Roman writer Apuleius' racy novel, *The Golden Ass,* it will slowly dawn on young students that they are not, in fact, the first people to discover sex. They will find, moreover, that they are mere babes in the woods when it comes to vice, that they are not nearly as depraved as they think they are. This is a disconcerting lesson for the young. A few pages of the Marquis de Sade or Petronius' *Satyricon* will send most people running back to church or synagogue far quicker than any sermon could ever do.

Thirdly, these stories of vice from the classics of Western literature teach young people that they are, in fact, part of an age-old community of iniquity. They are not alone! If they cast their eyes longingly at some nearly naked member of the opposite sex strolling down a beach, they can rest assured that others have done the same thing. If they find the idea of working twelve-hour days in mindless, repetitive labor utterly abhorrent, they can take comfort in knowing that generations before them have also found work something to be avoided at all costs.

THERE ARE A few notes and comments I feel compelled to make before we begin. First of all, although this book is *The Book of Vices,* some of the stories it contains do illustrate, if only indirectly, a virtue. I trust that readers will understand that sometimes an effective route to vice is through its opposite.

Also, the stories collected in this book are by no means the

final word on vice. There are literally hundreds of marvelous immoral novels, bawdy poems, and lewd and lascivious essays that
could not fit into this volume. I have done my best to include
portions of the great works that educated rakes and literary
lushes once knew by heart. But I have barely scratched the surface of the literature of vice, and so I encourage you, my readers,
to conduct more independent research in this area.

I must thank Cindy Spiegel, my editor at Riverhead Books,
who believed in this project and whose knowledge of vice can
only be called encyclopedic. When I was tempted to call it quits,
Cindy kept the project going by saying, "We'll discuss all that
next week."

Lisa Bankoff, my East Coast agent, deserves an enormous
amount of credit for convincing Cindy that I can be lucid for
whole days at a time and, what's more, could be trusted not to
hand her phone number out in bars. Also, I should thank
Dolores McMullan, an invaluable part of the Riverhead team,
who helped to keep the project on track; and Loretta G. Seyer,
who convinced me to investigate the lascivious material of the
eighteenth century. It goes without saying that I could never
have written this book without the living examples of vice ex-
hibited by my old friends, siblings, and in-laws. My friends Jay
Gilman, Chris Lynch, and Randy Remick taught me everything
I know about vice. My brother Tim Hutchinson, a student of
the Greek and Latin classics, pointed me in the direction of
lewd materials in the ancient world. My other brothers, Kelly,
Barney, and Barry, are never-ending inspirations for anyone
seriously pursuing a life of gluttony and sloth. And my sister,
Kathleen, whenever I weakened and thought about straighten-
ing my life out, encouraged me to keep writing. I also want to
thank, for their constant support and innumerable wild parties,
Helen and Leon Lis, John and Mary Brunson, John and Elisa

Duncan, James and Nancy Duncan, Bill and Cathy Duncan, Margaret Duncan, and Barbara Duncan. My father- and mother-in-law, John and Anne Duncan, deserve special thanks for not calling the wedding off when they discovered I'm a writer and don't work for a living. As for my parents, A'lan Hutchinson and Mary Jane Hutchinson, they are not responsible for any of the vices discussed herein: What they gave me, instead, was a love of books that has remained with me throughout my life.

Finally, my wife, Glenn Ellen, deserves most of the credit for this book. She edited and critiqued every word, as she does my general conversation.

My children, Robert John and James Timothy, who are now too young to read this book, will someday go off to college. It is my hope that the frolicking love of literature that lies behind this book will inspire them and keep them reading.

—Robert J. Hutchinson

One

…

Lust

*Da mihi castitatem et continentiam, sed noli
     modo.*
Give me chastity and continence—but not yet!
                    —*St. Augustine,* Confessions, *VIII, 7*

"I've looked on a lot of women with lust."
          —*President Jimmy Carter,* Playboy *magazine,*
                                        November 1976

"It was a blonde. A blonde to make a bishop kick
a hole in a stained glass window."
          —*Raymond Chandler,* Farewell, My Lovely

I t is one of the bizarre conceits of the modern age that, despite all evidence to the contrary, it discovered sex.

This is a curious delusion, when you think about it.

Human beings have been on the planet for well over a million years, or so our wizards inform us, and they have somehow managed to stumble their way through the basic operations of arousal and copulation without instruction from Dr. Ruth, Hugh Hefner, or Masters and Johnson.

They have even managed to think about it a bit, to reflect on what all that sweaty energy and desperate longing could possibly mean.

In the ancient Sumerian *Epic of Gilgamesh,* written on baked clay tablets around 2500 B.C., the tyrant Gilgamesh fears a wild child of nature, Enkidu, said to be roaming the fields and forests. Gilgamesh sends a trapper out into the forest with a woman in search of Enkidu. The trapper tells the woman, "There he is. Now, woman, make your breasts bare, have no shame, do not delay but welcome his love. Let him see you naked, let him possess your body. When he comes near uncover yourself and lie with him; teach him, the savage man, your woman's art, for when he murmurs love to you the wild beasts that shared his life in the hills will reject him."

The woman does this, she "makes herself naked and welcomes his eagerness," and in this way Enkidu's primal union with nature is broken: The wild creatures see him and flee. "Enkidu was grown weak, for wisdom was in him, and the thoughts of a man were in his heart."

This is a curious conclusion: Surrounded by machines and electronic gadgets, we tend to think of sex as an elemental union with nature, a reconnection with our animal selves. And surely it is that. Yet in this ancient epic, sex somehow *distances* man from nature. How can that be?

If there is one thing the literature of the ages teaches, it is that the primary human urge, almost from the time neolithic hunters began painting pictures of bison on the walls of their caves, has been to somehow deny, or try to overcome, our inevitable fate: We alone of all creatures see decay and death and have the self-awareness to realize that they, in fact, are our own destiny. With all of the vast inventiveness of the imagination, we human beings have thus sought to distract ourselves from unpleasant truths. The vast kaleidoscope of human culture, science, and religion has been one long attempt to evade the inevitable. This is the primal human drive, the quest for meaning and permanence, and it is, and always has been, intimately related to sex.

Human beings are preoccupied with sex, not solely because of some inner biological compulsion, but because sex is a primary symbol of the human condition. It is the ultimate reminder of who we really are. It pertains to the very mystery of life itself and is, by the very longing it imparts to men and women, a constant reaffirmation of humanity's physical nature.

The very first story about humanity in the Bible records this primal quest to rise above the human condition, to be, as Genesis says, "like God."

And the woman said to the serpent, "We may eat of the fruit of the trees of the garden; but God said, 'You shall not eat of the fruit of the tree which is in the midst of the garden, neither shall you touch it, lest you die.' " But the serpent said to the woman, "You shall not die. For God knows that when you eat of it your eyes will be opened, and you will be like God, knowing good and evil." So when the woman saw that the tree was good for food, and that it was a delight to the eyes, and that the tree was to be desired to make one wise, she took of its fruit and ate; and she also gave some to her husband, and he ate. Then the eyes of both were opened, and they knew that they were naked . . .

In our arrogance, we aspire to be angels or gods; our lust reminds us that we are only creatures, destined for dust. *Post coitum omne animal triste.*

That is why the modern attitude toward erotic love—simultaneously condescending and puritanical—is so perplexing. Modern technology masks all of the most natural of human experiences: wrinkles, disease, birth, death . . . and, to some degree, sex itself. By reducing sex to a mere electronic spectator sport, by making it cinematic and scientific and "safe," we seem to think we've somehow conquered nature at last. In fact, all we have done is to remove our last enduring connection to who we really are.

As the selections in this chapter demonstrate, earlier ages had a far more lighthearted, earthy, and yes, lusty, attitude toward sex. They saw sex as a fact of life, like eating or death, neither the beatific vision nor something to hide. Indeed, the medieval writers, such as Chaucer and Boccaccio—whom modern prejudice would believe puritanical—portrayed sex as pertaining

more to farce than anything else. In contrast, the modern attitude toward sex, like the modern attitude toward everything
else, is abrupt, utilitarian, lacking in any real abiding passion.
People who think ours is a lusty or even a lustful society just
because celebrities expose themselves on national television are
kidding themselves. The gauge of a society's erotic temperature
does not lie with nudity—*Playboy* doesn't have much on the
statues of Donatello, Michelangelo, or Rodin—but on the degree of emotional energy people put into their love affairs.

We suffer from an epidemic of narcoleptic libidos. If vice,
like virtue, is basically a habit, a natural inclination, it is safe to
say that many people have lost the habit of erotic love. Working
couples today report with increasing frequency that, what with
work and commuting and kids and grocery shopping, they end
up making love once a month . . . sometimes once every season.

The decline of authentic lust is a dangerous trend for the
human race. The reason is simple: Lust, like all of the vices—
from gluttony and sloth to envy and pride—is *vitally important*
for the survival of the human species.

As incredible as it may sound: no lust, no sex.

The stories found in this section represent an older approach
to lust, one which placed less emphasis on photographic
verisimilitude and more on, well, *euphemism,* discretion . . .
foreplay.

In the eighteenth-century erotic classic *Fanny Hill*—one of
the most sexually explicit novels ever written, by the way—there
is a startling absence of what we might call street language.

The reason why it seems so amazingly explicit is precisely because the writer was forced, by his policy of avoiding scatology,
to spend *entire pages* describing acts which, in our culture
today, we would convey with a single word.

The Decameron

Giovanni Boccaccio

Giovanni Boccaccio (c. 1313–1375) was the illegitimate son of a prosperous merchant who wanted his son to be a banker. The young Giovanni, however, was passionately interested in liter-ature and embarked, after failed attempts at commerce and law, on the somewhat unusual (for the middle ages) career of a professional writer. He was a talented and learned classicist but, rather than write in Latin, Boccaccio chose to write in the vernacular of his day. His most famous work, The Decameron, *written immediately after the Black Death swept through Europe, is still in print today. In it, ten young men and women, fleeing the plague, keep their spirits up by telling stories, many of them quite ribald. One of their stories follows below.*

Dioneo, observing that the queen's story, which he had fol-lowed with the closest attention, was now ended, and that only he remained to speak, did not wait to be asked but began with a smile:

"Gracious ladies, perhaps you have not yet heard how the devil is put into hell; therefore, without straying too far from the topic we have discussed all day, I will tell you how it's done. It may be that the lesson will prove to be inspiring, and besides you may learn from it that, although Love prefers the happy palace and the charming bedroom to the rustic cabin, yet, for all that, he may at times express his might in wilds cov-ered with forests, rugged with mountains, and desolate with caverns. You'll understand that all things are subject to Love's sway.

"Now, to come to my story, in the city of Capsa in Barbary there was once a very rich man, who, along with other children, had a fair and charming little daughter named Alibech. Now Alibech, not being a Christian, and hearing numerous Christians in the city speak in praise of the Christian Faith and the service of God, one day asked one of them the best way to serve God. She was told that they served God best who most completely renounced the world and its affairs and who made their abode in the wilds of the Thebaid desert.

"Without giving it serious reflection, but by childish impulse, the girl, who was very simple and about fourteen years of age, never said a word more about the matter but stole away the next day and, all alone, set out to walk to the Thebaid desert. By sheer force of resolution, and with no small suffering, she came after some days to the wilds, and there, spying a cabin a great way off, she went and found a holy man by the door. Marveling to see her, the holy man asked her why she had come. The girl answered that, guided by the spirit of God, she had come to discover how she might best serve Him and to find someone who might teach her how He ought to be served. Noticing her youth and her great beauty, the worthy man, fearing that if he allowed her to remain with him he would be ensnared by the devil, commended her good intentions, gave her a frugal meal of roots, herbs, crab apples and dates, and a little water with which to wash them down, and said to her: 'My daughter, there is a holy man not far from here who is much better able than I to teach you what you are seeking; go to him.' Then the holy man showed Alibech the way.

"But when Alibech went where she was directed she met with the same answer as before, and so, setting forth again, she at last came to the cell of a young hermit named Rustico, a very worthy and devout man, whom she interrogated as she had the others.

"Rustico had the idea of testing the firmness of his resolve and therefore did not send Alibech away, as the others had, but kept her with him in his cell. When night came, he made her a little bed of palm leaves and told her to ready herself for sleep. Hardly had she done so before the solicitations of the flesh joined battle with the powers of Rustico's spirit, and he, finding himself left in the lurch by the latter, endured not too many assaults before he retreated and offered an immediate and unconditional surrender: He said goodbye to holy meditation, prayer, and spiritual discipline and, instead, began musing on the youth and beauty of his companion. He soon fell into contemplation of how he might so direct their conversation that, without seeming to her to be a libertine, he might yet receive from her that which he now craved. By asking her many questions, Rustico discovered that the girl was as yet utterly ignorant of sex and as simple as she seemed. He therefore devised a plan for tricking her into giving him pleasure under the pretense of serving God.

"Rustico began by giving Alibech a long lecture on the great enmity that exists between God and the devil and by explaining that, God having condemned the devil to hell, to put him there was, of all the services human beings might do, the one most pleasing to God. The young girl then asked him how such a thing is done, and Rustico answered, 'You will know in a moment, but you must do exactly as I do.'

"Then, having thrown off what few clothes he had on, Rustico fell stark naked on his knees as though he were about to pray. Alibech followed his example and knelt down in front of him, also naked.

"As a result of all this, and with Rustico now being more than ever inflamed in his desire for a young girl so beautiful, there came the resurrection of the flesh. Alibech marveled at what she saw, and said, 'Rustico, what is that I see on you, thrusting itself forward, which I do not have?'

" 'My daughter,' Rustico replied, 'that is the devil of whom I spoke to you a moment ago. See, he gives me such agony that I can scarcely endure it.'

" 'Praise be to God,' Alibech answered back, 'I see I fare far better than you because I do not have such a devil.'

" 'That's true," rejoined Rustico, 'but you have something that I do not have and which you have instead of this.'

" 'What is that?' asked Alibech.

" 'You have hell, and I tell you that I believe God has sent you here for the welfare of my soul, so that, whenever this devil annoys me, you will have pity on me and help me to put him back into hell. In such a way, you will give me the utmost solace and will do God a very great pleasure and service, as indeed you said you came into this region to do.'

"The girl answered in good faith, 'Well, holy father, since I have a hell, let it be done as it pleases you.'

"Upon hearing this, Rustico said, 'Daughter, blessed are you; let us go then and put the devil back there, so he may leave me in peace.'

"So saying, Rustico laid Alibech on one of their little beds and taught her how she should imprison the thing accursed of God. The girl, who had never yet put any devil into hell, at first felt a little pain, and therefore said to Rustico, 'Certainly, father, this devil must indeed be an evil thing and an enemy of God, for he hurts hell itself whenever he is put back into it.'

" 'Daughter,' answered Rustico, 'it will not always be so.'

"Thereupon, they put the devil back into hell six times, and whenever they stirred from the bed they put him in hell again, so that, after a time, they took the desire to leave out of his head and he willingly stayed quiet.

"However, as the devil returned to Rustico again and again in the ensuing days and the obedient girl willingly lent herself to the task of putting him back into hell, it happened that the sport began to please her and she said to Rustico, 'I see now that those good people in Capsa spoke the truth when they said that it was the sweetest thing to serve God, for it's certain that I do not remember doing anything that gave me such pleasure and delight as putting the devil into hell. I therefore think that whoever applies himself to any other task than rendering service to God is a fool.'

"Accordingly, she often came to Rustico and said to him, 'My father, I came here to serve God and not be idle; let us go put the devil in hell.' While they were doing so, she said, 'Rustico, I do not know why the devil flees away from hell, for if he lived there as willingly as hell receives him and holds him, he would never come forth from there.'

"The girl, then, often invited Rustico and exhorted him to the service of God, so much so that she took the bombast out of his doublet and he felt cold when another time he had sweated. Therefore, he began to tell Alibech that the devil was not to be chastised nor put into hell except when he lifted up his head in pride. 'And we,' he added, 'by God's grace, have so defeated him that he prays to our Lord to allow him to lie in peace.' In this way, Rustico imposed a silence on the girl.

"However, when she saw that he no longer asked her to put the devil into hell, she said to him one day, 'Rustico, your devil may be defeated and give you no more pains, but my hell won't let me alone; therefore you will do well to aid me with your devil in lessening the raging of my hell, just as with my hell I have helped you take the pride out of your devil.'

"Rustico, who lived on roots and water, was ill-prepared to answer her calls and told her that she would need many devils to appease her hell, but he would do what he could. Accordingly, he satisfied her sometimes, but so seldom it was like throwing a bean into the lion's mouth. Alibech, feeling that she was not serving God nearly as much as she would like, began to complain. And while this struggle continued between Rustico and his devil and Alibech and her hell, over the desire on the one hand and the lack of power on the other, it happened that a fire broke out in Capsa and burnt down Alibech's father's house with himself in it and his wife and other children. As a result, Alibech inherited her father's entire estate. Therefore, a young man named Neerbale, who had squandered all his own money on gallantry, hearing that Alibech was still alive, set out in search of her and found her, before the court was able to lay hands upon her father's estate, as happened when a man died without an heir. To Rustico's great satisfaction, but against Alibech's own will, Neerbale brought her back to Capsa where he took her as his wife and then took control over the ample inheritance of her father.

"Once back in the city, Alibech was asked by the other women how she had served God in the desert. She answered, Neerbale not having yet slept with her, that she served Him by putting the devil into hell and that Neerbale had done a grievous sin by taking her away from such a service.

"The ladies asked, 'How do you put the devil into hell?' And the girl, with words and gestures, explained it all to them, whereupon the ladies began laughing to such an extent that they are still laughing to this day. They said to her, 'Don't worry too much about it, my girl, for that is done here also and Neerbale will serve our Lord very well with you at this.'

"And so, telling this story from one to another throughout

the city, the ladies brought it to a common saying that the most acceptable service one can render to God is to put the devil into hell. This saying has crossed the sea and is still common here. Therefore, all you young ladies, who have need of God's grace, learn to put the devil in hell, for that is highly acceptable to God and pleasing to both parties and much good may grow and come from it."

Nulla Puella Negat

Marcus Valerius Martialis

The Roman writer Martial was born in what is now Spain around the year A.D. 40. The selection below, Nulla Puella Negat *("No Girl Says No"), is taken from his famous* Epigrams.

> I've searched throughout the city,
> Safronius Rufus,
> to find a girl who says No.
> No girl
> says No.
> It's as though
> it were wrong,
> or disgraceful,
> or a sin,
> to say No.
> And so,
> no girl
> says No.

The Geranium

Richard Brinsley Sheridan

You have to be an English major to know who this guy is and not be one to have any clear understanding of what he is talking about. Richard Brinsley Sheridan (c. 1751–1816) is one of the funniest playwrights of the English language, best known for his plays The Rivals *and* The School for Scandal. *In the poem below, Sheridan compares sex to a geranium. Read it carefully. You'll never look at English poetry the same way again.*

In the close covert of a grove,
By nature formed for scenes of love,
Said Susan in a lucky hour,
Observe yon sweet geranium flower;
How straight upon its stalk it stands,
And tempts our violating hands:
Whilst the soft bud as yet unspread,
Hangs down its pale declining head:
Yet, soon as it is ripe to blow,
The stems shall rise, the head shall glow.
Nature, said I, my lovely Sue,
To all her followers lends a clue;
Her simple laws themselves explain,
As links of one continued chain;
For her the mysteries of creation,
Are but the works of generation:
Yon blushing, strong, triumphant flower,
Is in the crisis of its power:
But short, alas! its vigorous reign,

Lust
. . . . .

He sheds his seed, and drops again;
The bud that hangs in pale decay,
Feels not, as yet, the plastic ray;
Tomorrow's sun shall bid him rise,
Then, too, he sheds his seed and dies:
But words, my love, are vain and weak,
For proof, let bright example speak;
Then straight before the wondering maid,
The tree of life I gently laid;
Observe, sweet Sue, his drooping head,
How pale, how languid, and how dead;
Yet, let the sun of thy bright eyes,
Shine but a moment, it shall rise;
Let but the dew of thy soft hand
Refresh the stem, it straight shall stand:
Already, see, it swells, it grows,
Its head is redder than the rose,
Its shrivelled fruit, of dusky hue,
Now glows, a present fit for Sue:
The balm of life each artery fills,
And in o'erflowing drops distils.
Oh me! cried Susan, what is this?
What strange tumultuous throbs of bliss!
Sure, never mortal, till this hour,
Felt such emotion at a flower:
Oh, serpent! cunning to deceive,
Sure, 'tis this tree that tempted Eve;
The crimson apples hang so fair,
Alas! what woman could forbear?
Well hast thou guessed, my love, I cried,
It is the tree by which she died;
The tree which could content her,
All nature, Susan, seeks the centre;

Yet, let us still, poor Eve forgive,
It's the tree by which we live;
For lovely woman still it grows,
And in the centre only blows.
But chief for thee, it spreads its charms,
For paradise is in thy arms.—
I ceased, for nature kindly here
Began to whisper in her ear:
And lovely Sue lay softly panting,
While the geranium tree was planting.
'Til in the heat of amorous strife,
She burst the mellow tree of life.
'Oh, heaven!' cried Susan, with a sigh,
'The hour we taste—we surely die;
Strange raptures seize my fainting frame,
And all my body glows with flame;
Yet let me snatch one parting kiss
To tell my love I die with bliss:
That pleased, thy Susan yields her breath;
Oh! who would live if this be death!'

The Golden Ass

Lucius Apuleius

The Golden Ass, *or* Metamorphoses, *is renowned as one of the first full-fledged novels in the history of literature—and it is a racy one, at that! Apuleius was born around 125 A.D. in a country known as Madaura, in what is modern-day Algeria. When he wrote* The Golden Ass, *Apuleius was, according to his own autobiography, a tall, golden-haired youth of just twenty-five. The story relates the adventures of a young man named Lucius who is transformed into an ass by a Thessalian sorceress. Both before and after this event, the protagonist has many adventures which teach him the inner secrets of the human heart. The story below is merely one of the adventures from this ancient Roman novel.*

"My dearest Lucius, by the goddess beside us, I fear deeply for your safety, and I wish to put you on your guard as if you were my child of my own womb. Beware, I tell you. Beware with might and main of the wicked arts and vicious seductions of this Pamphile who is married to the Milo whose guest you say you are. She is a witch of the first rank, and is accounted Mistress of every Necromantic Chant. By merely breathing on twigs and pebbles and suchlike ineffectual things she knows how to drown the whole light of the starry universe in the depths of hell, back in its ancient chaos. For as soon as she sees an attractive youth, she is on tenterhooks of admiration, and she rivets her eyes and her lustful mind upon him. She sows her blandishment, she invades his spirit, she snares him in unbreakable bonds of bottomless love.

"And those who do not comply at once she loathes, and in a flash she whisks them into stones or cattle or any animal she chooses—or else she simply wipes them out. That is why I am alarmed for you, and consider that you ought to beware. For she inflames a man beyond redemption; and you, young and handsome as you are, are an apt victim."

Thus Byrrhaena warned me, apprehensively enough, but she merely excited my interest. For as soon as I heard her mention the Art of Magic, than which nothing was nearer to my heart's desire, I was so far from shuddering at Pamphile that a strong compulsion made me yearn to attain the described mastery, though I should have to pay heavy fees for it, though I should fling myself with a running jump into the very Abyss.

Trembling with distracted haste, I extricated myself from Byrrhaena's grasp as if from shackles, blushed, and bidding her farewell dashed excitedly off to the house of my host Milo. And while I scurried along like a madman, I was saying to myself, "Come now, Lucius, keep your wits about you, and look alive-O. Here is the desired chance. Put out your hand and take the thing you've prayed for so long. Satiate your heart with Marvels. Discard all puerile fears. Grapple as if you meant business. But renounce all amorous connexion wheresoever with your hostess, and respect the nuptial sofa of the upright Milo. On the other hand sue and woo the servant girl Fotis strenuously. For she is charmingly shaped, sportive in her ways, and decidedly talkative. Last evening when you retired to rest, she conducted you obligingly into the bedroom, and laid you soothingly in bed, and rather lovingly drew up the bedclothes. And then her reluctant face showed how little she liked leaving only that one goodnight kiss upon your brow. And on the doorstep she turned her head, and smiled again, and could not go. Good luck and speed to your need, my lad; and come what may, a breach must be made through Fotis."

Debating these matters, I reached Milo's front door and entered, with the question answered (as the saying goes) overwhelmingly in the affirmative. I did not, however, find Milo or his wife at home. My darling Fotis was alone in charge. She was preparing the stuffing for some black pudding, and was mincing the pigs' tripes, some of which stood finely shredded on the sideboard, ready for mixing with a gravy that tickled my nostrils with its succulently wafted steam.

She was neatly clad in a linen apron, with a shining scarlet stomacher which gathered her dress up high under her meeting breasts; and she was stirring the stock-pot with her rosy little hands moving round and round above it. As she stirred and turned the meat, she herself stirred and vibrated congruously all over her supple body. Her loins softly undulated, and her agile spine swayed and rippled in time, as she placidly stirred the pot.

I was entranced by the sight, and stood in mute admiration— as did that part of me which so far had not intruded. At last I addressed the girl, "How finely, my dear Fotis, how gaily you stir your buttocks as you stand over the pot. What a honeyed relish I see you getting ready. A happy man, a blessed man, is he that you will let dip finger there."

"Be off, you poor fellow," answered the young chatterbox, never at a loss for a repartee. "Be off from my fireplace. Keep your distance. For if the tiniest spark of that heat grazes you, you'll be scorched to the gizzard, and no one will be able to quench you but myself. For I'm very good at putting choice spice into pot or bed, and making them both equally stirring."

Chattering thus, she glanced at me and smiled; and I did not leave the room until I had diligently scrutinized every angle of her charm. But why divagate into detail? It has always been the prime concern of my life to observe in public the heads and tresses of beautiful women, and then to conjure up the image at home for leisurely enjoyment. This procedure is based on a clear and rationally determined proposition. Firstly, that Hair is the most important (visible) portion of the body, and that from its prominent position it provokes attention first. Secondly, that Hair by its natural hues provides that comeliness for the head which the gay tints of flowering dresses provide for the other limbs.

Moreover, most women, to commend their natural charms and graces, discard all mufflers, throw open their cloaks, and proudly delight in exhibiting their naked breasts, knowing that there is more delectation in the rosy gloss of the skin than in the golden sheen of a dress.

On the contrary (though even the supposition is irreligious, and I pray that there may never be an instance of so horrible a monstrosity) if you despoil the most surprisingly beautiful woman of her Hair, and denude her face of its natural accommodation—though she were dropped down from heaven, conceived of the sea foam, cradled among the waves—though she (I say) were Venus herself, though she were ringed-round by the three Graces, and environed with the whole mob of Cupids, and laced with her love-girdle, fragrant as cinnamon, and dewy with balsamum—yet if she came out bald, she would not be able to seduce even her own husband.

What satisfying hues and tangled lustres burn in woman's Hair. Sometimes it briskly repels the flash of the sun; sometimes it is absorbed into a softer penumbra, or glistens with varying toilettes of light. Now it coruscates with gold; now it deepens into honey-coloured shadows; now it is raven black; now it reflects the blue flower-tints of a dove's throat. And then when it has been anointed with Arabian nard, or parted by the fine teeth of the artful comb, or looped up at the nape of the neck, the lover looks upon it and sees there his own face, as in a mirror, enhanced by delight. O what beauty in Hair, whether in braided luxuriance it is twisted together and built up upon the head, or whether it is allowed to tumble in prolix curls down the back. Such, I conclude, is the dignity of Hair that no woman whosoever, though dressed-up with gold, tissues, gems and all other cosmetical apparatus, could be described, unless she had duly arranged her hair, as dressed at all.

But as far as my Fotis was concerned, it was not toilet-care but ringleted freedom that crowned her charms. Her plentiful hair, thrown loosely back and hanging down to her nape, was scattered over her shoulders and rested softly upon the swelling fringe of her dress, till at last it was gently collected and fastened up by a knot on the top of her head.

I could no longer bear the excruciation of such exquisite pleasure, and bending forwards I impressed a most delicious kiss on the spot where the hair was heaped on the crown of her head. She twisted away, and looked at me over her shoulder with sidelong and marrow-sucking glances.

"Hey now, my scholar," she said, "sweet and bitter is the sauce you lick. Take care that the sweetness of an overdose of honey doesn't choke you bitterly with bile for many a fine day."

"How is that, my Merriment?" I asked, "for I am ready to be laid flat for basting above that fire for as long as I am recruited every while by a tiny kiss." And, as good as my word, I embraced her more straitly and began kissing her.

With that her own desires kindled, and a mutually waxing ardour twined our bodies akin in love. Cinnamon was the exhalation of her opening mouth; and she succumbed to my kiss, while her quickening tongue ravished me nectarously.

"I am going," I said. "No, I'm a gone man already, unless you take pity on me."

Repeating the exploit of her kiss, she answered, "Raise up your spirits, man. I am fettered to you by the same legcuff of desire, and our pleasures won't be delayed very much longer. At the first flicker of torchtime I shall be in your bedroom. So be off, and gird yourself ready, for I mean to have a nightlong bone to pick with you, and there'll be no flinching on my side." And after some further (similarly pointed) remarks we separated.

About the hour of noon Byrrhaena sent me some guest-gifts—a fattened pig, five hens, and a winecask of choice vintage. I at once called Fotis.

"Look here," I said. "Bacchus, the abettor and squire of

Venus, has arrived of his own accord. Let us quaff all this wine today, so that we may lull the cowardice of shame in ourselves, and prick awake the lively courage of desire. For the voyage of Venus needs no other cargo than this—plenty of oil for the lamps through all the wakeful night, and plenty of wine for the cups."

I spent the rest of the day in the bathing-tubs, and then at supper. For I had been invited to share the neat tabloid meal of the worthy Milo. Mindful of Byrrhaena's counsel, I took my seat as safely sheltered from the gaze of his wife as possible, and turned my apprehensive eyes seldom towards her face—and then only as if towards the gulf of Avernus. But I kept looking round the room after the assiduously ministering Fotis, and by that means lifted up my heart.

Evening was already on us; and Pamphile, peering into a lamp, asserted, "It will rain heavily tomorrow." Her husband asked her how she could foretell the weather, and she replied that the lamp had thus prophesied.

When Milo heard this, he laughed and said, "So we are feeding a mighty Sibyl in this lamp which looks out from its socket as from a watch-tower on all the business of the Heavens and the Sun himself."

I interrupted here. "This is my first experience of this type of divination—though it is not so very mysterious that this Flamelet, trivial as it is, and produced by human agency, should yet possess an awareness of that greater and celestial Flame as of its Sire, and that it should know and announce to us by divine intuition what the latter will be doing up on the crest of the sky.

"Among us at Corinth there is a certain Chaldean stranger who is agitating the whole city with his marvellous responses, and exposing to any comer the Secrets of Fate for cash down. He declares to some what day strengthens the marriage twine, to others what day makes the foundations of buildings endure, what day is profitable for business, or best resorted-to for travel, or opportune for a sea-voyage. To me, when I consulted him as to the outcome of this journey of mine, he gave several answers curious in sooth, and sufficiently different.

"For he told me that I would win some fine bouquets of Fame, and also that I'd provide a great Tale, an incredible Plot, and material for Books."

"With what kind of appearance," asked Milo, guffawing again, "is this Chaldean blessed? and what is the name that he's ticketed with?"

"He's tall," I said, "and duskyish. Diophanes by name."

"That's the man," said Milo. "That's the very man. He gave the same sort of responses here, lots of them to lots of people— and at a good price too. Indeed he made an excellent thing out of it, till Fortune handed him a trick—or so I might rather say, landed him a kick."

ONE DAY WHEN he was the centre of a jostling crowd, and busy ladling out the Fates to the onlookers, a certain merchant by the name of Cerdo approached him with a query as to the most favourable day for a journey. After Diophanes had particularized a likely date, Cerdo lugged out his money-bag, emptied out the money, and counted a hundred denars which he meant to leave as the prophesying fee. At this moment a youth of the upper-class tiptoed up behind Diophanes and grasped him by the garment.

Diophanes swung round, and found himself clasped and kissed most dearly. Returning the salute, he desired the new-comer to take a seat at his side, for he was so blankly astonished at this sudden apparition that he forgot the business transaction in which he was engaged.

"Well now, I am glad to see you," he said. "How long ago did you arrive?"

"Jogged-in early last evening," the other answered. "But tell me in your turn, my dear friend, how you have sailed so rapidly to this city from the island of Euboea, and how you got along on land and sea."

Then Diophanes, this egregious Chaldean and scatter-brain, forgetting who he was, declared, "May all my enemies and ill-wishers light on such a chapter of accidents—as bad as the Odyssey! For the ship in which we embarked was smashed about by the veering cyclonic blasts. The rudders were carried away, and no sooner had we brought the hulk near to the farther shore than she sank like a stone. We saved our lives by swimming to land, but lost all else. And then whatever oddments we scraped together through the charity of strangers or the kindness of friends were stripped from us by a mob of robbers. My brother Arignotus was the only man to put up a resistance, and him they murdered before my very eyes."

While Diophanes was mournfully recounting his mishaps, the merchant Cerdo snatched up the money which he had paid out as fee for the prophecy, and showed the prophet a clean pair of heels. Then at last Diophanes collected his faculties and realized how he had blundered, while all of us that had stood round listening burst into salvoes of helpless laughter.

"HOWEVER, MASTER LUCIUS, I trust that the Chaldean hit on the truth in your case, if in no one else's, and that you may be fortunate and find nothing to mar your journey."

Thus Milo went on lengthily discoursing, while I sat silent, groaning internally and not a little irritated at myself for having started off a series of unseasonable anecdotes which threatened

to lay waste a good part of the evening and its delectable fruits.
But at last I gulped down my shame and said to Milo:

"Let Diophanes carry on with his Fortune, or miscarry with
his ill-gotten gains again on land or sea. I am still sore from the
exertions of yesterday. So please excuse me for going to bed
rather early."

As I spoke, I rose and went straight out, and reaching my
bedroom I discovered there a pleasant spread of toothsome tid-
bits. The servant-boys' bed was removed outside the door on
the ground a fair distance away—to prevent them from eaves-
dropping, I suppose, on our night-long babble.

Beside my bed a table was ranged, packed with the best of
the supper remnants, and generous cups already stained half-
full with wine that awaited only the tempering water, and a
flagon near by with gradually distending orifice to let the wine
gurgle out more freely—the whole advance guard of gladiatorial
Venus.

No sooner was I laid in bed than lo! Fotis. Her mistress had
now retired for the night; and the girl had come to me gaily gar-
landed with roses and with one rose in full blossom opening between her breasts. She embraced me with fast kisses, and tied a
wreath about my head, and strewed flowers over me; and then
she snatched a cup, and pouring warm water into it she prof-
fered me a draught; and before I had finished, she indulgently
took the cup away from my lips, and sipped the remainder of
the wine with little dainty birdlike sips, keeping her eyes intently
upon me all the while.

Another cup, and then a third, we shared thus, passing the
cup to and fro, until I was drenched in wine and every inch of
my body partook of my perturbed desire. I felt ticklishly ele-
vated, with all my energies keyed up; and now with one tweak I

demonstrated incontestably to my Fotis my straightforward intention.

"Pity me," I said, "come to my succor on the spot. For you can see that I am nervously taut with expectation of this pitched battle to which you challenged me without any go-between of a herald. Ever since the first arrow of pitiless Cupid twanged in my vitals, I have been standing to arms, and now I'm fairly scared that the bow-strings should snap with over-tension. But if you would humour me more richly, let down your wild hair, and while it falls about your shoulders undulatingly utter lovely embraces."

In less than a heartbeat she had pushed away with one sweep all the plates and dishes, and stripped herself of every stitch. Her hair tumbled down in blithe wantonness, and she stood before me metamorphosed into a Venus who rose beautifully from the trough of the sea—for a moment of coquettish craft shadowing (it could hardly be called modestly protecting) her depilated femininity with rosy palm.

"Fight," she said, "and fight stoutly. For I won't budge a hair's-breadth, nor turn my back. Face to face, I say, if you are a man, strike home, manœuvre into position busily, and die the death. Today the battle is waged without quarter."

With these words she leaped into bed, and saddling and bridling me she rode agilely into pleasure. In the process she showed herself to possess a spine of pliant lubricity, and she satiated me with the enjoyment of Venus-on-a-swing, until stretched at the last gasp of ecstasy with languid bodies we fell twined in a warm and mortal embrace, pouring out our souls.

In these and like entanglements, without a sigh of sleep, we came up to the confines of light, charming away moments of lassitude with the winecup, once more awakening desire and replenishing delight. And a good many more nights we spent in devices similarly pleasant.

The Country-Wife

William Wycherley

In the seventeenth-century comic masterpiece, The Country-Wife, *first performed in 1675, a rake by the name of Horner convinces a doctor, Quack, to let it be known around town that he had been made "as bad as a eunuch" by "an English-French disaster" of some kind. Horner's recent visit to France, and his two-week-long seclusion with the doctor, give credence to the rumor that he suffered some horrible wound leaving him impotent. Horner's plan is to feign such a condition, and such a hatred of women, so that the husbands of the town will trust him with their wives and he can merrily seduce anyone he chooses. The name "Horner," of course, means a man who makes horns—a reference to the ancient belief that a cuckold, a man whose wife cheats on him, grows horns on his head. This is also the origin of the modern term "horny."*

At first, Horner plays his part and spars verbally with three independent (but married) ladies—Lady Fidget, Mrs. Dainty Fidget, and Mrs. Squeamish—but before long he takes all three to bed. In the scene below, which takes place in Horner's lodgings, Sir Jaspar, Lady Fidget's husband, bursts through the door only to discover his wife embracing Horner. So strong is his belief in Horner's status as a eunuch, however, that Jaspar ignores the evidence of his own eyes and even allows Horner to take his wife away for a quick encounter next-door in the bed-

room under the pretext of examining Horner's collection of
china. Quack, hiding in another part of the room, watches the
proceedings unseen and in disbelief. When another of Horner's
bedmates, Mrs. Squeamish, arrives unexpectedly, she, too, de-
mands the opportunity to check out Horner's porcelain.

ACT IV, Scene III

SIR JASPAR How now!

LADY FIDGET *(Aside)* O my husband!—prevented!—and
what's almost as bad, found with my arms about another
man—that will appear too much—what shall I say?—Sir Jaspar, come hither. I am trying if Master Horner were ticklish,
and he's as ticklish as can be. I love to torment the con-
founded toad. Let you and I tickle him.

SIR JASPAR No, your ladyship will tickle him better without me,
I suppose. But is this your buying china? I thought you had
been at the china house?

HORNER *(Aside)* China house! That's my cue, I must take
it.—A pox! Can't you keep your impertinent wives at home?
Some men are troubled with the husbands, but I with the
wives. But I'd have you to know, since I cannot be your jour-
neyman by night, I will not be your drudge by day, to squire
your wife about and be your man of straw, or scarecrow, only
to pies and jays that would be nibbling at your forbidden
fruit. I shall be shortly the hackney gentleman-usher of the
town.

SIR JASPAR *(Aside)* He, he, he! Poor fellow, he's in the right
on't, faith! To squire women about for other folks is as un-
grateful an employment as to tell money for other folks.—
He, he, he! Ben't angry, Horner?

LADY FIDGET No, 'tis I have more reason to be angry, who am left by you to go abroad indecently alone; or, what is more indecent, to pin myself upon such ill-bred people of your acquaintance as this is.

SIR JASPAR Nay, prithee, what has he done?

LADY FIDGET Nay, he has done nothing.

SIR JASPAR But what d'ye take ill, if he has done nothing?

LADY FIDGET Ha, ha, ha! Faith, I can't but laugh, however. Why, d'ye think, the unmannerly toad would not come down to me to the coach. I was fain to come up to fetch him, or go without him, which I was resolved not to do; for he knows china very well, and has himself very good, but will not let me see it lest I should beg some. But I will find it out, and have what I came for yet.

Exit LADY FIDGET *and locks the door, followed by* HORNER *to the door.*

HORNER (*Apart to* LADY FIDGET) Lock the door, madam.—So, she has got into my chamber and locked me out. Oh, the impertinency of womankind! Well, Sir Jaspar, plain dealing is a jewel. If ever you suffer your wife to trouble me again here, she shall carry you home a pair of horns, by my Lord Mayor she shall! Though I cannot furnish you myself, you are sure, yet I'll find a way.

SIR JASPAR (*Aside*) Ha, ha, he! At my first coming in and finding her arms about him, tickling him it seems, I was half jealous, but now I see my folly.—He, he, he! Poor Horner.

HORNER (*Aside*) Nay, though you laugh now, 'twill be my turn ere long.—Oh, women, more impertinent, more cunning and more mischievous than their monkeys, and to me almost as ugly! Now is she throwing my things about, and rifling all I have, but I'll get into her the back way, and so rifle her for it.

SIR JASPAR Ha, ha, ha! Poor angry Horner.

HORNER Stay here a little, I'll ferret her out to you presently, I warrant.

Exit HORNER *at t'other door.*

SIR JASPAR Wife! My Lady Fidget! Wife! He is coming into you the back way!

SIR JASPAR *calls through the door to his wife; she answers from within.*

LADY FIDGET Let him come, and welcome, which way he will.

SIR JASPAR He'll catch you, and use you roughly, and be too strong for you.

LADY FIDGET Don't you trouble yourself, let him if he can.

QUACK *(Behind)* This indeed I could not have believed from him, nor any but my own eyes.

Enter MRS. SQUEAMISH

SQUEAMISH Where's this woman-hater, this toad, this ugly, greasy, dirty sloven?

SIR JASPAR *(Aside)* So the women all will have him ugly. Methinks he is a comely person, but his wants make his form contemptible to 'em; and 'tis e'en as my wife said yesterday, talking of him, that a proper handsome eunuch was as ridiculous a thing as a gigantic coward.

SQUEAMISH Sir Jaspar, your servant. Where is the odious beast?

SIR JASPAR He's within in his chamber, with my wife; she's playing the wag with him.

SQUEAMISH Is she so? And he's a clownish beast, he'll give her

no quarter, he'll play the wag with her again, let me tell you.
Come, let's go help her.—What, the door's locked?

SIR JASPAR Ay, my wife locked it.

SQUEAMISH Did she so? Let us break it open then.

SIR JASPAR No, no, he'll do her no hurt.

SQUEAMISH No. *(Aside)* But is there no other way to get into
'em? Wither goes this? I will disturb 'em.

Enter OLD LADY SQUEAMISH

OLD LADY SQUEAMISH Where is this harlotry, this impudent
baggage, this rambling tomrig? O Sir Jaspar, I'm glad to see
you here. Did you not see my wild grandchild come in hither
just now?

SIR JASPAR Yes.

OLD LADY SQUEAMISH Ay, but where is she then? where is she?
Lord, Sir Jaspar, I have e'en rattled myself to pieces in pursuit of her. But can you tell what she makes here? They say
below, no woman lodges here.

SIR JASPAR No.

OLD LADY SQUEAMISH No! What does she here then? Say, if it
be not a woman's lodging, what makes she here? But are you
sure no woman lodges here?

SIR JASPAR No, nor no man neither, this is Master Horner's
lodging.

OLD LADY SQUEAMISH Is it so, are you sure?

SIR JASPAR Yes, yes.

OLD LADY SQUEAMISH So—then there's no hurt in't, I hope.
But where is he?

SIR JASPAR He's in the next room with my wife.

OLD LADY SQUEAMISH Nay, if you trust him with your wife, I
may with my Biddy. They say he's a merry harmless man

now, e'en as harmless a man as ever came out of Italy with a good voice, and as pretty harmless company for a lady as a snake without his teeth.

SIR JASPAR Ay, ay, poor man.

Enter MRS. SQUEAMISH

SQUEAMISH I can't find 'em.—Oh, are you here, grandmother? I followed, you must know, my Lady Fidget hither. 'Tis the prettiest lodging, and I have been staring on the prettiest pictures.

Enter LADY FIDGET *with a piece of china in her hand, and* HORNER *following*

LADY FIDGET And I have been toiling and moiling for the prettiest piece of china, my dear.

HORNER Nay, she has been too hard for me, do what I could.

SQUEAMISH O Lord, I'll have some china too. Good Master Horner, don't think to give other people china, and me none. Come in with me too.

HORNER Upon my honour I have none left now.

SQUEAMISH Nay, nay, I have known you deny your china before now, but you shan't put me off so. Come.

HORNER This lady had the last there.

LADY FIDGET Yes, indeed, madam, to my certain knowledge he has no more left.

SQUEAMISH Oh, but it may be he may have some you could not find.

LADY FIDGET What, d'ye think if he had had any left, I would not have had it too? For we women of quality never think we have china enough.

HORNER Do not take it ill, I cannot make china for you all, but I will have a roll-wagon for you too, another time.

SQUEAMISH Thank you, dear toad.

LADY FIDGET *(To* HORNER, *aside)* What do you mean by that promise?

HORNER *(Apart to* LADY FIDGET*)* Alas, she has an innocent, literal understanding.

OLD LADY SQUEAMISH Poor Master Horner, he has enough to do to please you all, I see.

HORNER Ay, madam, you see how they use me.

OLD LADY SQUEAMISH Poor gentleman, I pity you.

HORNER I thank you madam. I could never find pity but from such reverend ladies as you are. The young ones will never spare a man.

SQUEAMISH Come, come, beast, and go dine with us, for we shall want a man at ombre after dinner.

HORNER That's all their use of me, madam, you see.

SQUEAMISH Come, sloven, I'll lead you, to be sure of you.

Pulls him by the cravat.

may i feel said he

e.e. cummings

This is one of edward estlin cummings's (c. 1894–1962) lesser-known but wonderfully playful poems.

> may i feel said he
> (i'll squeal said she

just once said he)
it's fun said she

(may i touch said he
how much said she
a lot said he)
why not said she

(let's go said he
not too far said she
what's too far said he
where you are said she)

may i stay said he
(which way said she
like this said he
if you kiss said she

may i move said he
is it love said she)
if you're willing said he
(but you're killing said she

but it's life said he
but your wife said she
now said he)
ow said she

(tiptop said he
don't stop said she
oh no said he)
go slow said she

(cccome? said he
ummm said she)
you're divine! said he
(you are Mine said she)

The Facetiae

Gian Francesco Poggio Bracciolini

Gian Francesco Poggio Bracciolini was born in 1380 in Ter-
ranuova, Italy, near Florence. Although he was very poor,
Poggio managed to finance his Latin education by duplicating
documents. He became so good at calligraphy that he invented
what was called the humanist script, based on the Caroline
style. In time, Poggio made a name for himself as a classicist of
some repute, discovering unknown manuscripts by such au-
thors as Cicero and Lucretius. But although Poggio was a scribe
for fifty years at the papal court, he was also the author of nu-
merous ribald tales of which The Facetiae *is a prime example.*
No one escaped his vituperative pen, with the clergy and schol-
ars receiving more than their fair share of his famous wit.
Below is just one of the many bawdy stories found in The
Facetiae, *originally written in Latin between 1438 and 1452.*

Of a Fool Who Thought His Wife Had Two
Openings

A rustic of our parts, a rather silly fool who was utterly ignorant about deeds of love, got married. Now it happened one
night that his wife turned her back to him in bed, so that her

buttocks rested in his lap, *renes versus virum volvens.* He had his arrow ready, the bow was bent, and by chance he landed right in the target. Amazed at his success, he inquired of his wife if she had two openings. And when she answered yes, he yelled: "Ho! ho! I am content with but one; the second is really superfluous." The woman, a sly hussy, who was secretly courted by the parish priest, replied: "The second one we can give away as a present to the Church and to our priest. He will find it most acceptable, and this won't hurt you in the least as you find one is enough." The peasant, anxious to please the priest, and to be rid of his unnecessary burden, agreed.

So, the priest was invited to supper and the matter was explained to him. The meal over, all three got into the same bed, the woman in the middle, the husband in front and the other behind, so as to avail himself of the gift made him. Full of desire, and lusting for the long-coveted present, the priest was the first to open fire. The woman, participating in the engagement, gave a few sighs. Fearing that his side of the fence was being trespassed upon, the peasant called out, "Observe our agreement, my friend. You stick to your own side, and let mine alone." But the priest had a ready reply: "God forbid!" he said. "I care nothing for what is yours, so long as I enjoy what belongs to the Church."

The ignorant peasant submitted quietly, and told the priest to use freely what he had conceded to the Church.

To His Mistress Going to Bed

John Donne

The Anglican divine John Donne (c. 1572–1631), like many deeply religious persons, was also sexually passionate. He is known both for his elegant sermons and his erotic love poetry.

Come, Madam, come, all rest my powers defie,
Until I labour, I in labour lie.
The foe oft-times having the foe in sight,
Is tir'd with standing though he never fight.
Off with that girdle, like heavens Zone glittering,
But a far fairer world incompassing.
Unpin that spangled breastplate which you wear,
That th'eyes of busie fooles may be stopt there.
Unlace your self, for that harmonious chyme,
Tells me from you, that now it is bed time.
Off with that happy busk, which I envie,
That still can be, and still can stand so nigh.
Your gown going off, such beautious state reveals,
As when from flowry meads th'hills shadow steales.
Off with that wyerie Coronet and shew
The haiery Diademe which on you doth grow:
Now off with those shooes, and then safely tread
In this loves hallow'd temple, this soft bed.
In such white robes, heaven's Angels us'd to be
Receavd by men; Thou Angel bringst with thee
A heaven like Mahomets Paradise; and though
Ill spirits walk in white, we easly know,
By this these Angels from an evil sprite
Those set our hairs, but these our flesh upright.

License my roaving hands, and let them go,
Before, behind, between, above, below.
O my America! my new-found-land,
My kingdome, safeliest when with one man man'd,
My Myne of precious stones, My Emperie,
How blest am I in this discovering thee!
To enter in these bonds, is to be free;
Then where my hand is set, my seal shall be.

Full nakedness! All joyes are due to thee,
As souls unbodied, bodies uncloth'd must be,
To taste whole joyes. Gems which you women use
Are like Atlanta's balls, cast in mens views,
That when a fools eye lighteth on a Gem,
His earthly soul may covet theirs, not them.
Like pictures, or like books gay coverings made
For lay-men, are all women thus array'd;
Themselves are mystick books, which only wee
(Whom their imputed grace will dignifie)
Must see reveal'd. Then since that I may know;
As liberally, as to a Midwife, shew
Thy self: cast all, yea, this white lynnen hence,
There is no pennance due to innocence.

To teach thee, I am naked first; why than
What needst thou have more covering then a man.

All's Well That Ends Well

William Shakespeare

There are numerous bawdy and earthy passages in the vast corpus of Shakespeare's work, but we will have to limit ourselves

*to merely one. William Shakespeare (c. 1564–1616) probably
wrote the comedy* All's Well That Ends Well *in his youth, and
it is based on Boccaccio's story of "Giletta of Narbova" from
the third day of* The Decameron. *In the scene below, Parolles
debates the relative value of virginity with Helena, a gentlewoman of Florence.*

Act 1, Scene 1
Enter Parolles.

PAR. Save you, fair queen!

HEL. And you, monarch!

PAR. No.

HEL. And no.

PAR. Are you meditating on virginity?

HEL. Ay. You have some stain of soldier in you; let me ask you a
    question: Man is enemy to virginity; how may we barricado it
    against him?

PAR. Keep him out.

HEL. But he assails; and our virginity, though valiant in the de-
    fence, yet is weak: unfold to us some warlike resistance.

PAR. There is none; man, sitting down before you, will under-
    mine you, and blow you up.

HEL. Bless our poor virginity from underminers, and blowers
    up! Is there no military policy, how virgins might blow up
    men?

PAR. Virginity, being blown down, man will quicklier be blown
    up: marry, in blowing him down again, with the breach your-
    selves made, you lose your city. It is not politic in the com-
    monwealth of nature to preserve virginity. Loss of virginity is
    rational increase; and there was never virgin got, till virginity
    was first lost. That, you were made of, is metal to make vir-

gins. Virginity, by being once lost, may be ten times found; by being ever kept, it is ever lost: 'tis too cold a companion: away with it.

HEL. I will stand for't a little, though therefore I die a virgin.

PAR. There's little can be said in't; 'tis against the rule of nature. To speak on the part of virginity, is to accuse your mothers; which is most infallible disobedience. He, that hangs himself, is a virgin: virginity murders itself; and should be buried in highways, out of all sanctified limit, as a desperate offendress against nature. Virginity breeds mites, much like a cheese; consumes itself to the very paring, and so dies with feeding his own stomach. Besides, virginity is peevish, proud, idle, made of self-love, which is the most inhibited sin in the canon. Keep it not; you cannot choose but lose by't: out with't: within ten year it will make itself ten, which is a goodly increase; and the principle itself not much the worse. Away with't.

HEL. How might one do, sir, to lose it to her own liking?

PAR. Let me see. Marry, ill, to like him that ne'er it likes. 'Tis a commodity will lose the gloss with lying; the longer kept, the less worth: off with't, while 'tis vendible: answer the time of request. Virginity, like an old courtier, wears her cap out of fashion; richly suited, but unsuitable: just like the brooch and the toothpick, which wear not now. Your date is better in your pie and your porridge, than in your cheek: and your virginity, your old virginity, is like one of our French withered pears: it looks ill, it eats drily; marry, 'tis a withered pear; it was formerly better, marry, yet 'tis a withered pear: will you any thing with it?

The Willing Mistriss

Aphra Behn

Aphra Behn (c. 1640–1689), whose colorful life included a stint as a spy, was one of England's first full-time professional women writers, earning her bread as a successful playwright. Many of her nineteen produced plays dealt frankly with women and sex. This poem is taken from her collection, Poems on Several Occasions, With a Voyage to the Island of Love, *first published in London in 1684.*

Amyntas led me to a Grove,
    Where all the Trees did shade us;
The Sun it self, though it had Strove,
    It could not have betray'd us:
The place secur'd from humane Eyes,
    No other fear allows,
But when the Winds that gently rise,
    Doe Kiss the yielding Boughs.

Down there we satt upon the Moss,
    And did begin to play
A Thousand Amorous Tricks, to pass
    The heat of all the day.
A many Kisses he did give:
    And I return'd the same
Which made me willing to receive
    That which I dare not name.

His Charming Eyes no Aid requir'd
    To tell their softning Tale;

On her that was already fir'd
    'Twas Easy to prevaile.
He did but Kiss and Clasp me round,
    Whilst those his thoughts Exprest:
And lay'd me gently on the Ground;
    Ah who can guess the rest?

The Spinach Song

Julia Lee

The jazz lyricist and entertainer Julia Lee (c. 1902–1958) spent her life in Kansas City. Like so much of jazz, Lee's lyrics were open to a variety of interpretations.

Spinach has vitamins A, B and D,
But spinach never appealed to me
But one day while having dinner
With a guy, I decided
To give it a try.

I didn't like it the first time
It was so new to me.
I didn't like it the first time
I was so young you see.
I used to run away from the stuff
But now somehow I can't get enough,

I didn't like it the first time
But O how it grew on me.

I didn't like it the first time
I had it on a date.
Although the first was the worst time,
Right now I think it's great.
Somehow it's always hitting the spot,
Especially when they bring it in hot.
I didn't like it the first time
But O how it grew on me.

I didn't like it the first time
I thought it was so strange.
I wasn't getting much younger,
So I just made the change.
No longer is the stuff on the shelf,
'Cause I make a pig of myself.
I didn't like it the first time
But O how it grew on me.

I didn't like it the first time
When I was just sixteen.
I didn't like it the first time
Guess I was mighty green.
But I've stocked up, 'cause I've gotten wise,
I've got enough for two dozen guys.
I didn't like it the first time
But O how it grew on me.

I didn't like it the first time
But O how it grew on me.

Fanny Hill

John Cleland

John Cleland's Fanny Hill *is perhaps one of the greatest cele-
brations of vice in the history of literature. Born in 1709, Cleland received a top-notch education at the Westminster School
and worked in India for the British East India Company. After
leaving India, he drifted around Europe and eventually ended
up in a debtors' prison. He made a famous bet with friends that
he could write the lewdest book in the English language without using a single "dirty" word. The result,* Fanny Hill, Mem-
oirs of a Woman of Pleasure, *was published in 1749 and was
an instant bestseller. The novel sprung Cleland from debtors'
prison and into court on obscenity charges, of which he was
acquitted. In 1821, the book was banned in the U.S., but in
1965 the U.S. Supreme Court ruled that the book could not be
legally prohibited and, to this day, it sells thousands of copies
each year. The narrator, Fanny, is a "kept woman" of a "Mr.
H . . . ," and in the scene below she recounts her attempts to
seduce a young servant-boy of nineteen, "fresh as a rose, well-
shaped and clever limb'd."*

I was then lying at length upon that very couch, the scene of
Mr. H . . .'s polite joys, in an undress, which was with all the art
of negligence flowing loose, and in a most tempting disorder: no
stays, no hoop, no encumbrance whatever. On the other hand,
he stood at a little distance, that gave me a full view of a fine
featur'd, shapely, healthy country lad, breathing the sweets of
fresh blooming youth; his hair, which was of a perfect shining
black, play'd to his face in natural side-curls, and was set out
with a smart tuck-up behind; new buckskin breeches, that, clip-

ping close, shew'd the shape of a plump, well made thigh; white stockings, garter-lac'd livery, shoulder-knot, altogether compos'd a figure in which the beauties of pure flesh and blood appeared under no disgrace from the lowness of a dress, to which a certain spruce neatness seems peculiarly fitted.

I bid him come towards me and give me his letter, at the same time throwing down, carelessly, a book I had in my hands. He colour'd, and came within reach of delivering me the letter, which he held out, awkwardly enough, for me to take, with his eyes riveted on my bosom, which was, through the design'd disorder of my blouse, sufficiently bare, and rather shaded than hid.

I, smiling in his face, took the letter, and immediately catching gently hold of his shirt sleeve, drew him towards me, blushing, and almost trembling; for surely his extreme bashfulness, and utter inexperience, call'd for, at least, all the advances to encourage him: his body was now conveniently inclin'd towards me, and, just softly chucking his smooth beardless chin, I asked him if he was afraid of a lady? . . . and with that took, and carrying his hand to my breasts, I prest it tenderly to them. They were now finely furnish'd, and rais'd, in flesh, so that, panting with desire, they rose and fell, in quick heaves, under his touch: at this, the boy's eyes began to lighten with all the fires of inflam'd nature, and his cheeks flush'd with a deep scarlet: tongue-tied with joy, rapture, and bashfulness, he could not speak, but then his looks, his emotion, sufficiently satisfy'd me that my train had taken, and that I had no disappointment to fear.

My lips, which I threw in his way, so as that he could not escape kissing them, fix'd, fir'd, and embolden'd him: and now, glancing my eyes towards that part of his dress which cover'd the essential object of enjoyment, I plainly discover'd the swell and commotion there; and as I was now too far advanc'd to stop in so fair a way, and was indeed no longer able to contain myself, or wait the slower progress of his maiden bashfulness (for such it seem'd, and really was), I stole my hand upon his thighs, down one of which I could see and feel a stiff hard body, confin'd by his breeches, that my fingers could discover no end to. Curious then, and eager to unfold so alarming a mystery, playing, as it were, with his buttons, which were bursting ripe from the active force within, those of his waistband and flore-flap flew open at a touch, when out it started; and now, disengag'd from the shirt, I saw, with wonder and surprise, what? not the play-thing of a boy, not the weapon of a man, but a maypole of so enormous a standard, that had proportions been observ'd, it must have belong'd to a young giant. Its prodigious size made me shrink again; yet I could not, without pleasure, behold, and even ventur'd to feel, such a length, such a breadth of animated ivory! perfectly well turn'd and fashion'd, the proud stiffness of which distended its skin, whose smooth polish and velvet softness might vie with that of the most delicate of our sex, and whose exquisite whiteness was not a little set off by a sprout of black curling hair round the root, through the jetty springs of which the fair skin shew'd as in a fine evening you may have remark'd the clear light ether through the branchwork of distant trees overtopping the summit of a hill: then the broad and blueish casted incarnate of the head, and blue serpentines of its veins, altogether compos'd the most striking assemblage of figure and colours in nature. In short, it stood an object of terror and delight.

But what was yet more surprising, the owner of this natural curiosity, through the want of occasions in the strictness of his home-breeding, and the little time he had been in town not having afforded him one, was hitherto an absolute stranger, in practice at least, to the use of all that manhood he was so nobly

stock'd with; and it now fell to my lot to stand his first trial of it,
if I could resolve to run the risks of its disproportion to that
tender part of me, which such an oversiz'd machine was very fit
to lay in ruins.

But it was now much too late to deliberate; for, by this time,
the young fellow, overheated with the present objects, and too
high mettled to be longer curb'd in by that modesty and awe
which had hitherto restrain'd him, ventur'd, under the strong
impulse and instructive promptership of nature alone, to slip his
hands, trembling with eager impetuous desires, under my petticoats; and seeing, I suppose, nothing extremely severe in my
looks to stop or dash him, he feels out, and seizes, gently, the
center-spot of his ardors. Oh then! the fiery touch of his fingers
determines me, and my fears melting away before the glowing
intolerable heat, my thighs disclose of themselves, and yield all
liberty to his hand: and now, a favourable movement giving my
petticoats a toss, the avenue lay too fair, too open to be miss'd.
He is now upon me: I had placed myself with a jet under him, as
commodious and open as possible to his attempts, which were
untoward enough, for his machine, meeting with no inlet, bore
and batter'd stiffly against me in random pushes, now above,
now below, now beside his point; till, burning with impatience
from its irritating touches, I guided gently, with my hand, this
furious engine to where my young novice was now to be taught
his first lesson of pleasure. Thus be nick'd at length, the warm
and insufficient orifice; but he was made to find no breach im-
practicable, and mine, tho' so often enter'd, was still far from
wide enough to take him easily in.

By my direction, however, the head of his unwieldy machine
was so critically pointed, that, feeling him foreright against the
tender opening, a favourable motion from me met his timely
thrust, by which the lips of it, strenuously dilated, gave way to

his thus assisted impetuosity, so that we might both feel that he had gain'd a lodgement. Pursuing then his point, he soon, by violent, and, to me, most painful piercing thrusts, wedges himself at length so far in, as to be now tolerably secure of his entrance: here he stuck, and I now felt such a mixture of pleasure and pain, as there is no giving a definition of. I dreaded alike his splitting me farther up, or his with-drawing; I could not bear either to keep or part with him. The sense of pain however prevailing, from his prodigious size and stiffness, acting upon me in those continued rapid thrusts, with which he furiously pursu'd his penetration, made me cry out gently: "Oh! my dear, you hurt me!" This was enough to check the tender respectful boy even in his mid-career; and he immediately drew out the sweet cause of my complaint, whilst his eyes eloquently express'd, at once, his grief for hurting me, and his reluctance at dislodging from quarters, of which the warmth and closeness had given him a wave of pleasure that he was now desire-mad to satisfy, and yet too much a novice not to be afraid of my withholding his relief, on account of the pain he had put me to.

But I was, myself, far from being pleas'd with his having too much regarded my tender exclamations; for now, more and more fir'd with the object before me, as it still stood with the fierce erection, unbonnetted, and displaying its broad vermilion head, I first gave the youth a re-encouraging kiss, which he repaid me with a fervour that seem'd at once to thank me, and bribe my further compliance; and soon replac'd myself in a posture to receive, at all risks, the renewal, which he did not delay an instant: for, being presently remounted, I once more felt the smooth hard gristle forcing an entrance, which he achiev'd rather easier than before. Pain'd, however, as I was, with his efforts of gaining a complete ad-

mission, which he was so regardful as to manage by gentle degrees, I took care not to complain. In the meantime, the soft
strait passage gradually loosens, yields, and stretch'd to its utmost bearing, by the stiff, thick, indriven engine, sensible, at
once, to the ravishing pleasure of the *feel* and the pain of the
distention, let him in about half way, when all the most nervous activity he now exerted, to further his penetration, gain'd
him not an inch of his purpose: for, whilst he hesitated there,
the crisis of pleasure overtook him, and the close compressure
of the warm surrounding fold drew from him the ecstatic
gush, even before mine was ready to meet it, kept up by the
pain I had endur'd in the course of the engagement, from the
insufferable size of his weapon, tho' it was not as yet in above
half its length.

I expected then, but without wishing it, that he would
draw, but was pleasingly disappointed: for he was not to be let
off so. The well breath'd youth, hot-mettled, and flush with
genial juices, was now fairly in for making me know my driver.
As soon, then, as he had made a short pause, waking, as it
were, out of the trance of pleasure (in which every sense
seem'd lost for a while, whilst, with his eyes shut, and short
quick breathing, he had yielded down his maiden tribute), he
still kept his post, yet unsated with enjoyment, and solacing in
these so new delights; till his stiffness, which had scarce per-
ceptibly remitted, being thoroughly recovered to him, who
had not once unsheath'd, he proceeded afresh to cleave and
open to himself an entire entry into me, which was not a little
made easy to him by the balsamic injection with which he had
just plentifully moisten'd the whole internals of the passage.
Redoubling, then, the active energy of his thrusts, favoured by
the fervid appetite of my motions, the soft oiled wards can no

longer stand so effectual a picklock, but yield, and open him an entrance. And now, with conspiring nature, and my industry, strong to aid him, he pierces, penetrates, and at length, winning his way inch by inch, gets entirely in, and finally a mighty thrust sheathes it up to the guard; on the information of which, from the close jointure of our bodies (insomuch that the hair on both sides perfectly interweav'd and incircl'd together), the eyes of the transported youth sparkl'd with more joyous fires, and all his looks and motions acknowledged excess of pleasure, which I now began to share, for I felt him in my very vitals! I was quite sick with delight, stir'd beyond bearing with its furious agitations within me, and gorged and cramm'd, even to surfeit. Thus I lay gasping, panting under him, till his broken breathings, faltering accents, eyes twinkling with humid fires, lunges more furious, and an increas'd stiffness, gave me to hail the approaches of the second period: it came . . . and the sweet youth, overpower'd with the ecstasy, died away in my arms, melting in a flood that shot in genial warmth into the innermost recesses of my body; every conduit of which, dedicated to that pleasure, was on flow to mix with it.

On Selecting a Mistress
Benjamin Franklin

Everyone knows who Benjamin Franklin (c. 1706–1790) was: printer, scientist, author, publisher, diplomat, statesman, inventor. What some people don't know is that he had a tremendous sense of humor, and an earthy one at that.

$\mathcal{L}$ust
· · · · ·

To ****

My Dear Friend:

I know of no medicine fit to diminish the violent natural inclinations you mention; and if I did, I think I should not communicate it to you. Marriage is the proper remedy. It is the most natural state of man, and therefore the state in which you are most likely to find solid happiness. Your reasons against entering into it at present appear to me not well founded. The circumstantial advantages you have in view by postponing it, are not only uncertain, but they are small in comparison with that of the thing itself, the being married and settled. It is the man and woman united that make the compleat human being. Separate, she wants his force of body and strength of reason; he, her softness, sensibility and acute discernment. Together they are more likely to succeed in the world. A single man has not nearly the value he would have in the state of union. If you get a prudent, healthy wife, your industry in your profession, with her good economy, will be a fortune sufficient.

But if you will not take this counsel and persist in thinking a commerce with the sex inevitable, then I repeat my former advice, that in all your amours you should prefer old women to young ones.

You call this a paradox and demand my reasons. They are these:

1. Because they have more knowledge of the world, and their minds are better stored with observations, their conversation is more improving, and most lastingly agreeable.

2. Because when women cease to be handsome they study to be good. To maintain their influence over men, they supply the diminution of beauty by an augmentation of utility. They learn to do a thousand services small and great, and are the most tender and useful of friends when you are sick. Thus

they continue amiable. And hence there is hardly such a thing to be found as an old woman who is not a good woman.

3. Because there is no hazard of children, which irregularly produced may be attended with much inconvenience.

4. Because through more experience they are more prudent and discreet in conducting an intrigue to prevent suspicion. The commerce with them is therefore safer with regard to your reputation. And with regard to theirs, if the affair should happen to be known, considerate people might be rather inclined to excuse an old woman, who would kindly take care of a young man, form his manners by her good counsels, and prevent his ruining his health and fortune among mercenary prostitutes.

5. Because in every animal that walks upright, the deficiency of the fluids that fill the muscles appears first in the highest part. The face first grows lank and wrinkled; then the neck; then the breast and arms; the lower parts continuing to the last as lump as ever: so that covering all above with a basket, and regarding only what is below the girdle, it is impossible of two women to know an old one from a young one. And as in the dark all cats are grey, the pleasure of corporal enjoyment with an old woman is at least equal, and frequently superior; every knack being, by practice, capable of improvement.

6. Because the sin is less. The debauching a virgin may be her ruin, and make her for life unhappy.

7. Because the compunction is less. The having made a young girl miserable may give you frequent bitter reflection; none of which can attend the making an old woman happy.

8thly & lastly. They are so grateful!

Thus much for my paradox. But still I advise you to marry directly; being sincerely

Your affectionate Friend,
Benjamin Franklin

A Woman Waits for Me

Walt Whitman

It's hard to believe today, but in its time The Leaves of Grass, *written by the preeminently American poet Walt Whitman (c. 1819–1892), was considered positively obscene. Its revolutionary free-verse poems, which were edited over Whitman's lifetime in nine editions, caused quite a stir—particularly this poem, "A Woman Waits for Me." Every high school teacher knows that, if you want to slap your dazed and confused students awake in a poetry class, give 'em a dose of Whitman.*

A woman waits for me, she contains all, nothing is
    lacking,
Yet all were lacking if sex were lacking, or if the moisture
    of the right man were lacking.

Sex contains all, bodies, souls,
Meanings, proofs, purities, delicacies, results,
    promulgations,
Songs, commands, health, pride, the maternal mystery,
    the seminal milk,
All hopes, benefactions, bestowals, all the passions, loves,
    beauties, delights of the earth,
All the governments, judges, gods, follow'd persons of
    the earth,
These are contain'd in sex as parts of itself and
    justifications of itself.

Without shame the man I like knows and avows the
    deliciousness of his sex,
Without shame the woman I like knows and avows hers.

Now I will dismiss myself from impassive women,
I will go stay with her who waits for me, and with those
    women that are warm-blooded and sufficient for
    me,
I see that they understand me and do not deny me,
I see that they are worthy of me, I will be the robust
    husband of those women.

They are not one jot less than I am,
They are tann'd in the face by shining suns and blowing
    winds,
Their flesh has the old divine suppleness and strength,
They know how to swim, row, ride, wrestle, shoot, run,
    strike, retreat, advance, resist, defend themselves,
They are ultimate in their own right—they are calm,
    clear, well-possess'd of themselves.

Loving Her Husband

Groucho Marx

*If the kids of today need reminding that they aren't nearly as
worldly wise as they think they are, someone should rent them
a Marx Brothers movie. Groucho (c. 1895–1977) was the comic
genius of the team, and his lightning-fast repartee, much of it
spontaneous, set the standard for generations of comics. Here is
just one example of Groucho's quick wit:*

A guest on Groucho's television show *You Bet Your Life* was
a woman who had given birth to twenty-two children. "I love
my husband," the woman explained shyly.

"I love my cigar too," Groucho said, "but I take it out once in a while."

Fear of Flying
Erica Jong

Erica Jong, while not the first woman to write bluntly about sex, caught the imagination of millions of women in the early 1970s. Her wildly popular novel Fear of Flying, *published in 1973, described a sexual fantasy believed, at that time, to be largely limited to men.*

Five years of marriage had made me itchy for all those things: itchy for men, and itchy for solitude. Itchy for sex and itchy for the life of a recluse. I knew my itches were contradictory—and that made things even worse. I knew my itches were un-American—and that made things *still* worse. It is heresy in America to embrace any way of life except as half of a couple. Solitude is un-American. It may be condoned in a man—especially if he is a "glamorous bachelor" who "dates starlets" during a brief interval between marriages. But a woman is always presumed to be alone as a result of abandonment, not choice. And she is treated that way: as a pariah. There is simply no dignified way for a woman to live alone. Oh, she can get along financially perhaps (though not nearly as well as a man), but emotionally she is never left in peace. Her friends, her family, her fellow workers never let her forget that her husbandlessness, her childlessness—her *selfishness,* in short—is a reproach to the American way of life.

Even more to the point: the woman (unhappy though she knows her married friends to be) can never let *herself* alone. She lives as if she were constantly on the brink of some great fulfillment. As if she were waiting for Prince Charming to take her away "from all this." All what? The solitude of living inside her own soul? The certainty of being herself instead of half of something else?

My response to all this was not (not yet) to have an affair and not (not yet) to hit the open road, but to evolve my fantasy of the Zipless Fuck. The zipless fuck was more than a fuck. It was a platonic ideal. Zipless because when you came together zippers fell away like rose petals, underwear blew off in one breath like dandelion fluff. Tongues intertwined and turned liquid. Your whole soul flowed out through your tongue and into the mouth of your lover.

For the true, ultimate zipless A-1 fuck, it was necessary that you never get to know the man very well. I had noticed, for example, how all my infatuations dissolved as soon as I really became friends with a man, became sympathetic to his problems, listened to him *kvetch* about his wife, or ex-wives, his mother, his children. After that I would like him, perhaps even love him—but without passion. And it was passion that I wanted. I had also learned that a sure way to exorcise an infatuation was to write about someone, to observe his tics and twitches, to anatomize his personality in type. After that he was an insect on a pin, a newspaper clipping laminated in plastic. I might enjoy his company, even admire him at moments, but he no longer had the power to make me wake up trembling in the middle of the night. I no longer dreamed about him. He had a face.

So another condition for the zipless fuck was brevity. And anonymity made it even better.

During the time I lived in Heidelberg I commuted to Frankfurt four times a week to see my analyst. The ride took an hour each way and trains became an important part of my fantasy life. I kept meeting beautiful men on the train, men who scarcely spoke English, men whose cliches and banalities were hidden by my ignorance of French, or Italian, or even German. Much as I had to admit it, there are some beautiful men in Germany.

One scenario of the zipless fuck was perhaps inspired by an Italian movie I saw years ago. As time went by, I embellished it to suit my head. It used to play over and over again as I shuttled back and forth from Heidelberg to Frankfurt, from Frankfurt to Heidelberg:

A grimy European train compartment (Second Class). The seats are leatherette and hard. There is a sliding door to the corridor outside. Olive trees rush by the windows. Two Sicilian peasant women sit together on one side with a child between them. They appear to be mother and grandmother and granddaughter. Both women vie with each other to stuff the little girl's mouth with food. Across the way (in the window seat) is a pretty young widow in a heavy black veil and tight black dress which reveals her voluptuous figure. She is sweating profusely and her eyes are puffy. The middle seat is empty. The corridor seat is occupied by an enormously fat woman with a mustache. Her huge haunches cause her to occupy almost half of the vacant center seat. She is reading a pulp romance in which the characters are photographed models and the dialogue appears in little puffs of smoke above their heads. The fivesome bounces along for a while, the widow and the fat woman keeping silent, the mother and grandmother talking to the child and each other about the food. And then the train screeches to a halt in a town called (perhaps) CORLEONE. A tall languid-looking soldier, unshaven, but with a beautiful mop of hair, a cleft chin, and somewhat devilish, lazy eyes, enters the compartment, looks insolently around, sees the empty half-seat between the fat woman and the widow, and, with many flirtatious apologies, sits down. He is sweaty and disheveled but basically a gorgeous hunk of flesh, only slightly rancid from the heat. The train screeches out of the station.

THEN WE BECOME aware only of the bouncing of the train and the rhythmic way the soldier's thighs are rubbing against the thighs of the widow. Of course, he is also rubbing against the haunches of the fat lady—and she is trying to move away from him—which is quite unnecessary because he is unaware of her haunches. He is watching the large gold cross between the widow's breasts swing back and forth in her deep cleavage. Bump. Pause. Bump. It hits one moist breast and then the other. It seems to hesitate in between as if paralyzed between two repelling magnets. The pit and the pendulum. He is hypnotized. She stares out the window, looking at each olive tree as if she had never seen olive trees before. He rises awkwardly, half-bows to the ladies, and struggles to open the window. When he sits down again his arm accidentally grazes the widow's belly. She appears not to notice. He rests his left hand on the seat between his thigh and hers and begins to wind rubber fingers around and under the soft flesh of her thigh. She continues staring at each olive tree as if she were God and had just made them and were wondering what to call them.

MEANWHILE THE ENORMOUSLY fat lady is packing away her pulp romance in an iridescent green plastic string bag full of smelly cheeses and blackening bananas. And the grandmother is rolling ends of salami in greasy newspaper. The mother is putting on the little girl's sweater and wiping her face with a handkerchief, lovingly moistened with maternal spittle. The train screeches to a stop in a town called (perhaps) PRIZZI, and the fat lady, the mother, the grandmother, and the little girl leave the compartment. Then the train begins to move again. The gold cross begins to bump, pause, bump between the widow's moist breasts, the fingers begin to curl under the widow's thighs, the widow continues to stare at the olive trees. Then the fingers are sliding between her thighs and they are parting her thighs, and they are moving upward into the fleshy gap between her heavy black stockings and her garters, and they are sliding up under her garters into the damp unpantied place between her legs.

THE TRAIN ENTERS a *galleria,* or tunnel, and in the semi-darkness the symbolism is consummated.

There is the soldier's boot in the air and the dark walls of the tunnel and the hypnotic rocking of the train and the long high whistle as it finally emerges. Wordlessly, she gets off at a town called, perhaps, BIVONA. She crosses the tracks, stepping carefully over them in her narrow black shoes and heavy black stockings. He stares after her as if he were Adam wondering what to name her. Then he jumps up and dashes out of the train in pursuit of her. At that very moment a long freight train pulls through the parallel track obscuring his view and blocking his way. Twenty-five freight cars later, she has vanished forever.

One scenario of the zipless fuck.

Two

···

AVARICE

"A feast is made for laughter,
and wine maketh merry:
but money answereth all things."
—*Ecclesiastes 10:19*

"Money is the wise man's religion."
—*Euripides,* The Cyclops

Avarice, or greed, is the desire to own things far out of proportion to a person's actual needs. The prototype of the avaricious person is the miser, someone who collects wealth simply to collect it, the way a kid collects baseball cards. When someone buys his fifth Ferrari, for example, some people might wonder if he couldn't get by with . . . just four.

But the problem with this definition is that it is too ambiguous. What, precisely, is a proportionate need? Needs are flexible—and they keep growing. The sanctimonious pundit or preacher who denounces suburban "greed" thinks nothing of owning his own stereo system, or a pair of $100 running shoes, or a VCR. There was a time, not too long ago, when owning a telephone was considered the height of luxury—and now the greedy denizens of Western societies have two, sometimes even *three* in their homes and, even worse, *feel no shame!*

Avarice is a difficult vice to discuss because it invariably entangles one in politics. Some of the vices, such as pride or sloth, usually affect people only on a local or, at most, a village level. If I lounge about most of the day, it may involve me in a dispute with my wife, or perhaps with my boss, but that is usually it. With avarice, however, all the world thinks it has a right to stick its long pointy nose into your affairs and offer not merely moral exhortations, but, what's worse, lengthy political as well as economic sermons as well.

And it is certainly true that avarice has been roundly denounced in history even as it has been more assiduously practiced than any other vice. As the selection from Geoffrey Chaucer's "Pardoner's Tale" in this chapter indicates, preaching against avarice has been, throughout the ages, one of the most prosperous careers an individual could undertake. Socrates, for example, didn't care about money because he was able to sponge off of the rich Athenian kids whom he corrupted and who later took over the city in a bloody coup d'état (and you thought they forced him to drink hemlock for jabbering about the Eternal Forms?). His last words, if you'll recall, were to ask his friend to repay the debt of a chicken he had borrowed. And Aristotle thought that money was a necessary but not sufficient condition for happiness; given that he was the personal tutor of Alexander the Great, who would shortly conquer the entire known world, he didn't have to worry too much about fulfilling that condition. The Roman poet Virgil spoke of the *auri sacra fames* (the "accursed love of gold") even though he was the Tom Clancy of his day and probably earned a million *sesterces* in royalties on every couplet he wrote, while St. Paul went so far as to declare, in his letter to Timothy, that "money is the root of all evil," although in his letter to the Romans he wasn't above begging for cash for his favorite charity (it seems *other people's* money is the root of all evil).

Much of the criticism of avarice comes from the Bible. The biblical prophets took a rather grim view of wealth: not because gold was bad in and of itself—Proverbs 22 says that fear of the Lord brings "wealth and honor and life"—but because human beings have an embarrassing tendency to bow down before it and begin offering *incense.* I have to admit that, if I had $100,000 stacked on my desk in neat piles of hundred-dollar bills, I would probably genuflect a few times myself and might even consider sacrificing a small goat.

All the world condemns poor Avarice while all the world is a living, breathing testament to its omnipresence.

This is strange. People who don't hesitate to describe their latest sexual indiscretion in graphic detail at a cocktail party would draw back in horror if they were asked to confess to particular acts of avarice. Whether they live in a hut or a hacienda, people are always convinced that the person three or four rungs above them on the economic ladder is guilty of avarice, but certainly not they. Their own economic aspirations have nothing to do with avarice. They are merely trying to make a living, to survive, to make do. It's the people down the street, the ones with the black Jag and the new pool, who are the truly greedy ones.

In the end, the problem with money does not lie in having it, but in spending it on the wrong stuff!

Like any good thing, money can be used badly, be put to idiotic purposes. Some people spend all of their spare cash on cocaine, or cloisonné vases, or football teams.

On the other hand, it's possible to spend money on useful things—a ski cabin, say, or a college education, or a wild week in Vegas. You could even spend a little cash on an actual good deed or two.

Money, spent wisely, may not buy happiness; but it sure as hell will make things easier—for yourself, your family, for anyone on the planet you happen to care about. As the great Joe Louis said, "I don't like money, actually, but it quiets my nerves."

The Satires

Decimus Junius Juvenalis

*The biting cynicism of the Roman satirist Juvenal (c. 60–
130 A.D.) is an acquired taste. His view of human nature is
dark, witty, and often hilarious. In this rant against avarice, he
fails to mention that, under the Emperor Hadrian, he himself
became quite rich.*

Young men need not be taught to imitate most of the
    vices,
Only avarice seems to oppose their natural instinct.
Here is a vice, for once, in the shape and shade of a
    virtue,
Gloomy of mien, and dour indeed in dress and
    expression.
The miserly man is praised, of course, as if he were
    frugal,
A saving soul, to be sure, a craftier keeper of fortunes
Than the dragon of Pontus or the Hesperidean gardens.
Add the fact that the people think of the man whom I
    mention
As an artist at gain: estates increase with such forge-men
And they increase every way, becoming bigger and
    bigger.
The anvil is never still and the furnace forever is blazing.

So when a father thinks that the avaricious are happy,
Looks openmouthed at wealth, and figures no poor man
    is blessed,
He is urging young men to follow along that highway,

To study in that same school. There are A B C's of the
vices;
These he indoctrinates first, compelling his pupils to
master
The meanest, the pettiest things, but before too long he
instructs them
In the insatiable hopes and passion for acquisition.

Fatigue
Hilaire Belloc

*Next to G. K. Chesterton, Hilaire Belloc (c. 1870–1953) was
perhaps the best-known Christian apologist of the early twentieth century. Like Chesterton, he was popular because much of
his witty writing, including his poetry, concerned more prosaic
matters—such as money and food.*

I'm tired of Love: I'm still more tired of Rhyme.
But Money gives me pleasure all the time.

The Bonfire of the Vanities
Tom Wolfe

*Novelist Tom Wolfe first wrote this searing portrait of 1980s
New York City in serial form in* Rolling Stone. *In the passage
that follows, he makes a convincing case for how difficult it is
to scrape by on a million bucks a year. The character is Sher-*

man McCoy, a top bond salesman at a major Wall Street bro-
kerage house, who was involved in a hit-and-run accident with
a young would-be mugger and who is now sweating over the
possibility that he'll get caught.

One breath of scandal, not only would the Giscard scheme
collapse but *his very career* would be finished! And what would
he do then? *I'm already going broke on a million dollars a year!*
The appalling figures came popping up into his brain. Last year
his income had been $980,000. But he had to pay out $21,000 a
month for the $1.8 million loan he had taken out to buy the
apartment. What was $21,000 a month to someone making a
million a year? That was the way he had thought of it at the
time—and in fact, it was merely a *crushing, grinding burden*—
that was all! It came to $252,000 a year, none of it deductible,
because it was a personal loan, not a mortgage. (The cooperative
boards in Good Park Avenue Buildings like his didn't allow you
to take out a mortgage on your apartment.) So, considering the
taxes, it required $420,000 in income to pay the $252,000. Of
the $560,000 remaining of his income last year, $44,400 was required for the apartment's monthly maintenance fees; $116,000
for the house on Old Drover's Mooring Lane in Southampton
($84,000 for mortgage payment and interest, $18,000 for heat,
utilities, insurance, and repairs, $6,000 for lawn and hedge cut-
ting, $8,000 for taxes). Entertaining at home and in restaurants
had come to $37,000. This was a modest sum compared to what
other people spent; for example, Campbell's birthday party in
Southampton had had only one carnival ride (plus, of course,
the obligatory ponies and the magician) and had cost less than
$4,000. The Taliaferro School, including the bus service, cost
$9,400 for the year. The tab for furniture and clothes had come
to about $65,000; and there was little hope of reducing that,

since Judy was, after all, a decorator and had to keep things up to par. The servants (Bonita, Miss Lyons, Lucille the cleaning woman, and Hobie the handyman in Southampton) came to $62,000 a year. That left only $226,200, or $18,850 a month, for additional taxes and this and that, including insurance payments (nearly a thousand a month, if averaged out), garage rent for two cars ($840 a month), household food ($1,500 a month), club dues (about $250 a month)—the abysmal truth was that he had spent *more* than $980,000 last year. Well, obviously he could cut down here and there—but not nearly enough—*if the worst happened!* There was no getting out from under the $1.8 million loan, the crushing $21,000-a-month nut, without paying it off or selling the apartment and moving into one far smaller and more modest—an *impossibility!* There was no turning back! Once you had lived in a $2.6 million apartment on Park Avenue—it was impossible to live in a $1 million apartment! Naturally, there was no way to explain this to a living soul. Unless you were a complete fool, you couldn't even make the words come out of your mouth. Nevertheless—*it was so!* It was . . . *an impossibility!* Why, his building was one of the great ones built just before the First World War! Back then it was still not entirely proper for a good family to live in an apartment (instead of a house). So the apartments were built like mansions, with eleven-, twelve-, thirteen-foot ceilings, vast entry galleries, staircases, servants' wings, herringbone-parquet floors, interior walls a foot thick, exterior walls as thick as a fort's, and fireplaces, fireplaces, fireplaces, even though the buildings were all built with central heating. A mansion!—except that you arrived at the front door via an elevator (opening upon your own private vestibule) instead of the street. That was what you got for $2.6 million, and anyone who put one foot in the entry gallery of the McCoy duplex on the tenth floor knew he was in . . . *one of those fabled apartments that the world,* le monde, *died for!* And what did a million get you today? At most, at most, at *most:* a three-bed-room apartment—no servants' rooms, no guest rooms, let alone dressing rooms and a sunroom—in a white-brick high-rise built east of Park Avenue in the 1960s with 8½-foot ceilings, a dining room but no library, an an entry gallery the size of a closet, no fireplace, skimpy lumberyard moldings, if any, plasterboard walls that transmit whispers, and no private elevator stop. Oh no; instead, a mean windowless elevator hall with at least five pathetically plain bile-beige metal-sheathed doors, each pro-tected by two or more ugly drop locks, opening upon it, one of those morbid portals being *yours.*

Patently . . . *an impossibility!*

Liar's Poker

Michael Lewis

While Wolfe wrote about the world of junk-bond salesmen in fictional form in The Bonfire of the Vanities, *a young trader at Solomon Brothers named Michael Lewis wrote a very funny real-life memoir of that same world. Lewis gave up the big money at Solomon Brothers and now writes regularly for* The New Republic.

A new employee, once he reached the trading floor, was handed a pair of telephones. He went on-line almost immedi-ately. If he could make millions of dollars come out of those phones, he became that most revered of all species: a Big Swing-ing Dick. After the sale of a big block of bonds and the deposit of a few hundred thousand dollars into the Salomon till, a managing director called whoever was responsible to confirm his identity: "Hey, you Big Swinging Dick, way to be." To this day the phrase brings to mind the image of an elephant's trunk swaying from side to side. Swish. Swash. Nothing in the jungle got in the way of a Big Swinging Dick.

That was the prize we coveted. Perhaps the phrase didn't stick in everyone's mind the way it did in mine; the name was less important than the ambition, which was common to us all. And of course, no one actually said, "When I get out onto the trading floor, I'm going to be a Big Swinging Dick." It was more of a private thing. But everyone wanted to be a Big Swinging Dick, even the women. Big Swinging Dickettes.

Spectator Ab Extra

Arthur Hugh Clough

The poet Arthur Hugh Clough (c. 1819–1861) was widely admired and copied in his own day, and one of his most famous poems is this pleasant hymn to mammon.

As I sat at the Cafe I said to myself,
They may talk as they please about what they call pelf,
They may sneer as they like about eating and drinking,
But help it I cannot, I cannot help thinking
  How pleasant it is to have money, heigh-ho!
  How pleasant it is to have money.

I sit at my table *en grand seigneur,*
And when I have done, throw a crust to the poor;

Not only the pleasure itself of good living,
But also the pleasure of now and then giving:
    So pleasant it is to have money, heigh-ho!
    So pleasant it is to have money.

They may talk as they please about what they call pelf,
And how one ought never to think of one's self,
How pleasures of thought surpass eating and drinking,
My pleasure of thought is the pleasure of thinking
    How pleasant it is to have money, heigh-ho!
    How pleasant it is to have money.

Texas-Style Ethics

Molly Ivins

*Molly Ivins and P. J. O'Rourke really should get together and
have a drink, because although they are from opposite ends of
the political spectrum—Ivins is a regular columnist for* The
Progressive, *O'Rourke for* The American Spectator—*they
share the same fundamental worldview. Both are too cynical to
be indignant, and would rather laugh at human weakness than
scold it. This essay is taken from Ivins's collection,* Molly Ivins
Can't Say That, Can She?

Jeez, just because Jim Wright is in trouble, now they're saying everybody in Texas politics is a crook. David Broder wrote a
column saying Jim Wright is just a product of his environment,
and everybody knows Lyndon Johnson was outrageous, and
now they've taken to quoting the old saw about how an honest

man in the Texas Legislature is one who stays bought. Our name is mud.

Actually, the criterion for being considered an honest politician in Texas is as follows: If you can't take their money, drink their whiskey, screw their women, and vote against 'em anyway, you don't belong in Texas politics.

The late Woody Bean of El Paso, one of our more memorable pols, used to tell about the time he had a client who had stuck up a grocery store. The perpetrator was inept and the law was hot on his heels right after the heist, so he ditched the loot in a brown paper bag (double-bagged for safety) by an oil well out in the country. He was then apprehended. Bean interviewed him at the local hoosegow and asked, "Son, what'd you do with the money?" The perp gave detailed directions to the boodle, and Bean promptly went and found it and helped himself to a generous fee. As he drove away he said to himself, "Woodrow Wilson Bean, you are skatin' on the thin edge of ethics."

Some of Bean's friends recall him adding, "Woodrow Wilson Bean, ethics is for young lawyers."

I wouldn't say our public servants here in the Great State are without ethics. Governor Bill Clements, when asked why he had repeatedly lied about the Southern Methodist University football scandal, replied reasonably enough, "Well, there was never a Bible in the room."

State Senator Bill ("the Bull of the Brazos") Moore once defended himself against the charge that he would personally profit from a bill he was backing by saying, "I'd just make a bit of money, I wouldn't make a whole lot."

One official with a colorful past felt so honored upon finding himself elected to statewide office that he called his staff together and said, "Boys, stealin's out."

House Speaker Gib Lewis recently found himself under attack because the Parks and Wildlife Department has been stocking his ranches with deer, elk, turkey, and bass without charging him for it. Lewis felt the complaints were unfair. "I have been helping Parks and Wildlife for seventeen years," he explained. "If they owe anyone a favor, they owe me a favor."

Lewis is not a crook; he just has the ethical sensitivity of a walnut. When he was first elected, he forgot to put some stuff on his financial-disclosure statement—a little oil well, a little airplane, a little bidness he happens to be in with some lobbyist friends. He explained that he ran out of room on the paper.

Lewis did make a mistake one time: He went to Ruidoso to watch the horseracing and let some horseracing lobbyists pay for the trip. Caught hell. So the next time he took a trip, to play golf at Pebble Beach, California, he let the taxpayers pay for it. Caught hell for that, too. So the next time he took a trip, he carefully pointed out to the press that it was not paid for by lobbyists and it was not paid for by the taxpayers: He was going as guest of the government of South Africa. Hunting is Gib Lewis's passion, and his office is covered with the stuffed and mounted heads of the assorted endangered species that he has knocked off over the years. His four-year-old granddaughter was recently in the office and stood solemnly looking at an Indian war bonnet that also graces the room. "When did you shoot the Indian, Grandpa?" she inquired.

Sid Richardson, the late Fort Worth oilman, once said to John Connally, "I'm gonna put you in the way to make a little money, John." And that's the way it has always been done in Texas. The rising politician is cut in on deals. The deals are legitimate, the profits are legitimate. It's just that the pol is never asked to put up money—his collateral is the value of his cut. When and whether there is a quid pro quo for this bidness opportunity is between the donor, the donee, and God.

I know a number of pols I count as honest who never did anything in return for such favors. Is it any ranker than getting a large compaign contribution from someone with a special interest in legislation? For virtue, try Minnesota.

The Pardoner's Tale

Chaucer

The Canterbury Tales *of Geoffrey Chaucer (c. 1343–1400) is a living monument to how much human beings have remained the same over the centuries. If anyone believes that people in the Middle Ages were all pious prudes, he or she should read what the Wife of Bath has to say about her five husbands. In the selection below, taken from the prologue to "The Pardoner's Tale," the priest describes his motives in preaching against avarice.*

"All my preaching is about avarice
and such cursed sins, in order to make them
give freely of their pennies—namely, to me;
for my intention is to win money,
not at all to cast out sins.
I don't care, when they are buried,
if their souls go a-blackberrying!
Certainly, many a sermon
proceeds from an evil intention;
some are intended to please and flatter folk,
To gain advancement through hypocricy,
and some are for vanity, and some for hate.
For when I do not dare to argue any other way,

then I will sting my opponent smartly with my tongue
in preaching, so that he can't escape
being falsely defamed, if he
has offended my brethren or me.
For, though I don't tell his proper name,
People will easily know it is he
by signs and other circumstances.
Thus I repay folk that displease us;
thus I spit out my venom under the color
of holiness, to seem holy and true.

But I shall explain my intention briefly:
I preach for no cause but covetousness.
Therefore my theme is still, and ever was,
'Radix malorum est cupiditas.'
Thus I can preach against the same vice
which I practice, and that is avarice.
But though I myself am guilty of that sin,
yet I can make other folk turn
from avarice, and repent sorely.
But that is not my principal intention.
I preach for no reason except covetousness:
but that ought to be enough of this matter.

Then I give them many instances
from old stories of long ago:
for ignorant people love old tales;
such things they can easily repeat and remember.
What! Do you think that while I can preach
and win gold and silver for my teaching,
that I will intentionally live in poverty?
No, no, I certainly never considered that!
For I will preach and beg in various lands;
I will not labor with my hands,
or live by making baskets

in order to keep from being an idle beggar.
I don't want to imitate any of the apostles;
I want to have money, wool, cheese, and wheat,
even if it is given by the poorest page,
or the poorest widow in a village,
although her children die of starvation.
No! I will drink liquor of the vine
and have a jolly wench in every town.
But listen, my lords, in conclusion;
Your wish is for me to tell a tale.
Now that I have had a drink of strong ale,
by God, I hope that I shall tell you something
that shall, with good reason, be to your liking.
For although I am myself a very vicious man,
yet I can tell you a moral tale,
which I am accustomed to preach for profit.
Now hold your peace, I will begin my tale."

Volpone

Ben Jonson

*Ben Jonson (c. 1572–1637) was regarded in his day as the most
brilliant playwright England had yet produced. In the selection
below from* Volpone, *Jonson expressed in a few deft lines the
true object of human worship, from the days of the golden calf
to today.*

Act One
(Volpone's house.)
(Volpone in a large bed. Enter MOSCA. VOLPONE *awakes.)*

VOLPONE: Good morning to the day; and next, my gold! Open
the shrine, that I may see my saint.

(MOSCA *draws a curtain, revealing piles of gold.*)

Hail the world's soul, and mine! More glad than is
The teeming earth to see the longed-for sun
Peep through the horns of the celestial Ram,
Am I, to view thy splendour darkening his;
That lying here, amongst my other hoards,
Show'st like a flame by night, or like the day
Struck out of chaos, when all darkness fled
Unto the centre. O, thou son of Sol
(But brighter than thy father) let me kiss,
With adoration, thee, and every relic
Of sacred treasure in this blessed room.
Well did wise poets by thy glorious name
Title that age which they would have the best,
Thou being the best of things, and far transcending
All style of joy in children, parents, friends,
Or any other waking dream on earth.
Thy looks when they go to Venus did ascribe,
They should have giv'n her twenty thousand Cupids,
Such are thy beauties and our loves! Dear saint,
Riches, the dumb god that giv'st all men tongues,
That canst do nought, and yet mak'st men do all things;
The price of souls; even hell, with thee to boot,
Is made worth heaven! Thou art virtue, fame,
Honour, and all things else. Who can get thee,
He shall be noble, valiant, honest, wise—
MOSCA: And what he will, sir. Riches are in fortune
A greater good than wisdom is in nature.

VOLPONE: True, my beloved Mosca. Yet, I glory
 More in the cunning purchase of my wealth
 Than in the glad possession, since I gain
 No common way: I use no trade, no venture.

Lines Indited with All
The Depravity of Poverty

Ogden Nash

Ogden Nash (c. 1902–1971) was one of the more financially successful poets of the twentieth century, all things considered. But he knew what it was like to be broke, as the lines below attest.

One way to be very happy is to be very rich
For then you can buy orchids by the quire and bacon by
    the flitch.
And yet at the same time
People don't mind if you only tip them a dime.
Because it's very funny
But somehow if you're rich enough you can get away
    with spending water like money
While if you're not rich you can spend in one evening
    your salary for the year
And everybody will just stand around and jeer.
If you are rich you don't have to think twice about
    buying a judge or a horse,
Or a lower instead of an upper, or a new suit, or a
    divorce,
And you never have to say When,

And you can sleep every morning until nine or ten,
All of which
Explains why I should like very, very much to be very,
    very rich.

The Inferno

Dante

Dante Alighieri (c. 1265–1321) had a sick, twisted sense of humor that should appeal to most of the readers of this book. His favorite pastime was to put all of his most bitter enemies, and a few in-laws, into various torture pits in hell. I've remembered this passage from The Inferno *all of my adult life. You'll see why.*

Thus we descended the dark scarp of Hell
to which all the evil of the Universe
comes home at last, into the Fourth Great Circle

and ledge of the abyss. O Holy Justice,
who could relate the agonies I saw!
What guilt is man that he can come to this?

Just as the surge Charybdis hurls to sea
crashes and breaks upon its countersurge,
so these shades dance and crash eternally.

Here, too, I saw a nation of lost souls,
far more than were above: they strained their chests
against enormous weights, and with mad howls

rolled them at one another. Then in haste
they rolled them back, one party shouting out:
"Why do you hoard?" and the other: "Why do you
    waste?"

So back around that ring they puff and blow,
each faction to its course, until they reach
opposite sides, and screaming as they go

the madmen turn and start their weights again
to crash against the maniacs. And I,
watching, felt my heart contract with pain.

"Master," I said, "what people can these be?
And all those tonsured ones there on our left—
is it possible they all were of the clergy?"

And he: "In the first life beneath the sun
they were so skewed and squinteyed in their minds
their misering or extravagance mocked all reason.

The voice of each clamors its own excess
when lust meets lust at the two points of the circle
where opposite guilts meet in their wretchedness.

These tonsured wraiths of greed were priests indeed,
and popes and cardinals, for it is in these
the weed of avarice sows its rankest seed."

And I to him: "Master, among this crew
surely I should be able to make out
the fallen image of some soul I knew."

And he to me: "This is a lost ambition.
In their sordid lives they labored to be blind,
and now their souls have dimmed past recognition.

All their eternity is to butt and bray:
one crew will stand tight-fisted, the other stripped
of its very hair at the bar of Judgment Day.

Hoarding and squandering wasted all their light
and brought them screaming to this brawl of wraiths.
You need no words of mine to grasp their plight.

Now may you see the fleeting vanity
of the goods of Fortune for which men tear down
all that they are, to build a mockery.

Not all the gold that is or ever was
under the sky could buy for one of these
exhausted souls the fraction of a pause."

Los Angeles Days

Joan Didion

*The essayist and novelist Joan Didion moved to New York City
in the early 1990s, but she is best known as a chronicler of Los
Angeles and its burnt-out dreamers. The essay below comes
from her collection,* After Henry, *and is certainly apropos of
our topic.*

This entire question of houses and what they were worth (and what they should be worth, and what it meant when the roof over someone's head was also his or her major asset) was, during the spring and summer of 1988, understandably more on the local mind than it perhaps should have been, which was one reason why a certain house then under construction just west of the Los Angeles Country Club became the focus of considerable attention, and of emotions usually left dormant on the west side of Los Angeles. The house was that being built by the television producer ("Dynasty", "Loveboat", "Fantasy Island") Aaron Spelling and his wife Candy at the corner of Mapleton and Club View in Holmby Hills, on six acres the Spellings had bought in 1983, for $10,250,000, from Patrick Frawley, the chairman of Schick.

At the time of the purchase there was already a fairly impressive house on the property, a house once lived in by Bing Crosby, but the Spellings, who had become known for expansive domestic gestures (crossing the country in private railroad cars, for example, and importing snow to Beverly Hills for their children's Christmas parties), had decided that the Crosby/Frawley house was what is known locally as teardown. The progress of the replacement, which was rising from the only residential site I have ever seen with a two-story contractor's office and a sign reading CONSTRUCTION AREA: HARD HATS REQUIRED, became over the next several months not just a form of popular entertainment but, among inhabitants of a city without much common experience, a unifying, even a political, idea.

At first the project was identified, on the kind of site sign usually reserved for office towers in progress, as "THE MANOR"; later "THE MANOR" was modified to what seemed, given the resemblance of the structure to a resort Hyatt, the slightly nutty discretion of "594 SOUTH MAPLETON DRIVE." It was said that the structure ("house" seemed not entirely to cover it) would have 56,500 square feet. It was said that the interior plan would include a bowling alley, and 560 square feet of extra closet space, balconied between the second and the attic floors. It was said, by the owner, that such was the mass of the steel frame construction that to break up the foundation alone would take a demolition crew six months, and cost from four to five million dollars.

Within a few months the site itself had become an established attraction, and evening drive-bys were enlivened by a skittish defensiveness on the part of the guards, who would switch on the perimeter floods and light up the steel girders and mounded earth like a prison yard. The *Los Angeles Times* and *Herald Examiner* published periodic reports on and rumors about the job ("Callers came out of the woodwork yesterday in the wake of our little tale about Candy Spelling having the foundation of her $45-million mansion-in-progress lowered because she didn't want to see the Robinson's department store sign from where her bed-to-be was to sit"), followed by curiously provocative corrections, or "denials," from Aaron Spelling. "The only time Candy sees the Robinson's sign is when she's shopping" was one correction that got everyone's attention, but in many ways the most compelling was this: "They say we have an Olympic-sized swimming pool. Not true. There's no gazebo, no guesthouse . . . When people go out to dinner, unless they talk about their movies, they have nothing else to talk about, so they single out Candy."

In that single clause, "unless they talk about their movies", there was hidden a great local truth, and the inchoate heart of the matter: this house was, in the end, that of a television producer, and people who make movies did not, on the average evening, have dinner with people who make television. People who make television had most of the money, but people who make movies had most of the status, and believed themselves the keepers of the community's unspoken code, of the rules, say, about what constituted excess on the housing front. This was a distinction usually left tacit, but the fact of the Spelling house was making people say things out loud. "There are people in this town worth hundreds of millions of dollars," Richard Zanuck, one of the most successful motion picture producers in the business, once said to my husband, "and they can't get a table at Chasen's." This was a man whose father had run a studio and who had himself run a studio, and his bewilderment was that of someone who had uncovered an anomaly in the wheeling of the stars.

Rabbit Is Rich

John Updike

There is a large portion of the American reading populace which has grown old, through a succession of novels from Rabbit, Run *through* Rabbit at Rest, *with John Updike's quirky character Rabbit Angstrom. In our selection, taken from* Rabbit Is Rich, *Rabbit has finally made it into the big money as the owner of a car dealership—and, as with most things for Updike and Angstrom, wealth carries with it a distinctly sexual component.*

When Janice comes back from the bathroom naked and damp inside her terrycloth robe, he has locked their bedroom door and arranged himself in his underpants on the bed. He calls in a husky and insinuating voice, "Hey, Janice. Look. I bought us something today."

Her dark eyes are glazed from all that drinking and parenting downstairs; she took the shower to help clear her head. Slowly her eyes focus on his face, which must show an intensity of pleasure that puzzles her.

He tugs open the sticky drawer and is himself startled to see the two tinted cylinders sliding toward him, still upright, still there. He would have thought something so dense with preciousness would broadcast signals bringing burglars like dogs to a bitch in heat. He lifts one roll out and places it in Janice's hand; her arm dips with the unexpected weight, and her robe, untied, falls open. Her thin brown used body is more alluring in this lapsed sheath of rough bright cloth than a girl's; he wants to reach in, to where the shadows keep the damp fresh.

"What is it, Harry?" she asks, her eyes widening.

"Open it," he tells her, and when she fumbles too long at the transparent tape holding on the toilet-seat-shaped little lid he pries it off for her with big fingernails. He removes the wad of tissue paper and spills out upon the quilted bedspread the fifteen Krugerrand. Their color is redder than gold in his mind had been. "Gold," he whispers, holding up close to her face, paired in his palm, two coins, showing the two sides, the profile of some old Boer on one and a kind of antelope on the other. "Each of these is worth about three hundred sixty dollars," he tells her. "Don't tell your mother or Nelson or anybody."

She does seem bewitched, taking one into her fingers. Her nails scratch his palm as she lifts the coin off. Her brown eyes pick up flecks of yellow. "Is it all right?" Janice asks. "Where on earth did you get them?"

"A new place on Weiser across from the peanut store that sells precious metals, buys and sells. It was simple. All you got to do is produce a certified check within twenty-four hours after they quote you a price. They guarantee to buy them back at the going rate any time, so all you lose is their six per cent commission and the sales tax, which at the rate gold is going up I'll have made back by next week. Here. I bought two stacks. Look." He takes the other thrillingly hefty cylinder from the drawer and undoes the lid and spills those fifteen antelopes slippingly upon the bedspread, thus doubling the riches displayed. The spread is a lightweight Pennsylvania Dutch quilt, small rectangular patches sewed together by patient biddies, graded from pale to dark to form a kind of dimensional effect, of four large boxes having a lighter and darker side. He lies down upon its illusion and places a Krugerrand each in the sockets of his eyes. Through the chill red pressure of the gold he hears Janice say, "My God. I thought only the government could have gold. Don't you need a license or anything?"

"Just the bucks. Just the fucking bucks, Wonder Woman."

Blind, he feels amid the pure strangeness of the gold his prick firming up and stretching the fabric of his Jockey shorts.

"Harry. How much did you spend?"

He wills her to lift down the elastic of his underpants and suck, suck until she gags. When she fails to read his mind and do this, he removes the coins and gazes up at her, a dead man reborn and staring. No coffin dark greets his open eyes, just his wife's out-of-focus face, framed in dark hair damp and stringy from the shower and fringy across the forehead so that Mamie Eisenhower comes to mind. "Eleven thousand five hundred more or less," he answers. "Honey, it was just sitting in the savings account drawing a lousy six per cent. At only six per cent these days you're losing money, inflation's running about twelve. The beauty of gold is, it loves bad news. As the dollar sinks, gold goes up. All the Arabs are turning their dollars into gold. Webb Murkett told me all about it, the day you wouldn't come to the club."

She is still examining the coin, stroking its subtle relief, when he wants her attention to turn to him. He hasn't had a hard-on just blossom in his pants since he can't remember when. Lotty Bingaman days. "It's pretty," Janice admits. "Should you be supporting the South Africans though?"

"Why not, they're making jobs for the blacks, mining the stuff. The advantage of the Krugerrand, the girl at this fiscal alternatives place explained, is it weighs one troy ounce exactly and is easier to deal with. You can buy Mexican pesos if you want, or that little Canadian maple leaf, though there she said it's so fine the gold dust comes off on your hands. Also I liked the look of that deer on the back. Don't you?"

"I do. It's exciting," Janice confesses, at last looking at him, where he lies tumescent amid scattered gold. "Where are we going to keep them?" she asks. Her tongue sneaks forward in thought, and rests on her lower lip. He loves her when she tries to think.

"In your great big cunt," he says, and pulls her down by the lapels of her rough robe. Out of deference to those around them in the house—Ma Springer just a wall's thickness away, her television a dim rumble, the Korean War turned into a joke—Janice tries to suppress her cries as he strips the terrycloth from her slippery body and the coins on the bedspread come in contact with her skin. The cords of her throat tighten; her face darkens as she strains in the grip of indignation and glee. His underwear off, the overhead light still on, his prick up like a jutting piece of pink wreckage, he calms her into lying motionless and places a Krugerrand on each nipple, one on her navel, and a number on her pussy, enough to mask the hair with a triangle of unsteady coins overlapping like snake scales. If she laughs and her belly moves the whole construction will collapse. Kneeling at her hips, Harry holds a Krugerrand by the edge as if to insert it in a slot. "No!" Janice protests, loud enough to twitch Ma Springer awake through the wall, loud enough to jar loose the coins so some do spill between her legs. He hushes her mouth with his and then moves his mouth south, across the desert, oasis to oasis, until he comes to the ferny jungle, which his wife lays open to him with a humoring toss of her thighs. A kind of interest compounds as, seeing red, spilled gold pressing on his forehead, he hunts with his tongue for her clitoris. He finds what he thinks is the right rhythm but doesn't feel it take; he thinks the bright overhead light might be distracting her and risks losing his hard-on in hopping from the bed to switch it off over by the door. Turning then in the half-dark he sees she has turned also, gotten up onto her knees and elbows, a four-legged moonchild of his, her soft cleft ass held high to him in the gloom as her face peeks around one shoulder. He fucks her in this position gently, groaning in the effort of keeping his jism in, letting his thoughts fly far. The pennant race, the recent hike in the factory base price of Corollas. He fondles her underside's defenseless slack flesh, his own belly massive and bearing down. Her back looks so breakable and brave and narrow—the long dent of its spine, the cross-bar of pallor left by her bathing-suit bra. Behind him his bare feet release a faraway sad odor. Coins jingle, slithering in toward their knees, into the depressions their interlocked weights make in the mattress. He taps her ass and asks, "Want to turn over?"

"Uh-huh." As an afterthought: "Want me to sit on you first?"

"Uh-huh." As an afterthought: "Don't make me come."

Harry's skin is bitten by ice when he lies on his back. The coins: worse than toast crumbs. So wet he feels almost nothing,

Janice straddles him, vast and globular in the patchy light that filters from the streetlight through the copper beech. She picks up a stray coin and places it glinting in her eye, as a monocle. Lording it over him, holding him captive, she grinds her wet halves around him; self to self, bivalve to tuber, this is what it comes to. "Don't come," she says, alarmed enough so that her mock-monocle drops to his tense abdomen with a thud. "Better get underneath," he grunts. Her body then seems thin and black, silhouetted by the scattered circles, reflecting according to their tilt. Gods bedded among stars, he gasps in her ear, then she in his.

After this payoff, regaining their breaths, they can count in the semi-dark only twenty-nine Krugerrands on the rumpled bedspread, its landscape of ridged green patches. He turns on the overhead light. It hurts their eyes. By its harshness their naked skins seem also rumpled. Panic encrusts Harry's drained body; he does not rest until, naked on his knees on the rug, a late strand of spunk looping from his reddened glans, he finds, caught in the crack between the mattress and the bed side-rail, the precious thirtieth.

In Praise of Debtors

Rabelais

You can't top François Rabelais (c. 1494–1553) for absurd satire. Here he has one of Pantagruel's numerous interlocutors explain why debtors are one of the most generous benefactors of mankind.

"But," asked Pantagruel, "when will you be out of debt?"

"At the Greek Kalends," replied Panurge, "when all the world will be content, and you will be your own heir. God forbid that I should be debt-free. For then I shouldn't find anyone to lend me a penny. A man who leaves no leaven overnight will never raise the dough in the morning. Always owe something to someone. Then there will be prayers continually offered up to God to grant you a long and happy life. Through fear of losing his money, your creditor will always speak well of you in all company. He will always gain new creditors for you, so that by borrowing from them you may pay him, and fill his ditch with other men's soil. When, by the Druidical law of ancient Gaul, slaves, servants, and attendants were burnt alive at the funerals of their lords and masters, had they not fine reason to fear the deaths of these same lords and masters, since they must die with them? Did they not continuously pray to their great god Mercury, and Dis, the father of wealth, to preserve their health for long years? Were they not careful to serve and look after them well? For together they could live, at least till death.

"Believe me, your creditors will pray to God for your life and fear your death even more fervently and devotedly, since they are fonder of the open palm than of the whole right arm, and love pennies better than their lives. Remember the usurers of Landerousse, who hanged themselves not long ago when they saw the prices of wine and corn falling and the good times returning."

As Pantagruel gave no answer, Panurge continued, "Lord bless me, now I come to think of it, when you twit me with my debts and creditors you're challenging my trump card. Why, by that achievement alone I thought I had earned respect, reverence, and awe. For notwithstanding the universal opinion of philosophers, who say that out of nothing nothing is made—

although I possessed nothing and had no prime substance, in this I was a maker and creator.

"And what had I created? So many good, fine creditors. Creditors are fine, good creatures—and I'll maintain that to everything short of the stake. The man who lends nothing is an ugly, wicked creature, created by the great ugly devil of hell. And what had I made? Debts. Rare and excellent things! Debts, I say, exceeding in number the syllables resulting from the combination of all the consonants with the vowels; a number once computed by the noble Xenocrates. If you judge of the perfection of debtors by the multitude of their creditors, you will not be far out in your practical arithmetic.

"Don't you suppose I'm pleased when, every morning, I see these debtors around me so humble, serviceable, and profuse in their bows? And when I notice that if I show a pleasanter face and a warmer welcome to one than to another, the fellow imagines he will be the first to get a settlement, that his payment will be first in date, and deduces from my smile that he will be paid cash? Then I seem to be playing God in the Saumur Passion-play, in the company of his angels and cherubim. These are my fawners, my parasites, my saluters, my sayers of 'Good day,' my perpetual speechifiers.

"I truly used to think that debts were the material of that hill of heroic virtues described by Hesiod, on which I hold the first degree of my licentiate, and towards which all human beings seem to aim and aspire, but which few climb owing to the difficulty of the path. For I see the whole world to-day in a fervent desire and vehement hunger to make fresh debts and creditors."

Three

...

SLOTH

"Death is the end of life; ah, why
Should life all labor be?"

—*Alfred, Lord Tennyson,*
The Lotus-Eaters

"Thus *Belial* with words cloth'd in reason's garb
Counsell'd ignoble ease, and peaceful sloth."

—*Milton,* Paradise Lost, *ii, 226*

O f all the many neglected vices of our age, none is as totally ignored as sloth.

There was a time when humanity understood and appreciated sloth—but that was long ago, in an era when lounging about, being a no-account, lazy, fit-for-nothin' bum, was a plausible calling.

In ages past, sloth resulted in a lower standard of living, perhaps, but if a man had few wants, and even fewer expectations, he could get by nicely. In our own day, the costs of modern living have multiplied at such a rate that sloth no longer seems like a vice: it seems more like suicide.

A slothful man or woman today—someone who, say, prefers only to work one or two days per week, so as not to let gainful employment interfere with fishing—must be cunning as well as lazy. What with the costs of medical care, housing, taxes, cable TV, and so on, a lazy man or woman has to worry more than is fitting. The only alternative open to a lazy person is to go into politics and feed off the public trough; but recently mean-spirited do-gooders have been insisting that politicians actually do a little work—which removes the attraction of public service in the first place.

It's difficult to determine precisely how we have arrived at such a sorry state, in which sloth is no longer considered an option even for the lowliest people in society. Even criminals, if you can believe this, no longer feel that they can be slothful, and if you can't lounge around in prison, where can you? Today, a typical prisoner will spend virtually all of his time in the joint lifting weights, studying law books, planning robberies, and performing other forms of useful activity that, in a more civilized age, would have been considered anathema for any self-respecting criminal. The whole idea behind crime, after all, is avoiding having to work.

The ancients, of course, had a saner view of sloth: They were all for it!

The Bible records that Adam and Eve, humanity's first role models, lounged around naked all day in their garden—an activity that would be frowned upon today by most priests, parsons, and aerobics instructors. Because of a little culinary indiscretion on their part, however, God punished Adam and Eve and declared that, from that moment forward, they and their descendants would have to—horror of horrors—work for a living.

But notice: work was considered a *punishment,* not something that should be sought out and actively encouraged. The Greeks and most ancient peoples recognized this and avoided work as much as possible. The noble Socrates, after all—the father of Western civilization—spent most of his time lounging around Athens corrupting the youth or having drinking contests with other Sophists. Socrates knew the value of sloth. According to historian Juliet Schor, the ancient Athenians had sixty holidays a year and the ancient Romans designated 109 of 355 days as *nefasti,* or "unlawful for judicial and political business." By the mid-fourth century, she says, "the number of *feriae publicae* (public festival days) reached 175."

Throughout the centuries, in other words, people worked

only as much as they had to in order to stay warm, well-fed, and supplied with sufficient quantities of ale. As we can tell from such histories as *The Canterbury Tales* or Rabelais's *Gargantua and Pantagruel,* ordinary people spent the rest of their time seducing each other's spouses, feasting, going on pilgrimages, jousting, and generally having a good time. The attitude of the ages was best expressed by Charles Lamb (c. 1775–1834). He wrote, in a letter to Barton:

> Who first invented Work—and tied the free
> And holy-day rejoicing spirit down
> To the ever-haunting importunity
> Of business, in the green fields, and the town—
> To plough—loom—anvil—spade—and, oh, most sad,
> To this dry drudgery of the desk's dead wood?

Then we come to the so-called modern age.

Somewhere along the line, modern men and women got it into their heads that the goal of a healthy and happy life was to stay as busy as possible. Thus, once the basic necessities of life were provided for, modern people, instead of going fishing like all the generations before them, began thinking up new occupations to eat up their time. Thus, we now have entire industries that do nothing except figure out new ways to keep people overscheduled and sweating at various "leisure activities"—from the latest aerobics craze to refurbishing unfixable "fixer-uppers."

Moreover, we now have so many useless gadgets and so-called services—from automatic toast-butterers to medical insurance for goldfish—that we can now plausibly maintain that we need to work twenty-four hours a day in order to pay for everything.

This is silly.

The time has come for a national crusade for sloth, for bringing back the ancient vice of laziness.

What the world needs now more than anything else is a good long nap.

The selections below celebrate the vice of sloth. They illustrate that earlier ages knew the importance of avoiding work as much as possible in order to pursue other, more satisfying pastimes . . . such as life.

The Adventures of Tom Sawyer
Mark Twain

Mark Twain (c. 1835–1910) was the pseudonym for Samuel Langhorne Clemens, perhaps America's greatest humorist and one of her most original novelists. If there were ever a man who appreciated vice and the underside of human nature, it was Twain. In the selection here, a famous scene from The Adventures of Tom Sawyer, *first published in 1872, Twain demonstrates his keen insight into human nature.*

Saturday morning was come, and all the summer world was bright and fresh, and brimming with life. There was a song in every heart; and if the heart was young the music issued at the lips. There was cheer in every face and a spring in every step. The locust trees were in bloom and the fragrance of the blossoms filled the air. Cardiff Hill, beyond the village and above it, was green with vegetation; and it lay just far enough away to seem a delectable land, dreamy, reposeful, and inviting.

♫loth
· · · · ·

Tom appeared on the sidewalk with a bucket of whitewash and a long-handled brush. He surveyed the fence, and all gladness left him and a deep melancholy settled down upon his spirit. Thirty yards of board fence nine feet high. Life to him seemed hollow, and existence but a burden. Sighing he dipped his brush and passed it along the topmost plank; repeated the operation; did it again; compared the insignificant whitewashed streak with the far-reaching continent of unwhitewashed fence, and sat down on a tree-box discouraged. Jim came skipping out at the gate with a tin pail, and singing, "Buffalo Gals." Bringing water from the town pump had always been hateful in Tom's eyes before, but now it did not strike him so. He remembered that there was company at the pump. White, mulatto, and Negro boys and girls were always there waiting their turns, resting, trading playthings, quarreling, fighting, skylarking. And he remembered that, although the pump was only a hundred and fifty yards off, Jim never got back with a bucket of water under an hour—and even then somebody generally had to go after him. Tom said:

"Say, Jim, I'll fetch the water if you'll whitewash some."

Jim shook his head and said:

"Can't, Marse Tom. Ole missis, she tole me I got to go an' git dis water an' not stop foolin' round' wid anybody. She say she spec' Marse Tom gwine to ax me to white wash, an' so she tole me go'long an' 'tend to my own business—she 'lowed she'd 'tend to de whitewashin'."

"Oh, never you mind what she said, Jim. That's the way she always talks. Gimme the bucket—I won't be gone only a minute. *She* won't ever know."

"Oh, I dasn't, Marse Tom. Ole missis she'd take an' tar de head off'n me. 'Deed she would."

"*She!* She never licks anybody—whacks 'em over the head

109

with her thimble—and who cares for that, I'd like to know. She talks awful, but talk don't hurt—anyways it don't if she don't cry. Jim, I'll give you a marvel. I'll give you a white alley."

Jim began to waver.

"White alley, Jim! And it's a bully taw."

"My! Dat's a mighty gay marvel, I tell you! But Marse Tom, I's powerful 'fraid ole missis—"

"And besides, if you will I'll show you my sore toe."

Jim was only human—this attraction was too much for him. He put down his pail, took the white alley, and bent over the toe with absorbing interest while the bandage was being unwound. In another moment he was flying down the street with his pail and a tingling rear, Tom was whitewashing with vigor, and Aunt Polly was retiring from the field with a slipper in her hand and triumph in her eye.

But Tom's energy did not last. He began to think of the fun he had planned for this day, and his sorrows multiplied. Soon the free boys would come tripping along on all sorts of delicious expeditions, and they would make a world of fun of him for having to work—the very thought of it burnt him like fire. He got out his worldly wealth and examined it—bits of toys, marbles, and trash; enough to buy an exchange for *work,* maybe, but not half enough to buy so much as half an hour of pure freedom. So he returned his straitened means to his pocket and gave up the idea of trying to buy the boys. At this dark and hopeless moment an inspiration burst upon him! Nothing less than a great, magnificent inspiration.

He took up his brush and went tranquilly to work. Ben Rogers hove in sight presently—the very boy, of all boys, whose ridicule he had been dreading. Ben's gait was the hop-skip-and-jump—proof enough that his heart was light and his anticipations high. He was eating an apple, and giving a long, melodious whoop, at intervals, followed by a deep-toned ding-dong-dong, ding-dong-dong, for he was personating a steamboat. As he drew near, he slackened speed, took the middle of the street, leaned far over to starboard and rounded too ponderously and with laborious pomp and circumstance—for he was personating the *Big Missouri,* and considered himself to be drawing nine feet of water. He was boat and captain and engine bells combined, so he had to imagine himself standing on his own hurricane deck giving the orders and executing them:

"Stop her, sir! Ting-a-ling-ling!" His arms straightened and stiffened down his sides.

"Set her back on the stabboard! Ting-a-ling-ling! Chow! Ch-chow-wow! Chow!" His right hand, meantime, describing stately circles—for it was representing a forty-foot wheel.

"Let her go back on the labboard! Ting-a-ling-ling! Chow-ch-chow-chow!" The left hand began to describe circles.

"Stop the stabboard! Ting-a-ling-ling! Stop the labboard! Come ahead on the stabbord! Stop her! Let your outside turn over slow! Ting-a-ling-ling! Chow-ow-ow! Get out that head line! *Lively* now! Come—out with your spring line—what're you about there! Take a turn round that stump with the bight of it! Stand by that stage, now—let her go! Done with the engines, sir! Ting-a-ling-ling! *Sh't! s'h't! sh't!*" (trying the gauge cocks).

Tom went on whitewashing—paid no attention to the steamboat. Ben stared a moment and then said:

"Hi-*yi*! *You're* up a stump, ain't you!"

No answer. Tom surveyed his last touch with the eye of an artist, then he gave his brush another gentle sweep and surveyed the result, as before. Ben ranged up alongside of him. Tom's mouth watered for the apple, but he stuck to his work. Ben said:

"Hello, old chap, you got to work, hey?"

Tom wheeled suddenly and said:

"Why, it's you, Ben! I warn't noticing."

"*Say,* I'm going in a-swimming, *I* am. Don't you wish you could? But of course you'd druther *work*—wouldn't you? Course you would!"

Tom contemplated the boy a bit, and said:

"What do you call work?"

"Why, ain't *that* work?"

Tom resumed his whitewashing, and answered carelessly:

"Well, maybe it is, and maybe it ain't. All I know is, it suits Tom Sawyer."

"Oh, come, now, you don't mean to let on that you *like* it?"

The brush continued to move.

"Like it? Well, I don't see why I oughtn't to like it. Does a boy get a chance to whitewash a fence every day?"

That put the thing in a new light. Ben stopped nibbling his apple. Tom swept his brush daintily back and forth—stepped back to note the effect—added a touch here and there—criticized the effect again—Ben watching every move and getting more and more interested, more and more absorbed. Presently he said:

"Say, Tom, let *me* whitewash a little."

Tom considered, was about to consent; but he altered his mind:

"No—no—I reckon it wouldn't hardly do, Ben. You see, Aunt Polly's awful particular about this fence—right here on the street, you know—but if it was the back fence I wouldn't mind and *she* wouldn't. Yes, she's awful particular about this fence; it's got to be done very careful; I reckon there ain't one boy in a thousand, maybe two thousand that can do it the way it's got to be done."

"No—is that so? Oh come, now—lemme just try. Only just a little—I'd let *you,* if you was me, Tom."

Sloth
. . . . .

"Ben, I'd like to, honest Injun; but Aunt Polly—well, Jim wanted to do it, but she wouldn't let him; Sid wanted to do it, and she wouldn't let Sid. Now don't you see how I'm fixed? If you was to tackle this fence and anything was to happen to it—"

"Oh, shucks, I'll be just as careful. Now lemme try. Say—I'll give you the core of my apple."

"Well, here—No, Ben, now don't. I'm afeared—"

"I'll give you *all* of it!"

Tom gave up the brush with reluctance in his face, but alacrity in his heart. And while the late steamer *Big Missouri* worked and sweated in the sun, the retired artist sat on a barrel in the shade close by, dangled his legs, munched his apple, and planned the slaughter of more innocents. There was no lack of material; boys happened along every little while; they came to jeer, but remained to whitewash. By the time Ben was fagged out, Tom had traded the next chance to Billy Fisher for a kite, in good repair; and when he played out, Johnny Miller bought in for a dead rat and a string to swing it with—and so on, and so on, hour after hour. And when the middle of the afternoon came, from being a poor poverty-stricken boy in the morning, Tom was literally rolling in wealth. He had besides the things before mentioned, twelve marbles, part of a jew's-harp, a piece of blue bottle glass to look through, a spool cannon, a key that wouldn't unlock anything, a fragment of chalk, a glass stopper of a decanter, a tin soldier, a couple of tadpoles, six firecrackers, a kitten with only one eye, a brass doorknob, a dog collar—but no dog—the handle of a knife, four pieces of orange peel, and a dilapidated old window sash.

He had had a nice, good, idle time all the while—plenty of company—and the fence had three coats of whitewash on it! If he hadn't run out of whitewash, he would have bankrupted every boy in the village.

Tom said to himself that it was not such a hollow world, after all. He had discovered a great law of human action, without knowing it—namely, that in order to make a man or a boy covet a thing, it is only necessary to make the thing difficult to attain. If he had been a great and wise philosopher, like the writer of this book, he would now have comprehended that Work consists of whatever a body is *obliged* to do and that Play consists of whatever a body is not obliged to do. And this would help him to understand why constructing artificial flowers or performing on a treadmill is work, while rolling tenpins or climbing Mont Blanc is only amusement. There are wealthy gentlemen in England who drive four-horse passenger coaches twenty or thirty miles on a daily line, in the summer, because the privilege costs them considerable money; but if they were offered wages for the service, that would turn it into work and then they would resign.

The boy mused awhile over the substantial change which had taken place in his worldly circumstances, and then wended toward headquarters to report.

Pretty Halcyon Days

Ogden Nash

Ogden Nash (c. 1902–1971) is most famous for his doggerel verse, which he published first in The New Yorker *and then later in books. This is one of my favorites.*

> How pleasant to sit on the beach,
> On the beach, on the sand in the sun,
> With ocean galore within reach,

♪loth
· · · · ·

And nothing at all to be done!
No letters to answer,
No bills to be burned.
No work to be shirked,
No cash to be earned.
It is pleasant to sit on the beach
With nothing at all to be done.

How pleasant to look at the ocean,
Democratic and damp; indiscriminate;
It fills me with noble emotion
To think I am able to swim in it.
To lave in the wave,
Majestic and chilly,
Tomorrow I crave;
But today it is silly.
It is pleasant to look at the ocean;
Tomorrow, perhaps I shall swim in it.

How pleasant to gaze at the sailors,
As their sailboats they manfully sail
With the vigor of vikings and whalers
In the days of the viking and whale.
They sport on the brink
Of the shad and the shark;
If it's windy they sink;
If it isn't, they park.
It is pleasant to gaze at the sailors,
To gaze without having to sail.

How pleasant the salt anaesthetic
Of the air and the sand and the sun;
Leave the earth to the strong and athletic,

And the sea to adventure upon.
But the sun and the sand
No contractor can copy;
We lie in the land
Of the lotus and poppy;
We vegetate, calm and aesthetic,
On the beach, on the sand, in the sun.

On Lying in Bed

G. K. Chesterton

G[ilbert] K[eith] Chesterton (c. 1874–1936) was perhaps the foremost Christian apologist of his age. Primarily a journalist, humorist, and illustrator, he also wrote volumes of light-hearted, often hilarious essays, poetry, biographies, plays, and a succession of enormously popular Father Brown mystery novels. Chesterton is best known for his paradoxes: his favorite trick was to examine some particularly inflexible piece of modern dogma and to show how, in fact, the opposite is the case. In the selection below, Chesterton looks at the unexamined dogma that it is best to rise early in the morning and not waste any time lying about in bed.

Lying in bed would be an altogether perfect and supreme experience if only one had a coloured pencil long enough to draw on the ceiling. This, however, is not generally a part of the domestic apparatus on the premises. I think myself that the thing might be managed with several pails of Aspinall and a broom. Only if one worked in a really sweeping and masterly way, and laid on the colours in great washes, it might drop down again on one's face in floods of rich and mingled colour like some strange fairy rain; and that would have its disadvantages. I am afraid it would be necessary to stick to black and white in this form of artistic composition. To that purpose, indeed, the white ceiling would be of the greatest possible use; in fact it is the only use I think of a white ceiling being put to.

But for the beautiful experiment of lying in bed I might never have discovered it. For years I have been looking for some blank spaces in a modern house to draw on. Paper is much too small for any really allegorical design; as Cyrano de Bergerac says: "Il me faut des géants." But when I tried to find these fine clear spaces in the modern rooms such as we all live in I was continually disappointed. I found an endless pattern and complication of small objects hung like a curtain of fine links between me and my desire. I examined the walls; I found them to my surprise to be already covered with wall-paper, and I found the wall-paper to be already covered with very uninteresting images, all bearing a ridiculous resemblance to each other. I could not understand why one arbitrary symbol (a symbol apparently entirely devoid of any religious or philosophical significance) should thus be sprinkled all over my nice walls like a sort of small-pox. The Bible must be referring to wall-papers, I think, when it says, 'Use not vain repetitions, as the Gentiles do.' I found the Turkey carpet a mass of unmeaning colours, rather like the Turkish Empire, or like the sweetmeat called Turkish Delight. I do not exactly know what Turkish Delight really is; but I suppose it is Macedonian Massacres. Everywhere that I went with my pencil or my paint brush, I found that others had unaccountably been before me, spoiling the walls, the curtains, and the furniture with their childish and barbaric designs.

Nowhere did I find a really clear space for sketching until this occasion when I prolonged beyond the proper limit the pro-

cess of lying on my back in bed. Then the light of that white
heaven broke upon my vision, that breadth of mere white which
is indeed almost the definition of Paradise, since it means purity
and also means freedom. But alas! like all heavens, now that it is
seen it is found to be unattainable: it looks more austere and
more distant than the blue sky outside the window. For my proposal to paint on it with the bristly end of a broom has been
discouraged—never mind by whom; by a person debarred from
all political rights—and even my minor proposal to put the
other end of the broom into the kitchen fire and turn it into
charcoal has not been conceded. Yet I am certain that it was
from persons in my position that all the original inspiration
came for covering the ceilings of palaces and cathedrals with a
riot of fallen angels or victorious gods. I am sure that it was only
because Michael Angelo was engaged in the ancient and honourable occupation of lying in bed that he ever realised how the
roof of the Sistine Chapel might be made into an awful imitation
of a divine drama that could only be acted in the heavens.

The tone now commonly taken towards the practice of lying
in bed is hypocritical and unhealthy. Of all the marks of modernity that seem to mean a kind of decadence, there is none more
menacing and dangerous than the exaltation of very small and
secondary matters of conduct at the expense of very great and
primary ones, at the expense of eternal ties and tragic human
morality. If there is one thing worse than the modern weakening
of major morals it is the modern strengthening of minor morals.
Thus it is considered more withering to accuse a man of bad
taste than of bad ethics. Cleanliness is not next to godliness
nowadays, for cleanliness is made an essential and godliness is
regarded as an offence. A playwright can attack the institution
of marriage so long as he does not misrepresent the manners of
society, and I have met Ibsenite pessimists who thought it wrong

to take beer but right to take prussic acid. Especially this is so in matters of hygiene; notably such matters as lying in bed. Instead of being regarded, as it ought to be, as a matter of personal convenience and adjustment, it has come to be regarded by many as if it were a part of essential morals to get up early in the morning. It is, upon the whole, part of practical wisdom; but there is nothing good about it or bad about its opposite.

Misers get up early in the morning; and burglars, I am informed, get up the night before. It is the great peril of our society that all its mechanism may grow more fixed while its spirit grows more fickle. A man's minor actions and arrangements ought to be free, flexible, creative; the things that should be unchangeable are his principles, his ideals. But with us the reverse is true; our views change constantly; but our lunch does not change. Now, I should like men to have strong and rooted conceptions, but as for their lunch, let them have it sometimes in the garden, sometimes in bed, sometimes on the roof, sometimes in the top of a tree. Let them argue from the same first principles, but let them do it in a bed, or a boat, or a balloon.

An Apology for Idlers

Robert Louis Stevenson

Robert Louis Stevenson (c. 1850–1894) is not generally considered a humorist but a novelist best known for his adventure stories Kidnapped, Treasure Island, *and* The Strange Case of Dr. Jekyll and Mr. Hyde. *The essay below, however, illustrates another side to Stevenson, and shows him to be a man who can appreciate what life is really all about.*

The greatest difficulty with most subjects is to do them well; therefore, please to remember this is an apology. It is certain that much may be judiciously argued in favour of diligence; only there is something to be said against it, and that is what, on the present occasion, I have to say. To state one argument is not necessarily to be deaf to all others, and that a man has written a book of travels in Montenegro, is no reason why he should never have been to Richmond.

It is surely beyond a doubt that people should be a good deal idle in youth. For though here and there a Lord Macaulay may escape from school honours with all his wits about him, most boys pay so dear for their medals that they never afterwards have a shot in their locker, and begin the world bankrupt. And the same holds true during all the time a lad is educating himself, or suffering others to educate him. It must have been a very foolish old gentleman who addressed Johnson at Oxford in these words: "Young man, ply your book diligently now, and acquire a stock of knowledge; for when years come upon you, you will find that poring upon books will be but an irksome task." The old gentleman seems to have been unaware that many other things besides reading grow irksome, and not a few become impossible, by the time a man has to use spectacles and cannot walk without a stick. Books are good enough in their own way, but they are a mighty bloodless substitute for life. It seems a pity to sit, like the Lady of Shalott, peering into a mirror, with your back turned on all the bustle and glamour of reality. And if a man reads very hard, as the old anecdote reminds us, he will have little time for thoughts.

If you look back on your own education, I am sure it will not be the full, vivid, instructive hours of truantry that you regret; you would rather cancel some lack-lustre periods between sleep and waking in the class. For my own part, I have attended a good many lectures in my time. I still remember that the spinning of a top is a case of Kinetic Stability. I still remember that Emphyteusis is not a disease, nor Stillicide a crime. But though I would not willingly part with such scraps of science, I do not set the same store by them as by certain other odds and ends that I came by in the open street while I was playing truant. This is not the moment to dilate on that mighty place of education, which was the favourite school of Dickens and Balzac, and turns out yearly many inglorious masters in the Science of the Aspects of Life. Suffice it to say this: if a lad does not learn in the streets, it is because he has no faculty of learning. Nor is the truant always in the streets, for if he prefers, he may go out by the gardened suburbs into the country. He may pitch on some tuft of lilacs over a burn, and some innumerable pipes to the tune of the water on the stones. A bird will sing in the thicket. And there he may fall into a vein of kindly thought, and see things in a new perspective. Why, if this be not education, what is? We may conceive Mr. Worldly Wiseman accosting such an one, and the conversation that should thereupon ensue:—

"How now, young fellow, what dost thou here?"

"Truly, sir, I take mine ease."

"Is not this the hour of the class? and should'st thou not be plying thy Book with diligence, to the end thou mayest obtain knowledge?"

"Nay, but thus also I follow after Learning, by your leave."

"Learning, quotha! After what fashion, I pray thee? Is it mathematics?"

"No, to be sure."

"Is it metaphysics?"

"Nor that."

"Is it some language?"

"Nay, it is no language."

"Is it a trade?"

"Nor a trade neither."

"Why, then, what is't?"

"Indeed, sir, as a time may soon come for me to go upon Pilgrimage, I am desirous to note what is commonly done by persons in my case, and where are the ugliest Sloughs and Thickets on the Road; as also, what manner of Staff is of the best service. Moreover, I lie here, by this water, to learn by root-of-heart a lesson which my master teaches me to call Peace, or Contentment."

Hereupon Mr. Worldly Wiseman was much commoved with passion, and shaking his cane with a very threatful countenance, broke forth upon this wise: "Learning, quotha!" said he; "I would have all such rogues scourged by the Hangman!"

And so he would go his way, ruffling out his cravat with a crackle of starch, like a turkey when it spread its feathers.

Now this, of Mr. Wiseman's, is the common opinion. A fact is not called a fact, but a piece of gossip, if it does not fall into one of your scholastic categories. An inquiry must be in some acknowledged direction, with a name to go by; or else you are not inquiring at all, only lounging; and the work-house is too good for you. It is supposed that all knowledge is at the bottom of a well, or the far end of a telescope. Saint-Beuve, as he grew older, came to regard all experience as a single great book, in which to study for a few years ere we go hence; and it seemed all one to him whether you should read in Chapter xx., which is the differential calculus, or in Chapter xxxix., which is hearing the band play in the gardens. As a matter of fact, an intelligent person, looking out of his eyes and hearkening in his ears, with a smile on his face all the time, will get more true education than many another in a life of heroic vigils. There is certainly some chill and arid knowledge to be found upon the summits of formal and laborious science; but it is all round about you, and for the trouble of looking, that you will acquire the warm and palpitating facts of life. While others are filling their memory with a lumber of words, one-half of which they will forget before the week be out, your truant may learn some really useful art: to play the fiddle, to know a good cigar, or to speak with ease and opportunity to all varieties of men. Many who have "plied their book diligently," and know all about some one branch or another of accepted lore, come out of the study with an ancient and owl-like demeanour, and prove dry, stockish, and dyspeptic in all the better and brighter parts of life. Many make a large fortune, who remain underbred and pathetically stupid to the last. And meantime there goes the idler, who began life along with them—by your leave, a different picture. He has had time to take care of his health and his spirits; he has been a good deal in the open air, which is the most salutary of all things for both body and mind; and if he has never read the great Book in very recondite places, he has dipped into it and skimmed it over to excellent purpose. Might not the student afford some Hebrew roots, and the business man some of his half-crowns, for a share of the idler's knowledge of life at large, and Art of Living? Nay, and the idler has another and more important quality than these. I mean his wisdom. He who has much looked on at the childish satisfaction of other people in their hobbies, will regard his own with only a very ironical indulgence. He will not be heard among the dogmatists. He will have a great and cool allowance for all sorts of people and opinions. If he finds not out of the way truths, he will identify himself with no very burning falsehood. His way takes him along a by-road, not much frequented, but very even and pleasant, which is called Commonplace Lane, and leads to the Belvedere of Commonsense. Thence he shall command an agreeable, if no very noble prospect; and while others behold the East and West, the Devil and the Sunrise, he will be contentedly aware of a sort of morning hour upon all sublunary things, with an army of shadows running speedily and in many different directions into the great daylight of Eternity. The shadows and the generations, the shrill doctors and the plangent wars, go by into ultimate silence and emptiness; but underneath all this, a man may see, out of the Belvedere windows, much green and peaceful landscape; many firelit parlours; good people laughing, drinking, and making love as they did before the Flood or the French Revolution; and the old shepherd telling his tale under the hawthorn.

A Confederacy of Dunces
John Kennedy Toole

A Confederacy of Dunces is one of the most remarkable and hilarious novels to come out of the 1960s. Its hero, Ignatius J. Reilly, is a self-proclaimed genius and irascible slob in open rebellion against the abominations of modernity, such as rationalism and a nine-to-five job. The author, Toole, died tragically at age thirty-two in 1969.

Mrs. Reilly stood in the hall looking at the DO NOT DISTURB sign printed on a sheet of Big Chief paper and stuck to the door by an old flesh-colored Band-Aid.

"Ignatius, let me in there, boy," she screamed.

"Let you in here?" Ignatius said through the door. "Of course I won't. I am occupied at the moment with an especially succinct passage."

"You let me in."

"You know you are never allowed in here."

Mrs. Reilly pounded at the door.

"I don't know what is happening to you, Mother, but I suspect that you are momentarily deranged. Now that I think of it, I am too frightened to open the door. You may have a knife or a broken wine bottle."

"Open this door, Ignatius."

"Oh, my valve! It is closing!" Ignatius groaned loudly. "Are you satisfied now that you have ruined me for the rest of the evening?"

Mrs. Reilly threw herself against the unpainted wood.

"Well, don't break the door," he said finally and, after a few moments, the bolt slid open.

"Ignatius, what's all this trash on the floor?"

"That is my worldview that you see. It still must be incorporated into a whole, so be careful where you step."

"And all the shutters closed. Ignatius, it's still light outside."

"My being is not without its Proustian elements," Ignatius said from the bed, to which he had quickly returned. "Oh, my stomach."

"It smells terrible in here."

"Well, what did you expect? The human body, when confined, produces certain odors which we tend to forget in this age of deodorants and other perversions. Actually, I find the atmosphere of this room rather comforting. Schiller needed the scent of apples rotting in his desk in order to write. I, too, have my needs. You may remember that Mark Twain preferred to lie supinely in bed while composing those rather dated and boring efforts which contemporary scholars try to prove meaningful. Veneration of Mark Twain is one of the roots of our current intellectual stalemate."

"If I know it was like this, I'd been in here a long time ago."

"I do not know why you are in here *now,* as a matter of fact, or why you have this sudden compulsion to invade my sanctuary. I doubt that it will ever be the same after the trauma of this intrusion by an alien spirit."

"I came to talk to you, boy. Get your face out of them pillows."

"This must be the influence of that ludicrous representative of the law. He seems to have turned you against your own child. By the way, he has left, hasn't he?"

"Yes, and I apologized to him over the way you acted."

"Mother, you are standing on my tablets. Will you please move a little? Isn't it enough that you have destroyed my digestion without destroying the fruits of my brain also?"

"Well, where I'm gonna stand, Ignatius? You want me to get in bed with you?" Mrs. Reilly asked angrily.

"Watch out where you're stepping, please!" Ignatius thundered. "My God, never has anyone been so totally and so literally stormed and besieged. What is it anyway that has driven you in here in this state of complete mania? Could it be the stench of cheap muscatel that is assaulting my nostrils?"

"I made up my mind. You gonna go out and get you a job."

Oh, what low joke was Fortuna playing on him now? Arrest, accident, job. Where would this dreadful cycle ever end?

"I see," Ignatius said calmly. "Knowing that you are congenitally incapable of arriving at a decision of this importance, I imagine that that mongoloid law officer put this idea into your head."

"Me and Mr. Mancuso talked the way I used to talk to your poppa. You poppa used to tell me what to do. I wish he was alive today."

"Mancuso and my father are alike only in that they both give

the impression of being rather inconsequential humans. However, your current mentor is apparently the type of person who
thinks that everything will be all right if everyone works continually."

"Mr. Mancuso works hard. He's got a hard road at the pre-
cinct."

"I am certain that he supports several unwanted children
who all hope to grow up to be policemen, the girls included."

"He's got three sweet chirren."

"I can imagine." Ignatius began to bounce slowly.

"Oh!"

"What are you doing? Are you fooling with that valve again?
Nobody else got him a valve but you. *I* ain't got no valve."

"*Everyone* has a valve!" Ignatius screamed. "Mine is simply
more developed. I am trying to open a passage which you have
succeeded in blocking. It may be permanently closed now for all
I know."

"Mr. Mancuso says if you work you can help pay off the man.
He says he thinks the man might take the money in install-
ments."

"Your friend the patrolman says a great deal. You certainly
bring people out, as they say. I never suspected that he could be
so loquacious or that he was capable of such perceptive com-
ment. Do you realize that he is trying to destroy our home? It
began the moment that he attempted that brutal arrest in front
of D. H. Holmes. Although you are too limited to comprehend
it all, Mother, this man is our nemesis. He's spun our wheel
downward."

"Wheel? Mr. Mancuso is a good man. You oughta be glad he
didn't take you in!"

"In my private apocalypse he will be impaled upon his own
nightstick. Anyway, it is inconceivable that I should get a job. I

am very busy with my work at the moment, and I feel that I am entering a very fecund stage. Perhaps the accident jarred and loosened my thought. At any rate, I accomplished a great deal today."

"We gotta pay that man, Ignatius. You wanna see me in jail? Wouldn't you be ashamed with your poor momma behind bars?"

"Will you please stop talking about imprisonment? You seem to be preoccupied with the thought. Actually, you seem to enjoy thinking about it. Martyrdom is meaningless at your age." He belched quietly. "I would suggest certain economies around the house. Somehow you will soon see that you have the required amount."

"I spend all the money on you for food and whatnots."

"I have found several empty wine bottles about lately, the contents of which I certainly did not consume."

"Ignatius!"

"I made the mistake of heating the oven the other day before inspecting it properly. When I opened it to put in my frozen pizza, I was almost blinded by a bottle of broiled wine that was preparing to explode. I suggest that you divert some of the monies that you are pouring into the liquor industry."

"For shame, Ignatius. A few bottles of Gallo muscatel, and you with all them trinkets."

"Will you please define the meaning of *trinkets*?" Ignatius snapped.

"All them books. That gramaphone. That trumpet I bought you last month."

"I consider the trumpet a good investment, although our neighbor, Miss Annie, does not. If she beats on my shutters again, I'll pour water on her."

"Tomorrow we looking at the want ads in the paper. You gonna dress up and go find a job."

"I am afraid to ask what your idea of 'dressing up' is. I will probably be turned into an utter mockery."

"I'm gonna iron you a nice white shirt and you gonna put on one of your poppa's nice ties."

"Do I believe what I am hearing?" Ignatius asked his pillow.

"It's either that, Ignatius, or I gotta take out a mortgage. You wanna lose the roof over your head?"

"No! You will not mortgage this house." He pounded a great paw into the mattress. "The whole sense of security which I have been trying to develop would crumble. I will not have any disinterested party controlling my domicile. I couldn't stand it. Just the thought of it makes my hands break out."

He extended a paw so that his mother could examine the rash.

"That is out of the question," he continued. "It would bring all of my latent anxieties to a head, and the result, I fear, would be very ugly indeed. I would not want you to have to spend the remainder of your life caring for a lunatic locked away somewhere in the attic. We shall not mortgage the house. You must have some funds somewhere."

"I got a hundred fifty in the Hibernia Bank."

"My God, is that all? I hardly thought that we were existing so precariously. However, it is fortunate that you have kept this from me. Had I known how close we were to total penury, my nerves would have given out long ago." Ignatius scratched his paws. "I must admit, though, that the alternative for me is rather grim. I doubt very seriously whether anyone will hire me."

"What do you mean, babe? You a fine boy with a good education."

"Employers sense in me a denial of their values."

He rolled over onto his back. "They fear me. I suspect that they can see that I am forced to function in a century which I loathe. That was true even when I worked for the New Orleans Public Library."

"But Ignatius, that was the only time that you worked since you got out of college, and you was only there for two weeks."

"That is exactly what I mean," Ignatius replied, aiming a paper ball at the bowl of the milk glass chandelier.

"All you did was paste them little slips in the books."

"Yes, but I had my own esthetic about pasting those slips. On some days I could only paste in three or four slips and at the same time feel satisfied with the quality of my work. The library authorities resented my integrity about the whole thing. They only wanted another animal who could slop glue on their best sellers."

"You think maybe you could get a job there again?"

"I seriously doubt it. At the same time I said some rather cutting things to the woman in charge of the processing department. They even revoked my borrower's card. You must realize the fear and hatred which my *weltanschauung* instills in people." Ignatius belched. "I won't mention that misguided trip to Baton Rouge. That incident, I believe, caused me to form a mental block against working."

To Have and Do Not

Fran Lebowitz

Fran Lebowitz's quirky essays on life in New York City among the literati *first appeared in such publications as Andy Warhol's* Interview, Mademoiselle, *and* Vogue *and then in collections such as* Metropolitan Life *and* Social Studies, *from which the selection below is taken.*

Not too long ago a literary agent of my close acquaintance negotiated a book deal on behalf of a writer of very successful commercial fiction. The book in question has not yet been written. At all. Not one page. On the basis, however, of the reputation of the author and the expertise of the agent, the book-to-be was sold for the gratifying sum of one million dollars. The following week the same agent sold the same book *manqué* for the exact same figure to, as they say, the movies.

Soon thereafter I found myself seated at dinner beside the fellow who had purchased the movie rights to the book in question. I smiled at him politely. He smiled back. I broached the subject.

"I understand," said I, "that you have purchased A Writer of Very Successful Commercial Fiction's next book for one million dollars?"

"Yes," he said. "Why don't *you* write a movie for us?"

I explained that my schedule could not, at this time, accommodate such a task, seeing as how I was up to my ears in oversleeping, unfounded rumors and superficial friendships. We were silent for a moment. We ate. We drank. I had an idea.

"You just bought A Writer of Very Successful Commercial Fiction's book for one million dollars, right?"

His reply was in the affirmative.

"Well," I said, "I'll tell you what. My next book is also unwritten. And my unwritten book is exactly the same as A Writer of Very Successful Commercial Fiction's unwritten book. I know I have an agent and I'm not supposed to discuss business but I am willing to sell you *my* unwritten book for precisely the same price that you paid for A Writer of Very Successful Commercial Fiction's unwritten book."

My dinner companion declined courteously and then offered me, for my unwritten book, a sum in six figures.

"Call my agent," I replied, and turned to my right.

The next morning I was awakened by a telephone call from my agent, informing me that she had just received and rejected the offer of a sum in six figures for the movie rights to my unwritten book.

"I think we can get more," she said. "I'll talk to you later."

I mulled this over and called her back. "Look," I said, "last year I earned four thousand dollars for the things that I wrote. This year I've been offered two sums in six figures for the things that I have not written. Obviously I've been going about this whole business in the wrong way. Not writing, it turns out, is not only fun but also, it would appear, enormously profitable. Call that movie fellow and tell him that I have several unwritten books—maybe as many as twenty." I lit another cigarette, coughed deeply and accepted reality. "Well, at least ten, anyway. We'll clean up."

We chatted a bit more and I hung up reluctantly, being well aware of how important talking on the telephone was to my newly lucrative career of not writing. I forged ahead, though, and am pleased to report that by careful application and absolute imposition of will, I spent the entire day not writing a single word.

That evening I attended an exhibit of the work of a well-known artist. I inquired as to the prices of the attractively displayed pictures, stalwartly registered only mild surprise and spent the remainder of the evening filled with an uneasy greed.

The next day, immediately upon awakening, I telephoned my agent and announced that I wanted to diversify—become more visual. Not writing was fine for the acquisition of a little capital but the real money was, it seemed to me, in not painting. No longer was I going to allow myself to be confined to one form. I was now not going to work in two mediums.

I spent the next few days in happy contemplation of my impending wealth. While it was true that no actual checks were rolling in, I was not born yesterday and know that these things take time. Inspired by my discovery, I began to look at things in an entirely new light. One weekend while driving through the countryside, I was struck by the thought that among the things that I cultivate, land is not one of them.

First thing Monday morning, I called my agent. "Listen," I said, "I know this is a little outside your field, but I would appreciate it if you would contact the Department of Agriculture and notify them that I am presently, and have been for quite some time, not growing any wheat. I know that the acreage in my apartment is small, but let's see what we can get. And while you're at it, why don't you try the Welfare Department? I don't have a job, either. That ought to be worth a few bucks."

She said she'd see what she could do and hung up, leaving me to fend for myself.

I didn't paint—a piece of cake. I grew no wheat—a snap. I remained unemployed—nothing to it. And as for not writing, well, when it comes to not writing, I am the real thing, the genuine article, an old pro. Except, I must admit, when it comes to a deadline. A deadline is really out of my hands. There are others to consider, obligations to be met. In the case of a deadline I almost invariably falter, and as you can see, this time was no exception. This piece was due. I did it. But as the more observant of you may note, I exercised at least a modicum of restraint. This piece is too short—much too short. Forgive me, but I needed the money. If you are going to do something, do it halfway. Business is business.

King Henry IV, Part I

William Shakespeare

You know who Will was. One of his most successful and endearing characters was the indomitable Sir John Falstaff, highwayman, drunkard, raconteur, and, not least, mentor to the future king of England.

Fal. Now, Hal, what time of day is it, lad?
Prince. Thou art so fat-witted, with drinking of old sack and unbuttoning thee after supper and sleeping upon benches after noon, that thou hast forgotten to demand that truly which thou wouldst truly know. What a devil hast thou to do with the time of the day? Unless hours were cups of sack and minutes capons and clocks the tongues of bawds and dials the signs of leaping-houses and the blessed sun himself a fair hot wench in flame-coloured taffeta, I see no reason why thou shouldst be so superfluous to demand the time of the day.

$\mathcal{S}$loth
· · · · ·

Kinflicks

Lisa Alther

Lisa Alther's brilliant first novel Kinflicks *perfectly captured the spirit of the 1970s. In the selection below, Alther's heroine, Ginny Babcock, finds herself on a commune in Vermont with a lesbian lover whose strict revolutionary principles forbid such bourgeois activities as work.*

The summer sun shone down bright and hot on the pond. Shimmering heat waves rose up all around the cabin. Bees bumbled in the weed flowers that were thigh-high in the yard.

"I was wondering, Eddie," I said between hastily swallowed bites, "if we maybe shouldn't rent a power tiller for the garden down at the hardware store." The garden we had so carefully planted was now overrun with weeds. We had to do something quick—either get rid of the weeds, or get used to them in lieu of tomatoes.

"Are you *kidding?* A *power tiller?* Are you out of your mind? You don't actually want to patronize an economy that turns The People into interchangeable cogs in some vast assembly line, do you? You couldn't possibly want to participate in a system of production that makes medical supplies with one hand and bombs with the other. I mean, that's why we're up here, isn't it, to wean ourselves from that sort of hypocrisy, to become honest working-class people? Well, isn't it?"

I said nothing. I wasn't at all sure that that was why I was in Vermont. I reviewed my motives and concluded that I was mostly here because Eddie wanted to be, for reasons of her own, and I wanted to be with Eddie. Once again I was shamelessly allowing myself to be defined by another person. I was afraid it would sound at best hopelessly bougie (Eddie's shorthand for "bourgeois") if I admitted this—and counterrevolutionary at worst. So instead I asked meekly, "Yes, but what about the weeds?"

"We'll pull them by hand," Eddie announced grandly, "like *every* person in the Third World does!"

That afternoon, shirtless, sweat pouring out of our hairy armpits, we pulled weeds in the hot sun for about fifteen minutes, clearing a small corner of the tomato patch. Our bodies clammy with sweat, we lay under an apple tree and smoked a joint.

"If tomatoes can't prevail against the weeds, they don't deserve to live," Eddie concluded. "To pull weeds would be to weaken the tomatoes and make them dependent on us."

"Maybe it's too late. I think they're already corrupted. They appear to need us."

The apples hanging above us were tinged with pink. Because we had failed to prune the trees or to control the insects, they were tiny and deformed and riddled with worm holes. We turned over on our stomachs so that we wouldn't have to look at yet another tribute to our ineptitude.

"We may not be freeing up our former food supplies for shipment to the Third World," I said, "but we're sure providing a feast for the area insects."

When Eddie looked at me, I knew that my remark hadn't been amusing, it had been reactionary. "What do you expect?" she demanded. "We're just picking up on all this soil shit. We'll get it together for next summer."

We passed the joint and became less and less glum. We glanced off and on at a beehive under a neighboring tree. At least we would have honey. We had left the bees almost entirely alone, in keeping with our policy of letting things fend for themselves. Only the bees had come through under this regime. They were rushing in and out with loads of nectar and pollen. Talk about accountant mentalities . . .

"We should do more hives next year," Eddie said, yawning. "That's my kind of project." She rolled over and wrapped her arms around me and nibbled my neck.

Four

...

GLUTTONY

"The Son of Man came eating and drinking, and they say, 'Behold a glutton and a drunkard, a friend of tax-collectors and sinners.' Yet wisdom is justified by her deeds."

—*Matthew 11:19*

"One cannot think well, love well, sleep well, if one has not dined well."

—*Virginia Woolf,*
A Room of One's Own

Once upon a time, eating and drinking were considered, next to perhaps making love, to be the greatest of human pleasures. They were thought of not merely as physical activities, but as spiritual ones as well. The followers of Jesus Christ recognized him not in an ecstatic mystical trance high on a mountain top but in the breaking of the bread. The central ritual of Christian worship is, indeed, a *meal*. Philosophy was born during feasts in Athens when, as recorded in Plato's *Symposium* (also known as *The Drinking Party*), Socrates drank such callow louts as Alcibiades under the table. From Cicero to Montaigne, La Rochefoucauld to Thomas Jefferson, the wisdom of the ages has praised and celebrated a healthy gluttony while casting a suspicious eye toward anyone advocating a strict dietary asceticism. Chesterton even used the love of wine as an argument for Catholicism:

> Wherever the Catholic sun doth shine,
> There's always laughter and good red wine.
> Wherever I go I find it so,
> Benedïcamus, Domino.

Today, however, eating and drinking are in danger of being outlawed. Roast beef has been declared not only politically in-

141

correct (for a variety of reasons), but also—dare I say it?—*un-healthful.* And in a time when the language of vice (or even virtue) is no longer understood by ordinary people, "unhealthy" is the worst label that can be applied to an activity. Who would imagine it possible? Since when are humanity's greatest obsessions—from eating and drinking to winning at poker—supposed to be *healthy?* If humanity thought only of good health, no one would ever have ventured across the Atlantic, or wiggled his way into little tin cans and shot himself around the moon, or sat in even smaller Parisian apartments to pen great novels or paint great pictures. If good health were the ultimate end of man, Michelangelo would not have spent a decade of his life perched five stories above the ground, breathing fumes from oil lamps while specks of plaster and paint dropped in his eyes.

What little people the modern age has made us! We have lost our appetites, not merely for good food, but for life. As the mournful Dane Kierkegaard wrote:

> Let others complain that the age is wicked; my complaint
> is that it is wretched, for it lacks passion. Men's thoughts are
> thin and flimsy like lace, they are themselves pitiable like the
> lacemakers. The thoughts of their hearts are too paltry to be
> sinful. . . . Their lusts are dull and sluggish, their passions
> sleepy.

"Sin boldly," said John Calvin, and who could not agree? The sage of Baltimore, H. L. Mencken, complained in his writings that morality for many people is not merely lack of opportunity; it is far worse: a lack of courage. Men remain loyal to their wives, he said, not out of a great and abiding passion for them, but because they are too cowardly to risk an affair. They fancy themselves degenerate rakes if they flirt harmlessly with the hat-check girl.

As with the other vices, so too with gluttony: Before we can pursue virtue, we must first know vice. Before we can submit to asceticism, we must first know feasting. It is hardly a virtue to give up what you do not know.

If you want to know the truth, as Holden Caulfield used to say, it's not an easy lot to be a human being. We suddenly awaken in a universe we know nothing about, find ourselves working at tasks for which we did not volunteer, and then we ponder, without any certainty of an answer, what will become of us as we age and die. But there are some consolations, few as they might be, and they are chiefly what we call our vices. A tumbler of good Scotch after eighteen holes of golf on a cold day. A full house with a large pot. And a tureen of steaming clam chowder with an ice cold beer.

It is said that the angels envy human beings only their food. As the selections below prove beyond a doubt, *they have good reason.*

Among the Gastrolaters

Rabelais

François Rabelais (c. 1494–1553) was a Franciscan monk who left the monastery to become a doctor and then, later, a comic satirist of some skill. His classic work, from which the selection below is taken, is Gargantua and Pantagruel, *an immense and often vulgar comic epic that has delighted students for centuries. This is an indispensable resource for the study of vice.*

At the court of this great master of ingenuity, Pantagruel met with two sorts of tiresome and over-officious summoners, whom he greatly detested. One lot were called the Engastrimythes or Ventriloquists, and the other the Gastrolaters or Belly-worshippers. . . .

The Gastrolaters . . . always went about in close troops and bands. Some were gay, dainty, and delicate; others sad, serious, harsh, and gloomy. But all were idle, doing nothing and not attempting a stroke of work. They were a charge and a useless burden on the land, as Hesiod says. For, as far as one could judge, they were afraid of offending and reducing the belly. Moreover they were so strangely masked and disguised, indeed so oddly dressed, that they were a fine sight to see. . . . They all looked up to Gaster as their great God, worshipped him as a God, sacrificed to him as their God almighty, and recognized no other God but him. You would have supposed that it was really of him that the holy Apostle wrote in the third chapter of the Epistle to the Philippians: "For many walk, of whom I have told you often, and now tell you even weeping, that they are the enemies of the cross of Christ: whose end is destruction and whose God is their belly."

Pantagruel compared them to the Cyclops Polyphemus, into whose mouth Euripides put these words: "I only sacrifice to myself—to the gods never—and to this belly of mine, the greatest of all the gods."

The Salad

Virgil

If you had to spend your entire life writing in Latin, wouldn't you at least indulge, like Ovid, in a little erotic love poetry? Instead, Publius Vergilius Maro (c. 70–19 B.C.) wrote about lettuce. At least he spared a few lines for the lithesome Dido in The Aeneid.

Close to his cottage lay a garden-ground,
With reeds and osiers sparely girt around;
Small was the spot, but liberal to produce,
Nor wanted aught that serves a peasant's use;
And sometimes even the rich would borrow thence,
Although its tillage was his sole expense.
For oft, as from his toils abroad he ceased,
Homebound by weather or some stated feast,
His debt of culture here he duly paid,
And only left the plough to wield the spade.
He knew to give each plant the soil it needs,
To drill the ground, and cover close the seeds;
And could with ease compel the wanton rill
To turn, and wind, obedient to his will.
There flourished starwort, and the branching beet,
The sorrel acid, and the mallow sweet,
The skirret, and the leek's aspiring kind,
The noxious poppy—quencher of the mind!
Salubrious sequel of a sumptuous board,
The lettuce, and the long huge-bellied gourd;
But these (for none his appetite controlled
With stricter sway) the thrifty rustic sold;

With broom-twigs neatly bound, each kind apart
He bore them ever to the public mart;
Whence, laden still, but with a lighter load,
Of cash well earned, he took his homeward road,
Expending seldom, ere he quitted Rome,
His gains, in flesh meat for a feast at home,
There, at no cost, on onions, rank and red,
Or the curled endive's bitter leaf, he fed;
On scallions sliced, or with a sensual gust
On rockets—foul provocatives of lust;
Nor even shunned, with smarting gums, to press
Nasturtium, pungent face-distorting mess!
  Some such regale now also in his thought,
With hasty steps his garden-ground he sought;
There delving with his hands, he first displaced
Four plants of garlic, large, and rooted fast;
The tender tops of parsley next he culls,
Then the old rue-bush shudders as he pulls,
And coriander last to these succeeds,
That hangs on slightest threads her trembling seeds.
  Placed near his sprightly fire, he now demands
The mortar at his sable servant's hands;
When stripping all his garlic first, he tore
The exterior coats, and cast them on the floor,
When cast away with like contempt the skin,
Flimsier concealment of the cloves within.
These searched, and perfect found, he one by one
Rinsed and disposed within the hollow stone;
Salt added, and a lump of salted cheese,
With his injected herbs he covered these,
And tucking with his left his tunic tight,
And seizing fast the pestle with his right,
The garlic bruising first he soon expressed,

And mixed the various juices of the rest.
He grinds, and by degrees his herbs below
Lost in each other their own powers forgo,
And with the cheese in compound, to the sight
Nor wholly green appear, nor wholly white.
His nostrils oft the forceful fume resent;
He cursed full oft his dinner for its scent,
Or with wry faces, wiping as he spoke
The trickling tears, cried—"Vengeance on the
smoke!"
The work proceeds: not roughly turns he now
The pestle, but in circles smooth and slow;
With cautious hand that grudges what it spills,
Some drops of olive oil he next instills;
Then vinegar with caution scarcely less;
And gathering to a ball the medley mess,
Last, with two fingers frugally applied,
Sweeps the small remnant from the mortar's side:
And thus complete in figure and in kind,
Obtains at length the Salad he designed.
                              —Translated by William Cowper

The Seven Pillars of Wisdom

T. E. Lawrence

*Many people are unaware that Thomas Edward Lawrence
(c. 1888–1935), "Lawrence of Arabia," was a writer, and some
critics claim his most imaginative work was the recounting of
his own exploits. Lawrence had an eye for detail, however.*

The bowl was now brim-full, ringed round its edge by white rice in an embankment a foot wide and six inches deep, filled with legs and ribs of mutton till they toppled over. It needed two or three victims to make in the centre a dressed pyramid of meat such as honour prescribed. The centre-pieces were the boiled, upturned heads, propped on their severed stumps of neck, so that the ears, brown like old leaves, flapped out on the rice surface. The jaws gaped emptily upward, pulled open to show the hollow throat with the tongue, still pink, clinging to the lower teeth; and the long incisors whitely crowned the pile, very prominent about the nostrils' pricking hair and the lips which sneered away blackly from them.

This load was set down on the soil of the cleared space between us, where it steamed hotly, while a procession of minor helpers bore small cauldrons and copper vats in which the cooking had been done. From them, with much-bruised bowls of enamelled iron, they ladled out over the main dish all the inside and outside of the sheep; little bits of yellow intestine, the white tail-cushion of fat, brown muscles and meat and bristly skin, all swimming in the liquid butter and grease of the seething. The bystanders watched anxiously, muttering satisfactions when a very juicy scrap plopped out.

The fat was scalding. Every now and then a man would drop his baler with an exclamation, and plunge his burnt fingers, not reluctantly, in his mouth to cool them: but they persevered till at last their scooping rang loudly on the bottoms of the pots; and, with a gesture of triumph, they fished out the intact livers from their hiding place in the gravy and topped the yawning jaws with them.

Two raised each smaller cauldron and tilted it, letting the liquid splash down upon the meat till the rice-crater was full, and the loose grains at the edge swam in the abundance; and yet they poured, till, amid cries of astonishment from us, it was running over, and the little pool congealing in the dust. That was the final touch of splendour, and the host called us to come and eat.

We feigned a deafness, as manners demanded: at last we heard him, and looked surprised at one another, each urging his fellow to move first; till Nasir rose coyly, and after them we all came forward to sink on one knee round the tray, wedging in and cuddling up till the twenty-two for whom there were barely space were grouped around the food. We turned back our sleeves to the elbow, and, taking lead from Nasir with a low, "In the name of God the merciful, the loving-kind," we dipped together.

The first dip, for me, at least, was always cautious, since the liquid fat was so hot that my unaccustomed fingers could seldom bear it; and so I would toy with an exposed and cooling lump of meat till others' excavations had drained my rice-segment. We would knead between the fingers (not soiling the palm), neat balls of rice and fat and liver and meat cemented by gentle pressure, and project them by leverage of the thumb from the crooked forefinger into the mouth. With the right trick and the right construction the little lump held together and came clean off the hand; but when surplus butter and odd fragments clung, cooling, to the fingers, they had to be licked carefully to make the next effort slip easier away.

As the meat pile wore down (nobody really cared about rice: flesh was the luxury) one of the chief Howeitat eating with us would draw his dagger, silver hilted, set with turquoise, a signed masterpiece of Mohammed ibn Zari, of Jauf, and would cut criss-cross from the larger bones long diamonds of meat easily torn up between the fingers; for it was necessarily boiled very tender, since all had to be disposed of with the right hand, which alone was honourable.

Our host stood by the circle, encouraging the appetite with pious ejaculations. At top speed we twisted, tore, cut, and stuffed: never speaking, since conversation would insult a meal's quality; though it was proper to smile thanks when an intimate guest passed a select fragment, or when Mohammed el Dheilan gravely handed over a huge barren bone with a blessing. On such occasions I would return the compliment with some hideous impossible lump of guts, a flippancy which rejoiced the Howeitat, but which the gracious, aristocratic Nasir saw with disapproval.

At length some of us were nearly filled, and began to play and pick; glancing sideways at the rest till they too grew slow, and at last ceased eating, elbow on knee, the hand hanging down from the wrist over the tray edge to drip, while the fat, butter, and scattered grains of rice cooled into a stiff white grease which gummed the fingers together. When all had stopped, Nasir meaningly cleared his throat, and we rose up together in haste with an explosive "God requite it you, O host," to group ourselves outside among the tent-ropes while the next twenty guests inherited our leaving.

Breakfast with Gerard Manley Hopkins

Anthony Brode

The work below is a delightful parody of the poetry of the British Jesuit poet Gerard Manley Hopkins (c. 1844–1889), who perfected the art of "sprung rhythm" in such poems as "The Windhover" and "Pied Beauty."

*G*luttony
· · · · ·

Delicious heart-of-the-corn, fresh-from-the-oven flakes are spar-
kled and spangled with sugar for a can't-be-resisted flavour.
Legend on a packet of breakfast cereal

Serious over my cereals I broke one breakfast my fast
  With something-to-read-searching retinas retained by
    print on a packet;
Sprung rhythm sprang, and I found (the mind
    fact-mining at last)
  An influence Father-Hopkins-fathered on the copy-
    writing racket.
Parenthesis-proud, bracket-bold, happiest with hyphens,
  The writers stagger intoxicated by terms, adjective-
    unsteadied—
Describing in graceless phrases fizzling like soda siphons
  All things crisp, crunchy, malted, tangy, sugared and
    shredded.
Far too, yes, too early we are urged to be purged, to
    savour
  Salt, malt and phosphates in English twisted and torn,
As, sparkled and spangled with sugar for a can't-be-
    resisted flavour,
  Come fresh-from-the-oven flakes direct from the heart
    of the corn.

151

Notes from the Overfed

Woody Allen

*Before Woody Allen became an cinematic auteur, he was, of
course, a stand-up comedian and writer of witty little essays for
such publications as* The New Yorker. *The one below, written
in 1968, is taken from his collection* Getting Even.

(After reading Dostoevski and the new "Weight Watchers"
magazine on the same plane trip)

I am fat. I am disgustingly fat. I am the fattest human I know.
I have nothing but excess poundage all over my body. My fingers are fat. My wrists are fat. My eyes are fat. (Can you imagine
fat eyes?) I am hundreds of pounds overweight. Flesh drips
from me like hot fudge off a sundae. My girth has been an object
of disbelief to everyone who's ever seen me. There is no question about it, I'm a regular fatty. Now, the reader may ask, are
there advantages or disadvantages to being built like a planet? I
do not mean to be facetious or speak in paradoxes, but I must
answer that fat in itself is above bourgeois morality. It is simply
fat. That fat could have a value of its own, that fat could be, say,
evil or pitying, is, of course, a joke. Absurd! For what is fat after
all but an accumulation of pounds? And what are pounds? Simply an aggregate composite of cells. Can a cell be moral? Is a cell
beyond good or evil? Who knows—they're so small. Now, my
friend, we must never attempt to distinguish between good fat
and bad fat. We must train ourselves to confront the obese without judging, without thinking this man's fat is first-rate fat and
this poor wretch's is grubby fat.

Take the case of K. This fellow was porcine to such a degree that he could not fit through the average doorframe without the aid of a crowbar. Indeed, K. would not think to pass from room to room in a conventional dwelling without first stripping completely and then buttering himself. I am no stranger to the insults K. must have borne from passing gangs of young rowdies. How frequently he must have been stung by cries of "Tubby!" and "Blimp!" How it must have hurt when the governor of the province turned to him on the Eve of Michaelmas and said, before many dignitaries, "You hulking pot of *kasha*!"

Then one day, when K. could stand it no longer, he dieted. Yes, dieted! First sweets went. Then bread, alcohol, starches, sauces. In short K. gave up the very stuff that makes a man unable to tie his shoelaces without help from the Santini Brothers. Gradually he began to slim down. Rolls of flesh fell from his arms and legs. Where once he looked roly-poly, he suddenly appeared in public with a normal build. Yes, even an attractive build. He seemed the happiest of men. I say "seemed," for eighteen years later, when near death and fever raged throughout his slender frame, he was heard to cry out, "My fat! Bring me my fat! Oh, please! I must have my fat! Oh, somebody lay some avoirdupois on me! What a fool I've been. To part with one's fat! I must have been in league with the Devil!" I think that the point of the story is obvious.

Now the reader is probably thinking, Why, then, if you are Lard City, have you not joined the circus? Because—and I confess this with no small embarrassment—I cannot leave the house. I cannot go out because I cannot get my pants on. My legs are too thick to dress. They are the living result of more corned beef than there is on Second Avenue—I would say about twelve thousand sandwiches per leg. And not all lean, even though I specified. One thing is certain: If my fat could speak, it would probably speak of a man's intense loneliness—with, oh, perhaps a few additional pointers on how to make a sailboat out of paper. Every pound of my body wants to be heard from, as do Chins Four through Twelve inclusive. My fat is strange fat. It has seen much. My calves alone have lived a lifetime. Mine is not happy fat, but it is real fat. It is not fake fat. Fake fat is the worst fat you can have, although I don't know if the stores still carry it.

But let me tell you how it was that I became fat. For I was not always fat. It is the Church that has made me thus. At one time I was thin—quite thin. So thin, in fact that to call me fat would have been an error in perception. I remained thin until one day—I think it was my twentieth birthday—when I was having tea and cracknels with my uncle at a fine restaurant. Suddenly my uncle put a question to me. "Do you believe in God?" he asked. "And if so, what do you think He weighs?" So saying, he took a long and luxurious draw at his cigar and, in that confident, assured manner he has cultivated, lapsed into a coughing fit so violent I thought he would hemorrhage.

"I do not believe in God," I told him. "For if there is a God, then tell me, Uncle, why is there poverty and baldness? Why do some men go through life immune to a thousand mortal enemies of the race, while others get a migraine that lasts for a week. Why are our days numbered and not, say, lettered? Answer me, Uncle. Or have I shocked you?"

I knew I was safe in saying this, because nothing ever shocked the man. Indeed, he had seen his chess tutor's mother raped by Turks and would have found the incident amusing had it not taken so much time.

"Good nephew," he said, "there is a God, despite what you think, and He is everywhere. Yes? Everywhere!"

"Everywhere, Uncle? How can you say that when you don't even know for sure if we exist? True, I am touching your wart at this moment, but could that not be an illusion? Could not all life be an illusion? Indeed, are there not certain sects of holy men in the East who are convinced that nothing exists outside their minds except for the Oyster Bar at Grand Central Station? Could it not be simply that we are alone and aimless, doomed to wander in an indifferent universe, with no hope of salvation, nor any prospect except misery, death, and the empty reality of eternal nothing?"

I could see that I made a deep impression on my uncle with this, for he said to me, "You wonder why you're not invited to more parties! Jesus, you're morbid!" He accused me of being nihilistic and then said, in that cryptic way the senile have, "God is not always where one seeks Him, but I assure you, dear nephew, He is everywhere. In these cracknels, for instance." With that, he departed, leaving me his blessing and a check that read like a tab for an aircraft carrier.

I returned home wondering what it was he meant by that one simple statement "He is everywhere. In these cracknels, for instance." Drowsy by then, and out of sorts, I lay down on my bed and took a brief nap. In that time, I had a dream that was to change my life forever. In the dream, I am strolling in the country, when I suddenly notice I am hungry. Starved, if you will, I come upon a restaurant and I enter. I order the open-hot-roast-beef sandwich and a side of French. The waitress, who resembles my landlady (a thoroughly insipid woman who reminds one instantly of some of the hairier lichens), tries to tempt me into ordering the chicken salad, which doesn't look fresh. As I am conversing with this woman, she turns into a twenty-four piece starter set of silverware, I become hysterical with laughter, which suddenly turns to tears and then into a serious ear infection. The room is suffused with a radiant glow, and I see a shimmering figure approach on a white steed. It is my podiatrist, and I fall to the ground with guilt.

· · ·

SUCH WAS MY dream. I awoke with a tremendous sense of well-being. Suddenly I was optimistic. Everything was clear. My uncle's statement reverberated to the core of my very existence. I went to the kitchen and started to eat. I ate everything in sight. Cakes, breads, cereals, meat, fruits. Succulent chocolates, vegetables in sauce, wines, fish, creams and noodles, éclairs, and wursts totalling in excess of sixty thousand dollars. If God is everywhere, I had concluded, then He is in food. Therefore, the more I ate the godlier I would become. Impelled by this new religious fervor, I glutted myself like a fanatic. In six months, I was the holiest of holies, with a heart entirely devoted to my prayers and a stomach that crossed the state line by itself. I last saw my feet one Thursday morning in Vitebsk, although for all I know they are still down there. I ate and ate and grew and grew. To reduce would have been the greatest folly. Even a sin! For when we lose twenty pounds, dear reader (and I am assuming you are not as large as I), we may be losing the twenty best pounds we have! We may be losing the pounds that contain our genius, our humanity, our love and honesty or, in the case of one inspector general I knew, just some unsightly flab around the hips.

Now, I know what you are saying. You are saying this is in direct contradiction to everything—yes, everything—I put forth before. Suddenly I am attributing to neuter flesh, values! Yes, and what of it? Because isn't life that very same kind of contradiction? One's opinion of fat can change in the same manner that the seasons change, that our hair changes, that life itself changes. For life is change and fat is life, and fat is also death. Don't you see? Fat is everything! Unless, of course, you're overweight.

Madame Bovary

Gustave Flaubert

The French do know how to eat, and, if you can afford the prices, French food would make any glutton's heart sing new songs. Madame Bovary, of course, had other sensual delights on her mind than mere food, but in this scene from Flaubert's classic you can tell that the portly author himself (c. 1821–1880) knew his way around a dinner table.

It was under the cart shed that the table had been laid. On it were four sirloin roasts, six chickens fricasseed, a casserole of veal, three legs of mutton, and in the center a beautiful suckling pig flanked by four fresh-casing sausages flavored with sorrel. At the corners were carafes of brandy. The bottles of sweet cider swelled with the thick foam around the corks, and all the glasses, in anticipation, had been filled to the brim with wine. Large platters of yellow cream, that trembled at the slightest jarring of the table, were brought forward, their smooth surface decorated with the newlyweds' initials in arabesques of spun sugar. A pastry chef had been found at Yvetot for the pies and sweets. Since this was his début in the region he took particular care with the extravaganza which elicited cries of astonishment. First, at the base was a square of blue cardboard shaped like a porticoed temple, ringed round by colonnades and stucco statuettes, the niches set with constellations of gold paper stars; then, on the second level was a dungeon made of Savoy cake surrounded by delicate fortifications built of angelica, almonds, raisins and quartered oranges; finally, on the topmost layer, which was a green rocky meadow with jam lakes and nutshell boats, one could see a little Cupid balancing in a chocolate swing supported by poles terminating in two natural rose buds, for knobs, at the very peak.

A Song of Gluttony

E. O. Parrott

This poem, and the one following, were winners in a contest sponsored by the (late, lamented) Punch *magazine on the subject of gluttony.*

There's nothing so delightful as a gorgeous spot of
    gluttony:
Roast beefery, or porkery, or caper-sauce-and-muttony.
Not a thing I let intrude upon the sacred rite of food;
I've never ever had enough till I'm undoing the
    top-buttony.

I haven't any patience with this modern vice of snackery.
Meals ought to be Falstaffian, with venison and sackery.
I love to read accounts of the Pickwickian amounts
Of food they eat in novels, both Dickensian and
    Thackeray.

There's nothing quite so scrumptious as frying food,
    right batterly,

And following with creamy sweets, and cheeses on a
    platterly.
Had a certain fair young maid to this sin obeisance paid,
There'd have never been this scandal in the woods with
    Lady Chatterley.

The Jolly Glutton

Margaret Cresswell

I am a jolly glutton: none is greedier than I
For soup and stew and savories and steak and kidney pie,
And I am gay and cheerful as I polish off each platter,
For I can eat from morn to night without becoming
    fatter.

My friends who are on diets in their martyrdom take
    pride,
While envying the quantities of food I tuck inside,
And when it comes to anger, they get madder than a
    hatter
To see me stuffing creamy cakes and never getting fatter.

And so I sometimes ponder, as I pour out double gins,
On anger, pride, and envy—they are miserable sins,
But gluttony's a pleasant sin and does not seem to matter
To those whose metabolic rate prevents their getting
    fatter.

Hymn to the Belly

Ben Jonson

Ben Jonson (c. 1573–1637) was a playwright who understood the vices. A few miscreant critics believe he was the true author of Shakespeare's plays, and it is said he was considered superior to old Will in his own day.

Room! room! make room for the bouncing Belly,
First father of sauce and deviser of jelly;
Prime master of arts and the giver of wit,
That found out the excellent engine, the spit,
The plow and the flail, the mill and the hopper,
The hutch and the boulter, the furnace and copper,
The oven, the bavin, the mawkin, the peel,
The hearth and the range, the dog and the wheel.
He, he first invented the hogshead and tun,
The gimlet and vise too, and taught 'em to run;
And since, with the funnel and hippocras bag,
He's made of himself that now he cries swag;
Which shows, though the pleasure be but of four inches,
Yet he is a weasel, the gullet that pinches
Of any delight, and not spares from his back
Whatever to make of the belly a sack.
Hail, hail, plump paunch! O the founder of taste,
For fresh meats or powdered, or pickle or paste!
Devourer of broiled, baked, roasted or sod!
And emptier of cups, be they even or odd!
All which have now made thee so wide i' the waist,
As scarce with no pudding thou art to be laced;

But eating and drinking until thou dost nod,
Thou break'st all thy girdles and break'st forth a god.

I Had But Fifty Cents

Anonymous

Any young man who has ever taken a girl out to dinner, not knowing quite whether he could afford it, should appreciate this marvelous poem.

I took my girl to a fancy ball;
It was a social hop;
We waited till the folks got out,
And the music it did stop.
Then to a restaurant we went,
The best one on the street;
She said she wasn't hungry,
But this is what she eat:
A dozen raw, a plate of slaw,
A chicken and a roast,
Some applesass, and sparagrass,
And soft-shell crabs on toast.
A big box stew, and crackers too;
Her appetite was immense!
When she called for pie,
I thought I'd die,
For I had but fifty cents.

She said she wasn't hungry
And didn't care to eat,

But I've got money in my clothes
To bet she can't be beat;
She took it in so cozy,
She had an awful tank;
She said she wasn't thirsty,
But this is what she drank:
A whiskey skin, a glass of gin,
Which made me shake with fear,
A ginger pop, with rum on top,
A schooner then of beer,
A glass of ale, a gin cocktail;
She should have had more sense;
When she called for more,
I fell on the floor,
For I had but fifty cents.

Of course I wasn't hungry,
And didn't care to eat,
Expecting every moment
To be kicked into the street;
She said she'd fetch her family round,
And some night we'd have fun;
When I gave the man the fifty cents,
This is what he done:
He tore my clothes,
He smashed my nose,
He hit me on the jaw,
He gave me a prize
Of a pair of black eyes
And with me swept the floor.
He took me where my pants hung loose,
And threw me over the fence;

Take my advice, don't try it twice
If you've got but fifty cents!

Steak and Chips

Roland Barthes

*Roland Barthes (c. 1915–1980) was a controversial French in-
tellectual and literary critic whose work influenced the development of semiotics (the study of signs and symbols). This
essay on steak is taken from his 1957 work,* Mythologies.

Steak is a part of the same sanguine mythology as wine. It is
the heart of meat, it is meat in its pure state; and whoever par-
takes of it assimilates a bull-like strength. The prestige of steak
evidently derives from its quasi-rawness. In it, blood is visible,
natural, dense, at once compact and sectile. One can well imagine the ambrosia of the Ancients as this kind of heavy substance
which dwindles under one's teeth in such a way as to make one
keenly aware at the same time of its original strength and of its
aptitude to flow into the very blood of man. Full-bloodedness is
the *raison d'être* of steak; the degrees to which it is cooked are
expressed not in calorific units but in images of blood; rare steak
is said to be *saignant* (when it recalls the arterial flow from the
cut in the animal's throat), or *bleu* (and it is now the heavy, ple-
thoric blood of the veins which is suggested by the purplish colour—the superlative of redness). Its cooking, even moderate,
cannot openly find expression; for this unnatural state, a euphe-

mism is needed: one says that steak is *à point*, "medium," and this in truth is understood more as a limit than as a perfection.

To eat steak rare therefore represents both a nature and a morality. It is supposed to benefit all the temperaments, the sanguine because it is identical, the nervous and lymphatic because it is complementary to them. And just as wine becomes for a good number of intellectuals a mediumistic substance which leads them towards the original strength of nature, steak is for them a redeeming food, thanks to which they bring their intellectualism to the level of prose and exorcize, through blood and soft pulp, the sterile dryness of which they are constantly accused. The craze for steak tartare, for instance, is a magic spell against the romantic association between sensitiveness and sickliness; there are to be found, in this preparation, all the germinating states of matter: the blood mash and the glair of eggs, a whole harmony of soft and life-giving substances, a sort of meaningful compendium of the images of pre-parturition.

Like wine, steak is in France a basic element, nationalized even more than socialized. It figures in all the surroundings of alimentary life: flat, edged with yellow, like the sole of a shoe, in cheap restaurants; thick and juicy in the bistros which specialize in it; cubic, with the core all moist throughout beneath a light charred crust, in haute cuisine. It is a part of all the rhythms, that of the comfortable bourgeois meal and that of the bachelor's bohemian snack. It is a food at once expeditious and dense, it effects the best possible ratio between economy and efficacy, between mythology and its multifarious ways of being consumed.

Moreover, it is a French possession (circumscribed today, it is true, by the invasion of American steaks). As in the case of wine there is no alimentary constraint which does not make the Frenchman dream of steak. Hardly abroad, he feels nostalgia for it. Steak is here adorned with a supplementary virtue of elegance, for among the apparent complexity of exotic cooking, it is a food which unites, one feels, succulence and simplicity. Being part of the nation, it follows the index of patriotic values: it helps them to rise in wartime, it is the very flesh of the French soldier, the inalienable property which cannot go over to the enemy except by treason. In an old film *(Deuxième Bureau contre Kommandantur),* the maid of the patriotic *curé* gives food to the Boche spy disguised as a French underground fighter: *"Ah, it's you, Laurent! I'll give you some steak."* And then, when the spy is unmasked: *"And when I think I gave him some of my steak!"*—the supreme breach of trust.

Commonly associated with chips, steak communicates its national glamour to them: chips are nostalgic and patriotic like steak. *Match* told us that after the armistice in Indo-China *"General de Castries, for his first meal, asked for chips."* And the President of the Indo-China Veterans, later commenting on this information added: *"The gesture of General de Castries asking for chips for his first meal has not always been understood."* What we were meant to understand is that the General's request was certainly not a vulgar materialistic reflex, but an episode in the ritual of appropriating the regained French community. The General understood well our national symbolism; he knew that *la frite,* chips, are the alimentary sign of Frenchness.

Five
...
PRIDE

"It's a fine thing to rise above pride, but you must have pride in order to do so."

—*Georges Bernanos,*
The Diary of a Country Priest

"I am the greatest."

—*Muhammad Ali*

The wonderful thing about pride is that, unlike all of the other vices, people are willing to say a good word or two about it.

That is definitely not true of, say, lust or envy or sloth.

At high school and college commencement ceremonies, you'll not hear the distinguished speakers tell the graduates that they need to cultivate their innate avarice. No one will tell them that, now that they are going out into the world, what they really need is a little more . . . lust.

Doesn't happen.

But these same distinguished speakers won't hesitate to sing the praises of pride.

They'll speak about how you need to take pride in yourself, pride in your country, pride in your school, pride in your profession. "You should all be proud of yourselves," the speakers, parents, and other assorted well-wishers will say.

Apparently, even though pride is one of the traditional seven deadly sins—indeed, is denounced as the primordial, the original, sin—it is still considered a good thing.

Judging from what people say, we could all use a lot more pride.

And I couldn't agree more.

For Aristotle, perhaps the most influential philosopher in the

West, pride was an essential component to a truly human life: the word he used was *megalopsychia* (μεγαλοψχία), which literally means "largeness of soul" or "high-mindedness." This word was translated into Latin as *magnanimitas,* from which we get the English word "magnanimity," but which really means a confident self-respect.

In his *Nicomachean Ethics,* Aristotle complains that there is not, in fact, a word for the proper blend of humility and self-confidence that he has in mind. "A man is regarded as high-minded *(megalopsychos)* when he thinks he deserves great things and actually deserves them," he says. Someone "who thinks he deserves them but does not is a fool" and this is, in fact, what false pride, or vanity, is. However, someone who *underestimates* himself is not truly humble, either, but "small-minded" *(micropsychos).*

What Aristotle admires, therefore, is someone who strives for greatness, achieves it, and recognizes that whatever honor he receives for his efforts is truly deserved. This was indeed the Greek ideal: the confident warrior who knows his weaknesses but also knows his strengths, who neither boasts nor feigns false humility.

On the surface, of course, it appears that the modern age is full of pride.

We are overflowing with products and services that cater to our vanity: liposuction, tanning booths, personal fitness trainers, thong bikinis. We jog, do abdominal exercises, and consult personal stylists. We subject ourselves to every kind of physical torture and monetary expense to hone our "natural beauty." We pay big bucks for nutritionists, psychotherapists, cosmetic surgeons, weight-loss clinics, exercise videos, Thighmasters, and hair-restoration treatments.

As Oscar Wilde put it, "To love oneself is the beginning of a lifelong romance."

And yet all of this effort and expense, this preoccupation with ourselves, does not appear to have given modern men and women the confidence we seem to seek.

Nietzsche, for one, worried that underneath all of that modern bluster, that surface vanity, modern men and women were as timid as rabbits, too frightened of what other people would think to really live, and utterly lacking in the warrior self-confidence of ancient peoples. In his view, Christianity and Judaism sucked much of the pride out of Western man and what little was left was drained by the modern mega-state.

It has never been clearer, in fact, that human beings today desperately need an infusion of *megalopsychia* or authentic pride. Indeed, our survival as a society, or at least our happiness as individuals, may depend upon it.

We are in danger of becoming domesticated animals, herds of medicated sheep, blindly accepting what our government and media elites tell us—without challenge or protest or even *thought*.

Imagine . . . just imagine . . . what it would be like to turn off your television sets, throw away your newspapers, chuck *Newsweek* and *People* and *The New Republic,* and actually live your life as you feel it should be lived.

What an astounding thought!

Imagine having the kind of pride that would allow you to ignore the robotic routines and preprogrammed thoughts of your friends and their media masters.

Imagine dressing the way you feel like dressing, eating the foods you truly feel like eating, doing the activities that really interest you, educating your children the way you think they should be educated, voting for the candidates you truly like and ignoring the ones pundits say are "realistic," reading the books you think should be read, driving the car you like to drive (even if it is old or unfashionable), living where you want to live.

In short, imagine what it would be like if you were a truly proud, independent, free-thinking individual who didn't really give a hoot in hell what the media or Rush Limbaugh or the ACLU thought.

This is the strong and cheerful pride described below in Emerson's essay on "Self-Reliance," in Walt Whitman's entire personality, in the hilarious body-builder in Sam Fussell's *Muscle,* in Moll Flanders and Hunter Thompson and Tennyson's *Ulysses.* This authentic pride stands in dramatic contrast to the false pride of vanity, based on weakness and fear, which is illustrated by many of the other selections in this chapter.

Vanity depends upon the opinion of others; true pride could care less.

Miles Gloriosus

Plautus

Human beings have mocked the braggart from when time began, and the comic motif of the arrogant soldier is a mainstay of classical literature. The Roman playwright Titus Maccius Plautus (c. 254–184 B.C.) took up the motif in this play. Like all things Roman, Plautus's plays are merely reworkings of early Greek versions.

$\mathscr{P}$ride
·····

ACT I

The stage represents a street, ostensibly in Ephesus, but in fact not unlike a typical street in Rome. We see two houses, side by side. Although they are attached to each other by a common wall, it is clear that they are two distinct residences. The house on stage left belongs to Pyrgopolynices, the braggart warrior; its neighbor belongs to Periplectomenus, an urbane and elderly bachelor. Each house has a prominent door opening onto the street. Downstage center there is a low altar; otherwise the street is clear.

Enter Pyrgopolynices, preceded by several weird and dismally incompetent slaves; he is followed at a short distance by his parasite Artotrogus, who is well fed and well oiled.

Act I, Scene I

PYRGO (*Striking a pose and addressing his slaves*)
  Shine my shield till it glows and glitters and gleams
  Like the radiant rays of the sun from a summer sky;
  So, when its hour has come and the foe's at hand.
  Its dazzling light will dizzy the enemy line.
  My task will be to comfort this pining sword:
  My gay blade mustn't despair or get down in the mouth.
  Poor lad, he's lived so long with his nose in my belt
  That now he longs to give someone a belt in the nose.
  Where's Artotrogus?
ARTOT Here, beside a hero
  Audacious, tenacious, sagacious; good gracious, a *king*!
  And a warrior! Even Mars would hesitate
  To match his deeds of courage against yours.
PYRGO Who was that man I saved on Cockroach Plains,

Where the commander-in-chief was Neptune's grandson,
Bumbomachides Clutomestoridysarchides?
ARTOT I remember. The one with golden armor,
Whose troops you puffed apart with a breath of air,
As the wind blows leaves or scatters a house of straw.
PYRGO Great Pollux, that was nothing.
ARTOT Great Hercules,
It was nothing compared to other deeds
I could describe—(aside) except you never did them.
(Speaking directly to the audience)
If anyone knows a more colossal liar,
A man more stuffed with pride and vanity,
Then call me your slave; I'll put myself on the block.
Why do I stay? His cheese sauce is divine!
PYRGO Where are you?
ARTOT Here, sir. Remember, sir,
That poor elephant we met in India?
You forcefully flung your fist and fractured his arm!
PYRGO His "arm"?
ARTOT I actually meant to say his "leg."
PYRGO But I hit him a careless blow.
ARTOT By Pollux, if only
You'd really tried, you'd have transpenetrated your arm
Through hide and guts clear down to elephant marrow.
PYRGO Let's not discuss it now.
ARTOT Heavens to Hercules,
It's a waste of valuable breath for you to tell me:
I know what a great, strong man you are.
(Aside) This painful role is strictly from hunger, friends:
I've got to get an earful to keep my stomach cheerful,
So I'm forced to nod my head to all his lies.
PYRGO Now what was I saying?

ARTOT Aha! I know what you want
   To say. It's a fact, sir, you did! I remember, you did.
PYRGO Did what?
ARTOT Well, whatever it was that you did.
PYRGO Have you got—
ARTOT Wax tablets? Yes, and a stylus, too.
PYRGO How intelligent of you to read my mind!
ARTOT I'm a student of all your ways; that's only right.
   My mission is to sniff your every whim.
PYRGO How good's your memory?
ARTOT *(Madly improvising)* In Cilicia, I recall,
   A hundred and fifty, a hundred in Babblebaloneya,
   Thirty Sards, three score from Macedon—
   All men that you . . . killed off one afternoon.
PYRGO And what's the total sum?
ARTOT *(After a rapid mental calculation)* Seven thousand.
PYRGO That should be right. First-class arithmetic!
ARTOT It's not written down, but I still remember it.
PYRGO Great pollux, I love your memory!
ARTOT It runs on food.
PYRGO If you never change, you'll never miss a meal;
   You'll always be my table's closest friend.
ARTOT *(With renewed enthusiasm)*
   In Cappadocia, five hundred at once (if your sword
   Had not gone dull) you'd have slain with a single slice.
PYRGO Poor nonentities, I let them live.
ARTOT Why should I tell you what every mortal knows?
   Pyrgopolynices, you alone on earth
   In courage and beauty and action stand invincible.
   All the girls adore you, naturally,
   Because you're so handsome. Yesterday some of them
   Caught me by the sleeve.

PYRGO And what did they say?

ARTOT They grilled me. "Is he Achilles?" said one to me.
  "No," I replied; "his brother." Then the second
  Said, "Merciful Castor, what a gorgeous man!
  A real gentleman! Look at his dreamy hair!
  I envy the girls that climb into bed with him!"

PYRGO That's what they said?

ARTOT Didn't they both implore me
  To march you past on parade over there today?

PYRGO It's a pain to be painfully handsome.

ARTOT You're telling me.
  The girls are pests: they plead and badger and beg
  To see you, ordering me to bring you round.
  I can't attend to your business affairs.

PYRGO I think it's time for us to go to the forum,
  Where I ought to pay the salary
  Of those recruits I signed up yesterday.
  King Seleucus is awfully keen for me
  To round up and enlist recruits for him.
  (Solemnly) This day is dedicated to the king.

ARTOT Let's go then, sir.

PYRGO Follow on, attendant lords.

(They march out toward the forum, stage left.)

176

The Twelve Caesars

Suetonius

And you think our *glorious and exalted leaders have egos! In his classic work,* Lives of the Twelve Caesars, *the Roman writer Gaius Suetonius Tranquillus (c. A.D. 69–140) paints a portrait of arrogance and pride perhaps unmatched until our own century. The Caesars were a living monument to Lord Acton's remark about power corrupting, and absolute power corrupting absolutely.*

So much for Caligula the Emperor; the rest of this history must needs deal with Caligula the Monster.

He adopted a variety of titles: such as 'Pious', 'Son of the Camp', 'Father of the Army', 'Caesar, Greatest and Best of Men'. But when once, at the dinner table, some foreign kings who had come to pay homage were arguing which of them was the most nobly descended, Caligula interrupted the discussion by declaiming Homer's line:

Nay, let there be one master, and one king!

And he nearly assumed a royal diadem then and there, doing away with the pretence that he was merely the chief executive of a republic. However, after his courtiers reminded him that he already outranked any king or tribal chieftain, he insisted on being treated as a god—sending for the most revered or artistically famous statues of the Greek dieties (including Juppiter at Olympia), and having their heads replaced by his own.

Next, Caligula extended the Palace as far as the Forum; converted the shrine of Castor and Pollux into a vestibule; and would often stand beside these Divine Brethren to be worshipped by all visitants, some of whom addressed him as 'Latian Juppiter'. He established a shrine to himself as God, with priests, the costliest possible victims, and a life-sized golden image, which was dressed every day in clothes identical with those that he happened to be wearing. All the richest citizens tried to gain priesthoods here, either by influence or bribery. Flamingoes, peacocks, black grouse, guinea-hens, and pheasants were offered as sacrifices, each on a particular day of the month. When the moon shone full and bright he always invited the Moon-goddess to his bed; and during the day would indulge in whispered conversations with Capitoline Juppiter, pressing his ear to the god's mouth, and sometimes raising his voice in anger. Once he was overheard threatening the god: 'If you do not raise me up to Heaven I will cast you down to Hell.' Finally he announced that Juppiter had persuaded him to share his home; and therefore connected the Palace with the Capitol by throwing a bridge across the Temple of the God Augustus; after which he began building a new house inside the precincts of the Capitol itself, in order to live even nearer.

Paradise Lost

John Milton

When it comes to pride, you'd have a hard time topping Milton's Satan: attempting to overthrow the Creator and take over heaven. Still, there is something oddly stirring about Satan's defiance: his willingness to accept his fate and make the most of it. Milton (c. 1608–1674) knew that Satan was an attractive

*character, of course, and he made him so deliberately in order
to emphasize the "glamour of evil."*

> Is this the Region, this the Soil, the Clime,
> Said then the lost Arch-Angel, this the seat
> That we must change for Heav'n, this mournful gloom
> For that celestial light? Be it so, since he
> Who now is Sovran can dispose and bid
> What shall be right: fardest from him is best
> Whom reason hath equall'd, force hath made supreme
> Above his equals. Farewell happy Fields
> Where Joy for ever dwells: Hail horrors, hail
> Infernal world, and thou profoundest Hell
> Receive thy new Possessor: One who brings
> A mind not to be chang'd by Place or Time.
> The mind is its own place, and in itself
> Can make a Heav'n of Hell, a Hell of Heav'n.
> What matter where, if I be still the same,
> And what I should be, all but less than hee
> Whom thunder hath made greater? Here at least
> We shall be free; th' Almighty hath not built
> Here for his envy, will not drive us hence:
> Here we may reign secure, and in my choice
> To reign is worth ambition though in Hell:
> Better to reign in Hell, than serve in Heav'n.

The Misanthrope

Jean-Baptiste Molière

*Going from Milton to the French comic playwright Jean-Bap-
tiste Molière (c. 1622–1673) is like going from the sublime to
the ridiculous, yet Molière was far more than just a comedy
writer. His wry observations of human nature and biting satire
still haunt us today. In the selection below, two women, fierce
rivals, show to what lengths pride will go in the eternal game of
one-upmanship.*

Scene Five
Arsinoe, Celimene

ARSINOE It's just as well those gentlemen didn't tarry.
CELIMENE Shall we sit down?
ARSINOE That won't be necessary.
  Madam, the flame of friendship ought to burn
  Brightest in matters of the most concern,
  And as there's nothing which concerns us more
  Than honor, I have hastened to your door
  To bring you, as your friend, some information
  About the status of your reputation.
  I visited, last night, some virtuous folk,
  And, quite by chance, it was of you they spoke;
  There was, I fear, no tendency to praise
  Your light behavior and your dashing ways.
  The quantity of gentlemen you see
  And your by now notorious coquetry
  Were both so vehemently criticized

By everyone, that I was much surprised.
Of course, I needn't tell you where I stood;
I came to your defense as best I could
Assured them you were harmless, and declared
Your soul was absolutely unimpaired.
But there are some things, you must realize,
One can't excuse, however hard one tries,
And I was forced at last into conceding
That your behavior, Madam, is misleading,
That it makes a bad impression, giving rise
To ugly gossip and obscene surmise,
And that if you were more *overtly* good,
You wouldn't be so much misunderstood.
Not that I think you've been unchaste—no! no!
The saints preserve me from a thought so low!
But mere good conscience never did suffice;
One must avoid the outward show of vice.
Madam, you're too intelligent, I'm sure,
To think my motives anything but pure
In offering you this counsel—which I do
Out of zealous interest in you.
CELIMENE Madam, I haven't taken you amiss;
  I'm very obliged to you for this;
  And I'll at once discharge the obligation
  By telling you about *your* reputation.
  You've been so friendly as to let me know
  What certain people say of me, and so
  I mean to follow your benign example
  By offering you a somewhat similar sample.
  The other day I went to an affair
  And found some most distinguished people there
  Discussing piety, both false and true.

The conversation soon came round to you.
Alas! Your prudery and bustling zeal
Appeared to have a very slight appeal.
Your affectation of a grave demeanor,
Your endless talk of virtue and of honor,
The aptitude of your suspicious mind
For finding sin where there is none to find,
Your towering self-esteem, that pitying face
With which you contemplate the human race,
Your sermonizings and your sharp aspersions
On people's pure and innocent diversions—
All these were mentioned, Madam, and, in fact,
Were roundly and concertedly attacked.
"What good," they said, "are all those outward shows,
When everything belies her pious pose?
She prays incessantly; but then, they say,
She beats her maids and cheats them of their pay;
She shows her zeal in every holy place,
But still she's vain enough to paint her face;
She holds that naked statues are immoral,
But with a naked *man* she'd have no quarrel."
Of course, I said to everyone there
That they were being viciously unfair;
But still they were disposed to criticize you,
And all agreed that someone should advise you
To leave the morals of the world alone,
And worry rather more about your own.
They felt that one's self-knowledge should be great
Before one thinks of setting others straight;
That one should learn the art of living well
Before one threatens other men with hell,
And that the Church is best equipped, no doubt,

To guide our souls and root our vices out.
Madam, you're too intelligent, I'm sure,
To think my motives anything but pure
In offering you this counsel—which I do
Out of a zealous interest in you.

ARSINOE I dared not hope for gratitude, but I
Did not expect so acid a reply;
I judge, since you've been so extremely tart,
That my good counsel pierced you in the heart.

CELIMENE Far from it, Madam. Indeed, it seems to me
We ought to trade advice more frequently.
One's vision of oneself is so defective
That it would be an excellent corrective.
If you are willing, Madam, let's arrange
Shortly to have another frank exchange
In which we'll tell each other, *entre nous,*
What you've heard tell of me, and I of you.

ARSINOE Oh, people never censure you, my dear;
It's me they criticize. Oh so I hear.

CELIMENE Madam, I think we either blame or praise
According to our taste and length of days.
There is a time of life for coquetry,
And there's a season, too, for prudery.
When all one's charms are gone, it is, I'm sure,
Good strategy to be devout and pure:
It makes one seem a little less forsaken.
Some day, perhaps, I'll take the road you've taken:
Time brings all things. But I have time aplenty,
And see no cause to be a prude at twenty.

ARSINOE You give your age in such a gloating tone
That one would think I was an ancient crone;
We're not so far apart, in sober truth,

That you can mock me with a boast of youth!
Madam, you baffle me. I wish I knew
What moves you to provoke me as you do.

CELIMENE For my part, Madam, I should like to know
Why you abuse me everywhere you go.
Is it my fault, dear lady, that your hand
Is not, alas, in very great demand?
If men admire me, if they pay me court
And daily make me offers of the sort
You'd dearly love to have them make to you,
How can I help it? What would you have me do?
If what you want is lovers, please feel free
To take as many as you can from me.

ARSINOE Oh, come. D'you think the world is losing sleep
Over that flock of lovers which you keep,
Or that we find it difficult to guess
What price you pay for their devotedness?
Surely you don't expect us to suppose
Mere merit could attract so many beaux?
It's not your virtue that they're dazzled by;
Nor is it virtuous love for which they sigh.
You're fooling no one, Madam; the world's not blind;
There's many a lady heaven has designed
To call men's noblest, tenderest feelings out,
Who has no lovers dogging her about;
From which it's plain that lovers nowadays
Must be acquired in bold and shameless ways,
And only pay one court for such reward
As modesty and virtue can't afford.
Then don't be quite so puffed up, if you please,
About your tawdry little victories;
Try, if you can, to be a shade less vain,

And treat the world with somewhat less disdain.
If one were envious of your amours,
One soon could have a following like yours;
Lovers are no great trouble to collect
If one prefers them to self-respect.

CELIMENE Collect them then, my dear; I'd love to see
You demonstrate that charming theory;
Who knows, you might . . .

ARSINOE Now, Madam, that will do;
It's time to end this trying interview.
My coach is late in coming to your door,
Or I'd have taken leave of you before.

Muscle

Confessions of an Unlikely Bodybuilder

Samuel Wilson Fussell

I love this book! Sam Fussell was a pencil-necked literary geek, an American graduate of Oxford University, working in New York City at a publishing house and finding himself utterly terrified by the street hustlers of the city. He started working out in a gym, got hooked, and began an unlikely quest to become a professional bodybuilder. His inside look at "the disease" tells you more about human pride, and the illusions and longings it creates, than you'll probably want to know.

It was while I was on the seated calf machine that day that I first heard the ruckus. My head was down, my face contorted in agony. I'd been at it for a full hour, painfully isolating my soleus and gastrocnemius muscles. To really "get into" them, I was, of course, using the usual visualization procedure, in this case, seeing my calves as gigantic spinnakers close to bursting from the force of a raging sea squall. My concentration was broken by the roar of a deep voice.

"In the final arena, there will be no judges, only witnesses to my greatness!" proclaimed an immense figure in a New York accent, hopping over the turnstile at the front door. He proceeded to do "the Walk" over to the squat platform. And oh what a walk he did. I had never seen quads thrust so far apart in the eternal battle against chafing, or arms suspended at such a distance from the body. And the majestic motion—so slow it took him a good 45 seconds to travel 30 feet.

He wore a silk do-rag over his head, a kind of colorful kerchief popular among minority women and gang members in depressed urban pockets of the United States. Over his massive and heavily acned torso, he sported a Gold's Gym tank top and sweatshirt. The sweatshirt was ripped just enough around the collar to reveal a jutting and greasy pair of trapezius muscles. On his legs he wore, direct from Marrakesh, billowing genie pants the color of orange sherbert. The outfit was completed by purple socks and Reeboks.

"Oh yes!" he screamed at the top of his lungs, nodding his head up and down dramatically. "Oh yes, we have come to train today! May we say it?" Without waiting for an answer, he burst forth with "Yes, I think we may. This is *serious* business!" Most of the other lifters, especially the smaller ones, gave him wide clearance.

"Do the right thing, buddy!" the hulk bellowed to himself. He shook his head from side to side, revealing the feathered earring that reached down to tickle one of his traps. Tightening his belt and wrist straps, he strode to the mirror to arrange his do-rag. He lingered for a moment at the mirror before rushing to the deadlift bar to warm up with 225 pounds for 15 lightening-quick reps. On his last rep, with a great clatter, he threw the bar from him in disgust, and did "the Walk" to the water fountain. There he lollygagged to slowly lick his flexed bicep for Tara and Xandra.

Xandra shrieked and hid under the counter. Tara, bolt upright, mouth slightly open, hips pressed forward against the counter's edge, didn't take her eyes off him.

On his way back to the platform, the hulk caught a smaller man eyeing him in distaste. Walking right up to him, he sneered, "Yeah? Don't break your pencil case, geek. Why don't you go get Raoul, huh? I spit on the both of you, you little closet shits!"

The target of his vehemence turned completely red, and fled in fear to the locker room. Clearly, it made the hulk's day. His heavily muscled arm was raised in triumph; he flourished his clenched fist. He did "the Walk" back to the squat platform, where for ten brutal repetitions he deadlifted 405 pounds.

"Make haste slowly," I reminded myself, resisting the urge to run over and join him. His act was familiar to me. It reminded me of the free-weight section back at the Y. But it was clear that it didn't go over well in this California gym.

No wonder. Back in New York, lifting had been about war. Here, judging from the conversations around me, it was about networking. The hard-core builders were there, true; the Axles, the Bulldozers, the Guses (the usual nerds were in attendance as well—the Norberts and Nestors). But they were all swamped by the crowd of Kips and Corkys and Alistaires who flooded through the door after five o'clock. And that went for the women, too. The Ramonas, Desirees, and Dulcies were now few; the Catherines, and Jennifers, and Victorias many. Back at the Y, "opportunities for advancement" had meant the squat

The Book of Vices
• • • • •

rack and the bench press. Here, it seemed to mean vocational choices and personal investments. The air was heavy with speculation on the vagaries of CDs, IRAs, and prime rates.

The one throwback to an earlier era was this blustering bully. As I watched, he skipped from the water fountain to the deadlifting bar. He sang the following ditty at the top of his lungs, while he chalked his palms and fingers and adjusted his wrist straps in preparation for the lift:

> One, two, three, four,
> Every night I pray for war!
> Five, six, seven, eight,
> Rape, kill, mutilate!

As if it were nothing, he picked up the 500 pounds on the deadlift bar and brought it up to his hips, repeating the movement for 10 strict reps. I was amazed. His face bore a rapt expression, as if nothing could please him more than being here and doing this. When I did it, for one pathetic rep, my whole body shuddered from pain.

"We're talkin' big man muscles, goddamnit, I mean, serious muscles, I mean we're talking' *big*!" he yelled at the mirror again, his straining, screaming face one inch from the glass. His face and upper back bore the deep pits and craters of endless acne bombardments. His bulging traps were decorated with gigantic boils and cysts. He looked as happy as a pig in slop.

The workout as operatic drama, with all the peaks and sloughs known to each. In body and performance, he was lightyears beyond Sweepea and Mousie. Here was joy. Here was fierceness.

A Study in Scarlet

Sir Arthur Conan Doyle

*Arthur Conan Doyle (c. 1859–1930) was a British doctor who
gave up the practice of medicine to become a full-time writer.
His most famous creation, of course, was the arrogant but brilliant "consulting detective" Sherlock Holmes. This scene from
the first Holmes novel,* A Study in Scarlet, *published in 1887,
is a character study in pride.*

"Well, I have a trade of my own. I suppose I am the only one
in the world. I'm a consulting detective, if you can understand
what that is. Here in London we have lots of government detectives and lots of private ones. When these fellows are at fault,
they come to me, and I manage to put them on the right scent.
They lay all the evidence before me, and I am generally able, by
the help of my knowledge of the history of crime, to set them
straight. There is a strong family resemblance about misdeeds,
and if you have all the details of a thousand at your finger ends,
it is odd if you can't unravel the thousand and first. Lestrade is a
well-known detective. He got himself into a fog recently over a
forgery case, and that was what brought him here."

"And these other people?"

"They are mostly sent on by private inquiry agencies. They
are all people who are in trouble about something and want a
little enlightening. I listen to their story, they listen to my comments, and then I pocket my fee."

"But do you mean to say," I said, "that without leaving your
room you can unravel some knot which other men can make

nothing of, although they have seen every detail for themselves?"

"Quite so. I have a kind of intuition that way. Now and again a case turns up which is a little more complex. Then I have to bustle about and see things with my own eyes. You see I have a lot of special knowledge which I apply to the problem, and which facilitates matters wonderfully. Those rules of deduction laid down in that article which aroused your scorn are invaluable to me in practical work. Observation with me is second nature. You appeared to be surprised when I told you, on our first meeting, that you had come from Afghanistan."

"You were told, no doubt."

"Nothing of the sort. I *knew* you came from Afghanistan. From long habit the train of thoughts ran so swiftly through my mind that I arrived at the conclusion without being conscious of intermediate steps. There were such steps, however. The train of reasoning ran, 'Here is a gentleman of a medical type, but with the air of a military man. Clearly an army doctor, then. He has just come from the tropics, for his face is dark, and that is not the natural tint of his skin, for his wrists are fair. He has undergone hardship and sickness, as his haggard face says clearly. His left arm has been injured. He holds it in a stiff and unnatural manner. Where in the tropics could an English army doctor have seen much hardship and got his arm wounded? Clearly in Afghanistan.' The whole train of thought did not occupy a second. I then remarked that you came from Afghanistan, and you were astonished."

"It is simple enough as you explain it," I said smiling. "You remind me of Edgar Allan Poe's Dupin. I had no idea that such individuals did exist outside of stories."

Sherlock Holmes rose and lit his pipe. "No doubt you think that you are complimenting me in comparing me to Dupin," he observed. "Now, in my opinion, Dupin was a very inferior fellow. That trick of his of breaking in on his friends' thoughts with an apropos remark after a quarter of an hour's silence is really very showy and superficial. He had some analytical genius, no doubt; but he was by no means such a phenomenon as Poe appeared to imagine."

"Have you read Gaboriau's works?" I asked. "Does Lecoq come up to your idea of a detective?"

Sherlock Holmes sniffed sardonically. "Lecoq was a miserable bungler," he said, in an angry voice; "he had only one thing to recommend him, and that was his energy. That book made me positively ill. The question was how to identify an unknown prisoner. I could have done it in twenty-four hours. Lecoq took six months or so. It might be made a textbook for detectives to teach them what to avoid."

I felt rather indignant at having two characters whom I admired treated in this cavalier style. I walked over to the window and stood looking out into the busy street. "This fellow may be very clever," I said to myself, "but he is certainly very conceited."

"There are no crimes and no criminals in these days," he said, querulously. "What is the use of having brains in our profession? I know well that I have it in me to make my name famous. No man lives or has ever lived who has brought the same amount of study and of natural talent to the detection of crime which I have done. And what is the result? There is no crime to detect, or, at most, some bungling villainy with a motive so transparent that even a Scotland Yard official can see through it."

I was still annoyed at his bumptious style of conversation. I thought it best to change the topic.

"I wonder what that fellow is looking for?" I asked, pointing

to a stalwart, plainly dressed individual who was walking slowly
down the other side of the street, looking anxiously at the numbers. He had a large blue envelope in his hand, and was evidently the bearer of a message.

"You mean the retired sergeant of the Marines," said Sherlock Holmes.

"Brag and bounce!" thought I to myself. "He knows that I
cannot verify his guess."

The thought had hardly passed through my mind when the
man whom we were watching caught sight of the number on
our door, and ran rapidly across the roadway. We heard a
loud knock, a deep voice below, and heavy steps ascending the
stair.

"For Mr. Sherlock Holmes," he said, stepping into the room
and handing my friend the letter.

Here was an opportunity of taking the conceit out of him. He
little thought of this when he made that random shot. "May I
ask you, my lad," I said, in the blandest voice, "what your trade
may be?"

"Commissionaire, sir," he said, gruffly. "Uniform away for
repairs."

"And you were?" I asked, with a slightly malicious glance at
my companion.

"A sergeant, sir, Royal Marine Light Infantry, sir. No answer? Right, sir."

He clicked his heels together, raised his hand in salute, and
was gone.

and hollow-cheeked, and dull-eyed. You will suffer horribly. . . .
Ah! realize your youth while you have it. Don't squander the
gold of your days, listening to the tedious, trying to improve the
hopeless failure, or giving away your life to the ignorant, the common, and the vulgar. These are the sickly aims, the false ideals,
of our age. Live! Live the wonderful life that is in you! Let nothing be lost upon you. Be always searching for new sensations. Be
afraid of nothing. . . . A new hedonism—that is what our century
wants. You might be its visible symbol. With your personality
there is nothing you could not do. The world belongs to you for
a season. . . . The moment I met you I saw that you were quite
unconscious of what you really are, of what you really might be.
There was so much in you that charmed me that I felt I must tell
you something about yourself. I thought how tragic it would be
if you were wasted. For there is such a little time that your youth
will last—such a little time. The common hill-flowers wither,
but they blossom again. The laburnum will be as yellow next
June as it is now. In a month there will be purple stars on the
clematis, and year after year the green night of its leaves will
hold its purple stars. But we never get back our youth. The pulse
of joy that beats in us at twenty becomes sluggish. Our limbs
fail, our senses rot. We degenerate into hideous puppets,
haunted by the memory of the passions of which we were too
much afraid, and the exquisite temptations that we had not the
courage to yield to. Youth! Youth! There is absolutely nothing
in the world but youth!''

Dorian Gray listened, open-eyed and wondering. The spray
of lilac fell from his hand upon the gravel. A furry bee came and
buzzed round it for a moment. Then it began to scramble all
over the oval stellated globe of the tiny blossoms. He watched it
with that strange interest in trivial things that we try to develop

when things of high import make us afraid, or when we are stirred by some new emotion for which we cannot find expression, or when some thought that terrifies us lays sudden siege to the brain and calls on us to yield. After a time, the bee flew away. He saw it creeping into the stained trumpet of a Tyrian convolvulus. The flower seemed to quiver, and then swayed gently to and fro.

Suddenly the painter appeared at the door of the studio and made staccato signs for them to come in. They turned to each other and smiled.

"I am waiting," he cried. "Do come in. The light is quite perfect, and you can bring your drinks."

They rose up and sauntered down the walk together. Two green-and-white butterflies fluttered past them, and in the pear-tree at the corner of the garden a thrush began to sing.

"You are glad you have met me, Mr. Gray," said Lord Henry, looking at him.

"Yes, I am glad now. I wonder shall I always be glad?"

"Always! That is a dreadful word. It makes me shudder when I hear it. Women are so fond of using it. They spoil every romance by trying to make it last for ever. It is a meaningless word, too. The only difference between a caprice and a lifelong passion is that the caprice lasts a little longer."

As they entered the studio, Dorian Gray put his hand upon Lord Henry's arm. "In that case, let our friendship be a caprice," he murmured, flushing at his own boldness, then stepped up on the platform and resumed his pose.

Lord Henry flung himself into a large wicker arm-chair and watched him. The sweep and dash of the brush on the canvas made the only sound that broke the stillness, except when, now and then, Hallward stepped back to look at his work from a distance. In the slanting beams that streamed through the open doorway the dust danced and was golden. The heavy scent of the roses seemed to brood over everything.

After about a quarter of an hour Hallward stopped painting, looked for a long time at Dorian Gray, and then for a long time at the picture, biting the end of one of his huge brushes and frowning. "It is quite finished," he cried at last, and stooping down he wrote his name in long vermilion letters on the left-hand corner of the canvas.

Lord Henry came over and examined the picture. It was certainly a wonderful work of art, and a wonderful likeness as well.

"My dear fellow, I congratulate you most warmly," he said. "It is the finest portrait of modern times. Mr. Gray, come over and look at yourself."

The lad started, as if awakened from some dream. "Is it really finished?" he murmured, stepping down from the platform.

"Quite finished," said the painter. "And you have sat splendidly to-day. I am awfully obliged to you."

"That is entirely due to me," broke in Lord Henry. "Isn't it, Mr. Gray?"

Dorian made no answer, but passed listlessly in front of his picture and turned towards it. When he saw it he drew back, and his cheeks flushed for a moment with pleasure. A look of joy came into his eyes, as if he had recognized himself for the first time. He stood there motionless and in wonder, dimly conscious that Hallward was speaking to him, but not catching the meaning of his words. The sense of his own beauty came on him like a revelation. He had never felt it before. Basil Hallward's compliments had seemed to him to be merely the charming exaggerations of friendship. He had listened to them, laughed at them, forgotten them. They had not influenced his nature. Then had come Lord Henry Wotton with his strange panegyric on youth, his terrible warning of its brevity. That had stirred him at the time, and now, as he stood gazing at the shadow of his own loveliness, the full reality of the description flashed across him. Yes, there would be a day when his face would be wrinkled and wizen, his eyes dim and colourless, the grace of his figure broken and deformed. The scarlet would pass away from his lips, and the gold steal from his hair. The life that was to make his soul would mar his body. He would become dreadful, hideous, and uncouth.

As he thought of it, a sharp pang of pain struck through him like a knife, and made each delicate fibre of his nature quiver. His eyes deepened into amethyst, and across them came a mist of tears. He felt as if a hand of ice had been laid upon his heart.

"Don't you like it?" cried Hallward at last, stung a little by the lad's silence, not understanding what it meant.

"Of course he likes it," said Lord Henry. "Who wouldn't like it? It is one of the greatest things in modern art. I will give you anything you like to ask for it. I must have it."

"It is not my property, Harry."

"Whose property is it?"

"Dorian's, of course," answered the painter.

"He is a very lucky fellow."

"How sad it is!" murmured Dorian Gray with his eyes still fixed upon his own portrait. "How sad it is! I shall grow old, and horrible, and dreadful. But this picture will remain always young. It will never be older than this particular day of June. . . . If it were only the other way! If it were I who was to be always young, and the picture that was to grow old! For that—for that—I would give everything! Yes, there is nothing in the whole world I would not give! I would give my soul for that!"

Song of Myself

Walt Whitman

We've already encountered Whitman (c. 1819–1892). This selection from Leaves of Grass *is perhaps his best known work.*

I celebrate myself, and sing myself,
And what I assume you shall assume,
For every atom belonging to me as good belongs to you.

I loafe and invite my soul,
I lean and loafe at my ease observing a spear of summer
    grass.

My tongue, every atom of my blood, form'd from this
    soil, this air,
Born here of parents born here from parents the same,
  and their parents the same,
I, now thirty-seven years old in perfect health begin,
Hoping to cease not till death.

Creeds and schools in abeyance,
Retiring back a while sufficed at what they are, but never
    forgotten,
I harbor for good or bad, I permit to speak at every
    hazzard,
Nature without check with original energy.

Houses and rooms are full of perfumes, the shelves are
    crowded with perfumes,

I breathe the fragrance myself and know it and like it,
The distillation would intoxicate me also, but I shall not
    let it.

The atmosphere is not a perfume, it has no taste of the
        distillation,
    it is odorless,
It is for my mouth forever, I am in love with it,
I will go to the bank by the wood and become
        undisguised and naked,
I am mad for it to be in contact with me.

The smoke of my own breath,
Echoes, ripples, buzz'd whispers, love-root, silk-thread,
        crotch and vine,
My respiration and inspiration, the beating of my heart,
        the passing of blood and air through my lungs,
The sniff of green leaves and dry leaves, and of the shore
        and dark-color'd sea-rocks, and of hay in the barn,
The sound of the belch'd words of my voice loos'd to the
        eddies of the wind,
A few light kisses, a few embraces, a reaching around of
        arms,
The play of shine and shade on the trees as the supple
        boughs wag,
The delight alone or in the rush of the streets, or along
        the fields and hill-sides,
The feeling of health, the full-noon trill, the song of me
        rising from bed
        and meeting the sun.

Have you reckon'd a thousand acres much? Have you
        reckon'd the earth much?

Have you practis'd so long to learn to read?
Have you felt so proud to get at the meaning of poems?

Stop this day and night with me and you shall possess the
        origin of all poems,
You shall possess the good of the earth and sun, (there
        are millions of suns left,)
You shall no longer take things at second or third hand,
        nor look through
        the eyes of the dead, nor feed on the spectres in
        books,
You shall not look through my eyes either, nor take
        things from me,
You shall listen to all sides and filter them from your self.

Moll Flanders

Daniel Defoe

Daniel Defoe (1660–1731) is best known for his novel Robin-
son Crusoe, *but* Moll Flanders *is by far the more enjoyable
book: bawdy, insightful, and very, very funny, it is the tale of a
liberated woman who, with luck and a little cash, makes her
own way in the world.*

I was now, as above, left loose to the world, and being still
young and handsome, as everybody said of me, and I assure you
I thought myself so, and with a tolerable fortune in my pocket, I
put no small value upon myself. I was courted by several very
considerable tradesmen and particularly very warmly by one, a

linen-draper, at whose house after my husband's death I took a lodging, his sister being my acquaintance. Here I had all the liberty and opportunity to be gay and appear in company that I could desire, my landlord's sister being one of the maddest, gayest things alive, and not so much mistress of her virtue as I thought at first she had been. She brought me into a world of wild company and even brought home several persons, such as she liked well enough to gratify, to see her pretty widow. Now, as fame and fools make an assembly, I was here wonderfully caressed, had abundance of admirers, and such as called themselves lovers; but I found not one fair proposal among them all. As for their common design, that I understood too well to be drawn into more snares of that kind. The case was altered with me; I had money in my pocket and had nothing to say to them. I had been tricked once by that cheat called love, but the game was over; I was resolved now to be married or nothing, and to be well married or not at all.

I loved the company, indeed, of men of mirth and wit, and was often entertained with such, as I was also with others; but I found by just observation that the brightest men came upon the dullest errand, that is to say, the dullest as to what I aimed at. On the other hand, those who came with the best proposals were the dullest and most disagreeable part of the world. I was not averse to a tradesman; but then I would have a tradesman, forsooth, that was something of a gentleman too; that when my husband had a mind to carry me to the court or to a play, he might become a sword, and look as like a gentleman as another man, and not like one that had the mark of his apron-strings upon his coat or the mark of his hat upon his periwig; that should look as if he was set on his sword when his sword was put on to him, and that carried his trade in his countenance.

Well, at last I found this amphibious creature, this land-water thing, called a gentleman-tradesman; and as a just plague upon my folly, I was catched in the very snare which, as I might say, I laid for myself.

This was a draper too, for though my comrade would have bargained for me with her brother, yet when they came to the point, it was, it seems, for a mistress, and I kept true to this notion that a woman should never be kept for a mistress that had money to make herself a wife.

Thus my pride, not my principle, my money, not my virtue, kept me honest; though as it proved, I found I had much better have been sold by my she-comrade to her brother than have sold myself as I did to a tradesman that was rake, gentleman, shopkeeper, and beggar all together.

Pride and Prejudice

Jane Austen

Jane Austen (c. 1775–1817) had a dry wit that is perhaps too dry for many modern readers, but she knew all about the vices—and about pride most of all. In the selection below, the unbelievably vain and arrogant clergyman, Mr. Collins, proposes marriage to a young woman utterly uninterested in his offer. Women readers have commented that they know his type only too well.

The next day opened a new scene at Longbourn. Mr. Collins made his declaration in form. Having resolved to do it without loss of time, as his leave of absence extended only to the following Saturday, and having no feelings of diffidence to make it distressing to himself even at the moment, he set about it in a very orderly manner, with all the observances which he supposed a regular part of the business. On finding Mrs. Bennet, Elizabeth, and one of the younger girls together, soon after breakfast, he addressed the mother in these words,

"May I hope, Madam, for your interest with your fair daughter Elizabeth, when I solicit for the honour of a private audience with her in the course of this morning?"

Before Elizabeth had time for anything but a blush of surprise, Mrs. Bennet instantly answered.

"Oh dear!—Yes—certainly.—I am sure Lizzy will be very happy—I am sure she can have no objection.—Come, Kitty, I want you up stairs." And gathering her work together, she was hastening away, when Elizabeth called out.

"Dear Ma'am, do not go.—I beg you will not go.—Mr. Collins must excuse me.—He can have nothing to say to me that anybody need not hear. I am going away myself."

"No, no, nonsense, Lizzy.—I desire you will stay where you are."—And upon Elizabeth's seeming really, with vexed and embarrassed looks, about to escape, she added, "Lizzy, I *insist* upon your staying and hearing Mr. Collins."

Elizabeth would not oppose such an injunction—and a moment's consideration making her also sensible that it would be wisest to get it over as soon and as quietly as possible, she sat down again, and tried to conceal by incessant employment the feelings which were divided between distress and diversion. Mrs. Bennet and Kitty walked off, and as soon as they were gone Mr. Collins began.

"Believe me, my dear Miss Elizabeth, that your modesty, so far from doing you any disservice, rather adds to your other perfections. You would have been less amiable in my eyes had there *not* been this little unwillingness; but allow me to assure you that I have your respected mother's permission for this address. You can hardly doubt the purport of my discourse, however your natural delicacy may lead you to dissemble; my attentions have been too marked to be mistaken. Almost as soon as I entered the house I singled you out as the companion of my future life. But before I am run away with by my feelings on this subject, perhaps it will be advisable for me to state my reasons for marrying—and moreover for coming into Hertfordshire with the design of selecting a wife, as I certainly did."

The idea of Mr. Collins, with all his solemn composure, being run away with by his feelings, made Elizabeth so near laughing that she could not use the short pause he allowed in any attempt to stop him farther, and he continued:

"My reasons for marrying are, first, that I think it a right thing for every clergyman in easy circumstances (like myself) to set the example of matrimony in his parish. Secondly, that I am convinced it will add very greatly to my happiness; and thirdly,—which perhaps I ought to have mentioned earlier, that it is the particular advice and recommendation of the very noble lady whom I have the honour of calling patroness. Twice has she condescended to give me her opinion (unasked too!) on this subject; and it was but the very Saturday night before I left Hunsford—between our pools at quadrille, while Mrs. Jenkinson was arranging Miss de Bourgh's foot-stool, that she said, 'Mr. Collins, you must marry. A clergyman like you must marry.—Chuse properly, chuse a gentlewoman for *my* sake; and for your *own,* let her be an active, useful sort of person, not brought up high, but able to make a small income go a good way. This is my advice. Find such a woman as soon as you can, bring her to Hunsford, and I will visit her.' Allow me, by the way, to observe, my fair cousin, that I do not reckon the notice and kindness of Lady Catherine de Bourgh as among the least of the advantages in my power to offer. You will find her manners beyond any thing I can describe; and your wit and vivacity I think must be acceptable to her, especially when tempered with the silence and respect which her rank will inevitably excite. Thus much for my general intention in favour of matrimony; it remains to be told why my views were directed to Longbourn instead of my own neighbourhood, where I assure you there are many amiable young women. But the fact is, that being, as I am, to inherit this estate after the death of your honoured father, (who, however, may live many years longer), I could not satisfy myself without resolving to chuse a wife from among his daughters, that the loss to them might be as little as possible, when the melancholy event takes place—which, however, as I have already said, may not be for several years. This has been my motive, my fair cousin, and I flatter myself it will not sink me in your esteem. And now nothing remains for me but to assure you in the most animated language of the violence of my affection. To fortune I am perfectly indifferent, and shall make no demand of that nature on your father, since I am well aware that it could not be complied with; and that one thousand pounds in the 4 per cents, which will not be yours till after your mother's decease, is all that you may ever be entitled to. On that head, therefore, I shall be uniformly silent; and you may assure yourself that no ungenerous reproach shall ever pass my lips when we are married."

It was absolutely necessary to interrupt him now.

"You are too hasty, Sir," she cried. "You forget that I have made no answer. Let me do it without farther loss of time. Accept my thanks for the compliment you are paying me. I am very sensible of the honour of your proposals, but it is impossible for me to do otherwise than decline them."

"I am not now to learn," replied Mr. Collins, with a formal wave of the hand, "that it is usual with young ladies to reject the addresses of the man whom they secretly mean to accept, when he first applies for their favour; and that sometimes the refusal is repeated a second or even a third time. I am therefore by no means discouraged by what you have just said, and shall hope to lead you to the altar ere long."

"Upon my word, Sir," cried Elizabeth, "your hope is rather an extraordinary one after my declaration. I do assure you that I am not one of those young ladies (if such young ladies there are) who are so daring as to risk their happiness on the chance of being asked a second time. I am perfectly serious in my refusal.—You could not make *me* happy, and I am convinced that I am the last woman in the world who would make *you* so.— Nay, were your friend Lady Catherine to know me, I am persuaded she would find me in every respect ill qualified for the situation."

"Were it certain that Lady Catherine would think so," said Mr. Collins very gravely—"but I cannot imagine that her ladyship would at all disapprove of you. And you may be certain that when I have the honour of seeing her again I shall speak in the highest terms of your modesty, economy, and other amiable qualifications."

"Indeed, Mr. Collins, all praise of me will be unnecessary. You must give me leave to judge for myself, and pay me the compliment of believing what I say. I wish you very happy and very rich, and by refusing your hand, do all in my power to prevent your being otherwise. In making me the offer, you must have satisfied the delicacy of your feelings with regard to my family, and may take possession of Longbourn estate whenever it falls, without any self-reproach. This matter may be considered, therefore, as finally settled." And rising as she thus spoke, she would have quitted the room, had not Mr. Collins thus addressed her.

"When I do myself the honour of speaking to you next in this subject I shall hope to receive a more favourable answer than you have now given me; though I am far from accusing you of cruelty at present, because I know it to be the established custom of your sex to reject a man on the first application, and perhaps you have even now said as much to encourage my suit as would be consistent with the true delicacy of the female character."

"Really, Mr. Collins," cried Elizabeth with some warmth, "you puzzle me exceedingly. If what I have hitherto said can appear to you in the form of encouragement, I know not how to express my refusal in such a way as may convince you of its being one."

"You must give me leave to flatter myself, my dear cousin, that your refusal of my addresses is merely words of course. My reasons for believing it are briefly these:—It does not appear to me that my hand is unworthy your acceptance, or that the establishment I can offer would be any other than highly desirable. My situation in life, my connections with the family of De Bourgh, and my relationship to your own, are circumstances highly in my favour; and you should take it into farther consideration that in spite of your manifold attractions, it is by no means certain that another offer of marriage may ever be made you. Your portion is unhappily so small that it will in all likelihood undo the effects of your loveliness and amiable qualifications. As I must therefore conclude that you are not serious in your rejection of me, I shall chuse to attribute it to your wish of increasing my love by suspense, according to the usual practice of elegant females."

"I do assure you, Sir, that I have no pretension whatever to that kind of elegance which consists in tormenting a respectable man. I would rather be paid the compliment of being believed. I thank you again and again for the honour you have done me in your proposals, but to accept them is absolutely impossible. My feelings in every respect forbid it. Can I speak plainer? Do not consider me now as an elegant female intending to plague you, but as a rational creature speaking the truth from her heart."

"You are uniformly charming!" cried he, with an air of awkward gallantry; "and I am persuaded that when sanctioned by the express authority of both your excellent parents, my proposals will not fail of being acceptable."

To such perseverance in wilful self-deception Elizabeth would make no reply, and immediately and in silence withdrew; determined, if he persisted in considering her repeated refusals as flattering encouragement, to apply to her father, whose negative might be uttered in such a manner as must be decisive, and whose behaviour at least could not be mistaken for the affectation and coquetry of an elegant female.

Self-Reliance

Ralph Waldo Emerson

Emerson (c. 1803–1882) was a weird mixture of common sense and what we would call today New Age goofiness. Generations of readers, however, have cherished this little testament to being true to oneself and it certainly belongs in a chapter on pride.

To believe your own thought, to believe that what is true for you in your private heart is true for all men,—that is genius. Speak your latent conviction, and it shall be the universal sense; for the inmost in due time becomes the outmost,—and our first thought is rendered back to us by the trumpets of the Last Judgment. Familiar as the voice of the mind is to each, the highest merit we ascribe to Moses, Plato, and Milton is, that they set at naught books and traditions, and spoke not what men but what they thought. A man should learn to detect and watch that gleam of light which flashes across his mind from within, more than the lustre of the firmament of bards and sages. Yet he dismisses without notice his thought, because it is his. In every work of genius we recognize our own rejected thoughts: they come back to us with a certain alienated majesty. Great works of art have no more affecting lesson for us than this. They teach us to abide by our spontaneous impressions with good-humored inflexibility then most when the whole cry of voices is on the other side. Else, tomorrow a stranger will say with masterly good sense precisely what we have thought and felt all the time, and we shall be forced to take with shame our own opinion from another.

Six
...
ENVY

Whenever a friend succeeds, a little something in me dies.

—*Gore Vidal*

Puritanism is the haunting fear that someone, somewhere, may be happy.

—*H. L. Mencken*

I 've never really understood what's so bad about envy.

In the classical definition, at least according to Webster's, envy is the desire for some advantage or quality which another person has.

And what's so wrong with that?

If I wanted to be a lawyer, which I don't, I would naturally envy the law degrees which members of the bar possess. If I wanted to ski, I would envy the skiing ability of those who ski.

A friend of mine has a new Jeep, so why shouldn't I think that, all things considered, I'd like to have one, too? I don't want *his* Jeep: I'd just like one *like* his.

I'm not one of those people whose happiness depends on having *more* than other people. If I had $10 million in a Swiss bank account, it wouldn't bother me much if I knew that other people had a similar amount. I might even invite them over to the house for brandy and cigars after dinner.

In fact, envy is the spiritual foundation of our most important social enterprises, from the economy to education: Without envy, no one would desire material possessions of any kind, or, for that matter, an education, or good health, or any other good thing. We can convince students to learn to read, or to add up a column of numbers, because they see other kids reading books and get it into their heads that reading, or adding, might be a useful, fun skill to have. Businesses find that the best way to sell anything is to point out to you that Jones has a particular item or service and, what's more, it has made a tremendous difference in Jones' life.

So what do people have against envy?

St. Thomas Aquinas considered the matter in his usual thorough way and found that there are two basic types of envy.

The malicious kind of envy, Aquinas wrote, is when you are unhappy over some good thing happening to someone else because you believe he or she is unworthy of it. For example, if your drunken ex-brother-in-law suddenly inherits a million bucks from a long-lost uncle, you probably figure he doesn't deserve his good fortune. This, Aquinas says, is forbidden by the Bible: "Be not envious of evil-doers nor envy them that work iniquity" (Psalm 73).

It also sometimes happens that we envy good people their fortune, not because we necessarily want what they have, but because we don't want *them* to have it. This is true envy *(invidia),* and it is always a sin, according to Aquinas, because it involves grieving over what should make us rejoice—namely, our neighbor's good fortune. Envy of this type is exemplified by the seething hatred which the character Salieri bears toward the youthful Mozart in Peter Shaffer's play *Amadeus.*

However, Aquinas wrote that there is also a benevolent kind of envy: When we desire a good not because someone else has it but simply because we do not. This is what most people today mean by envy; but, Aquinas writes that this should actually be called zeal *(zelus).* If it concerns spiritual goods, this form of envy is always laudable, for the Bible says, "Be zealous for spiritual gifts." If it concerns material goods, Aquinas says, it may or may not be sinful.

It is clear that this kind of envy, the desire for some advantage or quality that another person has, is often a good thing. It is what drives the human spirit to be and to do, to strive for excellence. Human beings are not like angels: mere contemplation of an abstract ideal is not enough to motivate us. We have to see someone else actually benefiting from an education, or driving around in a new Jeep, or making more money, before we can want such advantages for ourselves.

The key, as always, is being envious of the right things. The problem with envy is that, like love, it is often blind. We may envy our neighbor his new boat, but we don't really know all the details involved in owning it: the endless cleaning, the extra expense, the hassles of putting it in and taking it out of the water. We may think we want such a seemingly good thing, but we may not. As the proverb puts it: Be careful of what you wish for, because you might get it.

The problem with human beings, generally speaking, is not that they are too envious but that they are not envious enough. People get comfortable, even lazy, and lose the desire, as Tennyson put it, "to strive, to seek, to find and not to yield."

We need more envy because, as another fine poet put it, "man's reach should exceed his grasp . . . or what's a heaven for?"

On Envy

Horace

Quintus Horatius Flaccus (c. 65–8 B.C.) was a Roman poet whose Odes *and* Satires *reflect the calm sanity of Roman*

*thought. His satire on envy is a gentle jibe at the notion that
the grass is always greener across the street.*

How comes it, Maecenas, that no man living is content with
the lot which either his choice has given him, or chance has
thrown in his way, but each has praise for those who follow
other paths? "O happy traders!" cries the soldier, as he feels the
weight of years, his frame now shattered with hard service. On
the other hand, when southern gales toss the ship, the trader
cries: "A soldier's life is better. Do you ask why? There is the
battle clash, and in a moment of time comes speedy death or
joyous victory." One learned in law and statutes has praise for
the farmer, when towards cockcrow a client comes knocking at
his door. The man yonder, who has given surety and is dragged
into town from the country cries that they only are happy who
live in town. The other instances of this kind—so many are
they—could tire out the chatterbox Fabius. To be brief with
you, hear the conclusion to which I am coming. If some god
were to say: "Here I am! I will grant your prayers forthwith.
You, who were but now a soldier, shall be a trader; you, but now
a lawyer, shall be a farmer. Change parts; away with you—and
with you! Well! Why standing still?" They would refuse. And
yet 'tis in their power to be happy. What reason is there why
Jove should not, quite properly, puff out both cheeks at them in
anger, and say that never again will he be so easy-going as to
lend ear to their prayers?

Furthermore, not to skim over the subject with a laugh like a
writer of witticisms—and yet what is to prevent one from telling
truth as he laughs, even as teachers sometimes give cookies to
children to coax them into learning their A B C?—still, putting
jesting aside, let us turn to serious thoughts: yon farmer, who
with tough plough turns up the heavy soil, our rascally host

here, the soldier, the sailors who boldly scour every sea, all say
that they bear toil with this in view, that when old they may re-
tire into secure ease, once they have piled up their provisions;
even as the tiny, hard-working ant (for she is their model) drags
all she can with her mouth, and adds it to the heap she is building, because she is not unaware and not heedless of the morrow.
Yet she, soon as Aquarius saddens the upturned year, stirs out
no more but uses the store she gathered beforehand, wise creature that she is; while as for you, neither burning heat, nor winter, fire, sea, sword, can turn you aside from gain—nothing
stops you, until no second man be richer than yourself.

Snow-White and the Seven Dwarfs
The Brothers Grimm

*For primal fables that cut to the very heart of the human soul,
you'd have a hard time topping Jacob (c. 1785–1863) and Wil-
helm (c. 1786–1859) Grimm, the German folklorists and phi-
lologists. Most of their stories in children's books have been
tidied up a bit for modern sensibilities. The tale of Snow
White, of course, is one of the most common motifs in literature: the envy of the old for the young.*

Once upon a time in the middle of winter, when the snow-
flakes were falling like feathers from the sky, a queen sat at her
window working, and her embroidery frame was of ebony. And
as she worked, gazing at times out on the snow, she pricked her
finger, and there fell from it three drops of blood on the snow.
And when she saw how bright and red it looked, she said to

herself, "Oh, that I had a child as white as snow, lips as red as blood, and hair as black as the wood of the embroidery frame!"

Not very long afterwards she had a daughter, with a skin as white as snow, lips as red as blood, and hair as black as ebony, and she was named Snow-White. And when she was born the Queen died.

After a year had gone by, the King took another wife, a beautiful woman, but proud and overbearing, and she could not bear to be surpassed in beauty by anyone. She had a magic looking glass, and she used to stand before it and look in it and say:

> "Looking glass upon the wall,
> Who is fairest of us all?"

And the looking glass would answer:

> "You are fairest of them all."

And she was contented, for she knew that the looking glass spoke the truth.

Now Snow-White was growing prettier and prettier, and when she was seven years old she was as beautiful as day, far more so than the Queen herself. So one day when the Queen went to her mirror and said:

> "Looking glass upon the wall,
> Who is fairest of us all?"

It answered:

"Queen, you are full fair, 'tis true,
But Snow-White fairer is than you."

This gave the Queen a great shock, and she became yellow and green with envy, and from that hour her heart turned against Snow-White and she hated her. And envy and pride like ill weeds grew higher in her heart every day until she had no peace day or night.

Reflections at Dawn

Phyllis McGinley

The poet Phyllis McGinley, unlike many modern commentators, confesses that she desires many things.

I wish I owned a Dior dress
    Made to order out of satin.
I wish I weighed a little less
    And could read Latin,
Had perfect pitch or matching pearls,
    A better head for street directions,
And seven daughters all with curls
    And fair complexions.
I wish I'd tan instead of burn.
    But most, on all the stars that glisten,
I wish at parties I could learn
    to sit and listen.

Vanity Fair

William Makepeace Thackeray

The British novelist William Thackeray (c. 1811–1863) is best known for his larger-than-life saga Vanity Fair. *In the selection below, the narrator indulges in that time-honored rite of envy: wondering how a neighbor can afford to live the way he or she does.*

I suppose there is no man in this Vanity Fair of ours so little observant as not to think sometimes about the worldly affairs of his acquaintances, or so extremely charitable as not to wonder how his neighbor Jones, or his neighbour Smith, can make both ends meet at the end of the year. With the utmost regard for the family, for instance (for I dine with them twice or thrice in the season), I cannot but own that the appearance of the Jenkinses in the park, in the large barouche with the grenadier-footmen, will surprise and mystify me to my dying day: for though I know the equipage is only jobbed, and all the Jenkins people are on board wages, yet those three men and the carriage must represent an expense of six hundred a year at the very least—and then there are the splendid dinners, the two boys at Eton, the prize governess and masters for the girls, the trip abroad, or to Eastbourne or Worthing, in the autumn, the annual ball with a supper from Gunter's (who, by the way, supplies most of the *first-rate* dinners which J. gives, as I know very well, having been invited to one of them to fill a vacant place, when I saw at once that these repasts are very superior to the *common* run of entertainments for which the *humbler* sort of J.'s acquaintances get cards)—who, I say, with the most good-natured feelings in the world, can help wondering how the Jenkinses make out matters? What *is* Jenkins? We all know—Commissioner of the Tape and Sealing Wax Office, with £1200 a year for a salary. Had his wife a private fortune? Pooh!—Miss Flint—one of eleven children of a small squire in Buckinghamshire. All she ever gets from her family is a turkey at Christmas, in exchange for which she has to board two or three of her sisters in the off season, and lodge and feed her brothers when they come to town. How does Jenkins balance his income? I say, as every friend of his must say, How is it that he has not been outlawed long since, and that he ever came back (as he did to the surprise of everybody) last year from Boulogne?

"I" is here introduced to personify the world in general—the Mrs. Grundy of each respected reader's private circle—every one of whom can point to some families of his acquaintance who live nobody knows how. Many a glass of wine have we all of us drunk, I have very little doubt, hob-and-nobbing with the hospitable giver and wondering how the deuce he paid for it.

Some three or four years after his stay in Paris, when Rawdon Crawley and his wife were established in a very small comfortable house in Curzon Street, May Fair, there was scarcely one of the numerous friends whom they entertained at dinner that did not ask the above question regarding them. The novelist, it has been said before, knows everything, and as I am in a situation to be able to tell the public how Crawley and his wife lived without any income, may I entreat the public newspapers which are in the habit of extracting portions of the various periodical works now published *not* to reprint the following exact narrative and calculations—of which I ought, as the discoverer (and at some expense, too), to have the benefit? My son, I would say, were I blessed with a child—you may by deep inquiry and constant intercourse with him learn how a man lives comfortably on nothing a year. But it is best not to be intimate with gentlemen of this profession and to take the calculations at second hand, as you do logarithms, for to work them yourself, depend upon it, will cost you something considerable.

Penis Envy

Sigmund Freud

Sigmund Freud (c. 1856–1939) was the father of a particular school of psychotherapy that was highly influential in the early twentieth century and that attempted to discover repressed sexual conflicts within the human psyche—such as, in the example below, the famous phenomenon of "penis-envy." Not only many feminists, but also many psychiatrists, now regard much of Freud's theory as "voodoo psychology."

You will note that we ascribe a castration-complex to the female sex as well as to the male. We have good grounds for doing so, but that complex has not the same content in girls as in boys. In the boy, the castration-complex is formed after he has learnt from the sight of the female genitals that the sexual organ which he prizes so highly is not a necessary part of every human body. He remembers then the threats which he has brought on himself by his playing with his penis, he begins to believe in them, and thence forward he comes under the influence of *castration-anxiety,* which supplies the strongest motive force for his further development. The castration-complex in the girl, as well, is started by the sight of the genital organs of the other sex. She immedi-

ately notices the difference, and—it must be admitted—its significance. She feels herself at a great disadvantage, and often declares that she would "like to have something like that too," and
falls a victim to *penis-envy,* which leaves ineradicable traces on
her development and character-formation, and, even in the
most favourable instances, is not overcome without a great ex-
penditure of mental energy. That the girl recognizes the fact that
she lacks a penis, does not mean that she accepts its absence
lightly. On the contrary, she clings for a long time to the desire
to get something like it, and believes in that possibility for an
extraordinary number of years; and even at a time when her
knowledge of reality has long since led her to abandon the fulfillment of this desire as being quite unattainable, analysis
proves that it still persists in the unconscious and retains a considerable charge of energy. The desire after all to obtain the
penis for which she so much longs may even contribute to the
motives that impel a grown-up woman to come to analysis; and
what she quite reasonably expects to get from analysis, such as
the capacity to pursue an intellectual career, can often be recognized as a sublimated modification of this repressed wish.

The Alchemist

Ben Jonson

*This is another sampling of the witty Ben Jonson (c. 1572–
1637). One of the principal motivations of the alchemist in this
play is to make enough gold so he will no longer have to "thirst
of satin."*

[*Outside* LOVEWIT'S *house.*]
[*Enter* SIR EPICURE MAMMON *and* PERTINAX SURLY.]

MAMMON: Come on, sir. Now you set your foot on shore
  In *Novo Orbe;* here's the rich Peru,
  And there within, sir, are the golden mines,
  Great Solomon's Ophir! He was sailing to 't
  Three years, but we have reached it in ten months.
  This is the day wherein, to all my friends,
  I will pronounce the happy word, 'Be rich!'
  This day you shall be *spectatissimi.*
  You shall no more deal with the hollow die,
  Or the frail card. No more be at charge of keeping
  The livery-punk for the young heir, that must
  Seal, at all hours, in his shirt; no more,
  If he deny, ha' him beaten to 't, as he is
  That brings him the commodity; no more
  Shall thirst of satin, or the covetous hunger
  Of velvet entrails for a rude-spun cloak,
  To be displayed at Madam Augusta's, make
  The sons of sword and hazard fall before
  The golden calf, and on their knees, whole nights
  Commit idolatry with wine and trumpets,
  Or go a-feasting after drum and ensign.
  No more of this. You shall start up young viceroys,
  And have your punks and punketees, my Surly.
  And unto thee I speak it first, 'Be rich!'
  Where is my Subtle there? Within, ho!
  [FACE *(within)*:] Sir,
  He'll come to you by and by.
MAMMON: That's his fire-drake,
  His Lungs, his Zephyrus, he that puffs his coals,

Till he firk nature up, in her own centre.
You are not faithful, sir. This night I'll change
All that is metal in my house to gold,
And, early in the morning, will I send
To all the plumbers and the pewterers
And buy their tin and lead up; and to Lothbury
For all the copper.

David Copperfield

Charles Dickens

Charles Dickens (c. 1812–1870) had a marvelous trick: he gave every character a kind of verbal tic so that, no matter what the situation, and regardless of whether the narrator identified who was speaking or not, the reader could tell who was speaking just by listening to his or her diction, the choice of words. One of Dickens's most memorable characters, the slimy Uriah Heep, constantly proclaimed that he was "very 'umble" but he was, in fact, filled with envy.

I have said that the company were all gone, but I ought to have excepted Uriah, whom I don't include in that denomination, and who had never ceased to hover near us. He was close behind me when I went downstairs. He was close beside me when I walked away from the house, slowly fitting his long skeleton fingers into the still longer fingers of a great Guy Fawkes pair of gloves.

It was in no disposition for Uriah's company, but in remembrance of the entreaty Agnes had made to me, that I asked him if he would come home to my rooms and have some coffee.

"Oh, really, Master Copperfield," he rejoined—"I beg your pardon, Mister Copperfield, but the other comes so natural—I don't like that you should put a constraint upon yourself to ask a humble person like me to your ouse."

"There is no constraint in the case," said I. "Will you come?"

"I should like to, very much," replied Uriah, with a writhe.

"Well, then, come along!" said I.

I could not help being rather short with him, but he appeared not to mind it. We went the nearest way, without conversing much upon the road; and he was so humble in respect of those scarecrow gloves, that he was still putting them on, and seemed to have made no advance in that labour, when we got to my place.

I led him up the dark stairs, to prevent his knocking his head against anything, and really his damp cold hand felt so like a frog in mine, that I was tempted to drop it and run away. Agnes and hospitality prevailed, however, and I conducted him to my fireside. When I lighted my candles, he fell into meek transports with the room that was revealed to him; and when I heated the coffee in an unassuming blocktin vessel in which Mrs. Crupp delighted to prepare it (chiefly, I believe, because it was not intended for the purpose, being a shaving-pot, and because there was a patent invention of great price mouldering away in the pantry), he professed so much emotion that I could joyfully have scalded him.

"Oh, really, Master Copperfield—I mean Mister Copperfield," said Uriah—"to see you waiting upon me is what I never could have expected! But, one way and another, so many things happen to me which I never could have expected, I am sure, in my umble station, that it seems to rain blessings on my ed. You have heard something, I des-say, of a change in my expectations, Master Copperfield—*I* should say, Mister Copperfield?"

ℰ n v y
· · · · ·

As he sat on my sofa, with his long knees drawn up under his coffee-cup, his hat and gloves upon the ground close to him, his spoon going softly round and round, his shadowless red eyes, which looked as if they had scorched their lashes off, turned towards me without looking at me, the disagreeable dints I have formerly described in his nostrils coming and going with his breath, and a snaky undulation pervading his frame from his chin to his boots, I decided in my own mind that I disliked him intensely. It made me very uncomfortable to have him for a guest, for I was young then, and unused to disguise what I so strongly felt.

"You have heard something, I des-say, of a change in my expectations, Master Copperfield—I should say, Mister Copperfield?" observed Uriah.

"Yes," said I, "something."

"Ah! I thought Miss Agnes would know of it!" he quietly returned. "I'm glad to find Miss Agnes knows of it. Oh, thank you, Master—Mister Copperfield!"

I could have thrown my boot-jack at him (it lay ready on the rug), for having entrapped me into the disclosure of anything concerning Agnes, however immaterial. But I only drank my coffee.

"What a prophet you have shown yourself, Mister Copperfield!" pursued Uriah. "Dear me, what a prophet you have proved yourself to be! Don't you remember saying to me once that perhaps I should be a partner in Mr. Wickfield's business, and perhaps it might be Wickfield and Heep? *You* may not recollect it; but when a person is umble, Master Copperfield, a person treasures such things up."

"I recollect talking about it," said I, "though I certainly did not think it very likely then."

"Oh! who *would* have thought it likely, Mister Copperfield!"

returned Uriah enthusiastically. "I am sure I didn't myself. I recollect saying with my own lips that I was much too umble. So I considered myself really and truly."

He sat, with that carved grin on his face, looking at the fire, as I looked at him.

"But the umblest persons, Master Copperfield,—" he presently resumed, "may be the instruments of good. I am glad to think I have been the instrument of good to Mr. Wickfield, and that I may be more so. Oh, what a worthy man he is, Mister Copperfield, but how imprudent he has been!"

"I am sorry to hear it," said I. I could not help adding, rather pointedly, "on all accounts."

"Decidedly so, Mister Copperfield," replied Uriah; "on all accounts. Miss Agnes's above all! You don't remember your own eloquent expressions, Master Copperfield, but *I* remember how you said one day that everybody must admire her, and how I thanked you for it! You have forgot that, I have no doubt, Master Copperfield?"

"No," said I dryly.

"Oh, how glad I am you have not!" exclaimed Uriah. "To think that you should be the first to kindle the sparks of ambition in my umble breast, and that you've not forgot it! Oh!— Would you excuse me asking for a cup more coffee?"

Something in the emphasis he laid upon the kindling of those sparks, and something in the glance he directed at me as he said it, had made me start as if I had seen him illuminated by a blaze of light. Recalled by his request, preferred in quite another tone of voice, I did the honours of the shaving-pot; but I did them with an unsteadiness of hand, a sudden sense of being no match for him, and a perplexed suspicious anxiety as to what he might be going to say next, which I felt could not escape his observation.

He said nothing at all. He stirred his coffee round and round, he sipped it, he felt his chin softly with his grisly hand, he looked at the fire, he looked about the room, he gasped rather than smiled at me, he writhed and undulated about in his deferential servility, he stirred and sipped again, but he left the renewal of the conversation to me.

"So Mr. Wickfield," said I at last, "who is worth five hundred of you—or me"—for my life, I think, I could not have helped dividing that part of the sentence with an awkward jerk—"has been imprudent, has he, Mr. Heep?"

"Oh, very imprudent indeed, Master Copperfield," returned Uriah, sighing modestly. "Oh, very much so! But I wish you'd call me Uriah, if you please. It's like old times."

"Well, Uriah," said I, bolting it out with some difficulty.

"Thank you," he returned, with fervour. "Thank you, Master Copperfield. It's like the blowing of old breezes or the ringing of old bellses to hear *you* say Uriah. I beg your pardon. Was I making any observation?"

"About Mr. Wickfield," I suggested.

"Oh! Yes, truly," said Uriah. "Ah! Great imprudence, Master Copperfield. It's a topic that I wouldn't touch upon to any soul but you. Even to you I can only touch upon it, and no more. If any one else had been in my place during the last few years, by this time he would have had Mr. Wickfield (oh, what a worthy man he is, Master Copperfield, too!) under his thumb. Under—his thumb," said Uriah, very slowly, as he stretched out his cruel-looking hand above my table, and pressed his own thumb down upon it, until it shook, and shook the room.

If I had been obliged to look at him with his splay foot on Mr. Wickfield's head, I think I could scarcely have hated him more.

"Oh dear, yes, Master Copperfield," he proceeded, in a soft voice, most remarkably contrasting with the action of his thumb, which did not diminish its hard pressure in the least degree; "there's no doubt of it. There would have been loss, disgrace, I don't know what all. Mr. Wickfield knows it. I am the umble instrument of umbly serving him; and he puts me on an eminence I hardly could have hoped to reach. How thankful should I be!" With his face turned towards me, as he finished, but without looking at me, he took his crooked thumb off the spot where he had planted it, and slowly and thoughtfully scraped his lank jaw with it, as if he were shaving himself.

I recollect well how indignantly my heart beat, as I saw his crafty face, with the appropriately red light of the fire upon it, preparing for something else.

"Master Copperfield," he began—"but am I keeping you up?"

"You are not keeping me up. I generally go to bed late."

"Thank you, Master Copperfield! I have risen from my umble station since first you used to address me, it is true, but I am umble still. I hope I never shall be otherwise than umble. You will not think the worse of my umbleness if I make a little confidence to you, Master Copperfield? Will you?"

"Oh, no," said I, with an effort.

"Thank you!" He took out his pocket-handkerchief, and began wiping the palms of his hands. "Miss Agnes, Master Copperfield—"

"Well, Uriah?"

"Oh, how pleasant to be called Uriah spontaneously!" he cried, and gave himself a jerk, like a convulsive fish. "You thought her looking very beautiful to-night, Master Copperfield?"

"I thought her looking as she always does—superior, in all respects, to everyone around her," I returned.

"Oh, thank you! It's so true!" he cried. "Oh, thank you very much for that!"

"Not at all," I said loftily; "there is no reason why you should thank me."

"Why that, Master Copperfield," said Uriah, "is, in fact, the confidence that I am going to take the liberty of reposing. Umble as I am" (he wiped his hands harder, and looked at them and at the fire by turns), "umble as my mother is, and lowly as our poor but honest roof has ever been, the image of Miss Agnes (I don't mind trusting you with my secret, Master Copperfield, for I have always overflowed towards you since the first moment I had the pleasure of beholding you in a pony-shay) has been in my breast for years. Oh, Master Copperfield, with what a pure affection do I love the ground my Agnes walks on!"

I believe I had a delirious idea of seizing the red-hot poker out of the fire and running him through with it. It went from me with a shock, like a ball fired from a rifle; but the image of Agnes, outraged by so much as a thought of this red-headed animal's, remained in my mind (when I looked at him, sitting all awry, as if his mean soul gripped his body), and made me giddy. He seemed to swell and grow before my eyes; the room seemed full of the echoes of his voice; and the strange feeling (to which, perhaps, no one is quite a stranger) that all this had occurred before, at some indefinite time, and that I knew what he was going to say next, took possession of me.

A timely observation of the sense of power that there was in his face did more to bring back to my remembrance the entreaty of Agnes, in its full force, than any effort I could have made. I asked him, with a better appearance of composure than I could have thought possible a minute before, whether he had made his feelings known to Agnes.

"Oh, no, Master Copperfield!" he returned; "oh dear, no! Not to any one but you. You see, I am only just emerging from my lowly station. I rest a good deal of hope on her observing how useful I am to her father (for I trust to be very useful to him indeed, Master Copperfield), and how I smooth the way for him, and keep him straight. She's so much attached to her father, Master Copperfield (oh, what a lovely thing it is in a daughter!), that I think she may come, on his account, to be kind to me."

I fathomed the depth of the rascal's whole scheme, and understood why he laid it bare.

"If you'll have the goodness to keep my secret, Master Copperfield," he pursued, "and not, in general, to go against me, I shall take it as a particular favour. You wouldn't wish to make unpleasantness. I know what a friendly heart you've got; but having only known me on my umble footing (on my umblest, I should say, for I am very umble still), you might, unbeknown, go against me rather with my Agnes. I call her mine, you see, Master Copperfield. There's a song that says, 'I'd crowns resign to call her mine!' I hope to do it one of these days."

Dear Agnes! So much too loving and too good for any one that I could think of, was it possible that she was reserved to be the wife of such a wretch as this?

"There's no hurry at present, you know, Master Copperfield," Uriah proceeded, in his slimy way, as I sat gazing at him, with this thought on my mind. "My Agnes is very young still; and mother and me will have to work our way upwards, and make a good many new arrangements, before it would be quite convenient. So I shall have time gradually to make her familiar with my hopes, as opportunities offer. Oh, I'm so much obliged to you for this confidence! Oh, it's such a relief, you can't think, to know that you understand our situation, and are certain (as you wouldn't wish to make unpleasantness in the family) not to go against me!"

He took the hand which I dared not withhold, and having given it a damp squeeze, referred to his pale-faced watch.

"Dear me!" he said, "it's past one. The moments slip away so, in the confidence of old times, Master Copperfield, that it's almost half-past one!"

I answered that I had thought it was later; not that I had really thought so, but because my conversational powers were effectually scattered.

"Dear me!" he said, considering. "The ouse that I am stopping at—a sort of a private hotel and boarding-ouse, Master Copperfield, near the New River ed—will have gone to bed these two hours."

"I am sorry," I returned, "that there's only one bed here, and that I—"

"Oh, don't think of mentioning beds, Master Copperfield!" he rejoined ecstatically, drawing up one leg. "But *would* you have any objections to my laying down before the fire?"

"If it comes to that," I said, "pray take my bed, and I'll lie down before the fire."

His repudiation of this offer was almost shrill enough, in the excess of its surprise and humility, to have penetrated to the ears of Mrs. Crupp, then sleeping, I suppose, in a distant chamber situated at about the level of low water-mark, soothed in her slumbers by the ticking of an incorrigible clock, to which she always referred me when we had any little difference on the score of punctuality, and which was never less than three-quarters of an hour too slow, and had always been put right in the morning by the best authorities. As no arguments I could urge, in my bewildered condition, had the least effect upon his modesty in inducing him to accept my bedroom, I was obliged to make the best arrangements I could for his repose before the fire. The mattress of the sofa (which was a great deal too short for his lank figure), the sofa pillows, a blanket, the table-cover, a clean breakfast-cloth, and a great-coat, made him a bed and covering, for which he was more than thankful. Having lent him a nightcap, which he put on at once, and in which he made such an awful figure that I have never worn one since, I left him to his rest.

I never shall forget that night. I never shall forget how I turned and tumbled; how I wearied myself with thinking about Agnes and this creature; how I considered what could I do, and what ought I to do; how I could come to no other conclusion than that the best course for her peace was to do nothing, and to keep to myself what I had heard. If I went to sleep for a few moments, the image of Agnes with her tender eyes, and of her father looking fondly on her (as I had so often seen him look), arose before me with appealing faces, and filled me with vague terrors. When I awoke, the recollection that Uriah was lying in the next room sat heavy on me, like a waking nightmare, and oppressed me with a leaden dread, as if I had had some meaner quality of devil for a lodger.

Memorabilia

Xenophon

Xenophon (c. 430–354 B.C.), the Greek soldier and historian, is known to generations of classics majors through his Anabasis, *the classic text that recounts the struggle of 10,000 Greek mercenaries to get back home after finding themselves aban-*

doned in Persia, their leaders killed, thousands of miles from home. But Xenophon is also the only major source scholars have for the life of Socrates, and he complements (and sometimes contradicts) Plato's version.

Considering the nature of Envy, [Socrates] found it to be a kind of pain, not, however, at a friend's misfortune, nor at an enemy's good fortune, but the envious are those only who are annoyed at their friends' successes. Some expressed surprise that anyone who loves another should be pained at his success, but he reminded them that many stand in this relation towards others, that they cannot disregard them in time of trouble, but aid them in misfortune, and yet they are pained to see them prospering. This, however, could not happen to a man of sense, but it is always the case with fools.

Envy

Yuri Olesha

Yuri Olesha (c. 1899–1960) was raised in Odessa, the son of an impoverished landowner, and became famous in 1927 with the publication of the short novel Envy. *At first, the Soviets heralded the novel, but after a time the implications of what it was saying began to make party censors nervous and the work was banned. It remains, however, one of the best psychological portraits of envy ever penned.*

Mornings, he sings in the lavatory. Imagine how pleased with life he is, how healthy. His singing is a reflex. These songs of his, which have neither melody nor words, just a single "ta-ra-ra" which he shouts out in different tunes, can be interpreted thus:

"How pleasant my life is . . . ta-ra, ta-ra . . . my bowels are elastic . . . ra-ta-ta-ta-ra-ree . . . my juices flow within me . . . ra-tee-ta-doo-da-ta . . . contract, guts, contract . . . tram-ba-ba-boom!"

In the morning, I pretend to be asleep as he passes me on the way from the bedroom to the door leading to the entrails of the apartment, to the lavatory. I follow him in imagination. I hear him moving in the small lavatory, which is narrow for his big body. His back bangs against the inside, shutting the door; his sides thrust against the walls; he shuffles his feet. In the lavatory door, there is an oval panel of opaque glass. He flicks the switch, the oval lights up from the inside and becomes a beautiful egg, the color of an opal. In my mind's eye, I see that egg, hanging in the dark of the corridor.

He weighs around 220 pounds. Recently, going downstairs somewhere, he noticed how his breasts quivered to the rhythm of his steps: And so he decided to add a new set to his daily calisthenics.

That's a real man for you.

Usually he does his gymnastics, not in his own bedroom, but in the room of undefined purpose that I occupy. It is roomier there, airier; there's more light, more radiance. Coolness pours in through the open door of the balcony. Moreover, this is where the washstand is. He brings a mat from the bedroom. He is stripped except for jersey drawers, done up by a single button in the middle of his stomach, a mother-of-pearl one in which the pale blue and pink world of the room spins around. When he lies on his back on the mat, raising first one leg then the other, the button comes undone. His groin is exposed. A splendid groin. A tender spot. A forbidden corner. The groin of a pro-

duction manager. I saw just such a velvety groin on a buck antelope once. Amorous currents must course through his young
secretaries and office girls at his mere glance.

He washes himself like a little boy: trumpets, dances around,
snorts, makes noises. He scoops up the water in the hollow of
his hands. Most of it splatters on the mat before it reaches his
armpits. The droplets of it that scatter are full and clean. The
lather, falling into the basin, hisses like a pancake. Sometimes
the soap blinds him; cursing, he tears at his eyelids with his
thumbs. He rinses his throat, gargling with such zest that, under
the balcony, people stop and raise their heads.

The morning is quiet and rosy. Spring is at its height. There
are flower boxes on all the window sills. The vermillion of this
year's blooms is already showing.

(THINGS DON'T LIKE me. Furniture tries to trip me up.
Once the sharp corner of some polished thing literally bit me.
My relations with my blanket are always complicated. Soup,
given to me, never cools. If some bit of junk—a coin or a collar
button—falls off the table, it usually rolls under some almost
unmovable piece of furniture. And when, crawling around on
the floor after it, I raise my head, I catch the sideboard laughing
at me.)

THE BLUE STRAPS of his suspenders hang at his sides. He
goes into his bedroom, takes his pince-nez from the chair, puts
it on in front of the mirror and comes back to my room. Here,
standing in the middle of the room, he lifts the suspender straps,
both at once, as if he were shouldering a load. He doesn't say a
word to me. I pretend to be asleep. In the metal clips of his suspenders there are two burning clusters of sunbeams. (Things
like him.)

He doesn't have to comb his hair or groom a mustache and beard. His hair is close-cropped and his mustache is small, right under his nose. He looks like a grown-up fat boy.

He takes the flask; the glass stopper squeaks. He pours eau de cologne on his palm and passes his palm over the globe of his head, from his forehead to the nape of his neck and back again.

For breakfast, he drinks two glasses of cold milk. He takes the little jug out of the sideboard, pours the milk, and drinks it, without sitting down.

MY FIRST IMPRESSION of him was flabbergasting. I would never have imagined anything like it. . . . He stood there in a well-tailored gray suit, smelling of eau de cologne. His lips were fresh, slightly pouted. He turned out to be a fancy dresser.

OFTEN, AT NIGHT, I am awakened by his snoring. In a daze, I don't know what's going on. Someone seems to keep repeating threateningly, over and over: "Krakatoo . . . kkra . . . ka . . . taooooooo . . ."

They have given him a wonderful apartment. It has a vase on a lacquered stand by the balcony door! A vase of the finest porcelain, rounded, tall, a tender blood-red, like a hand held against a light. It reminds you of a flamingo. The apartment is on the third floor. The balcony hangs over an ethereal space. A wide suburban street, looking like a highway. Across the street below, there is a garden: a garden thick and heavy with trees, like so many in the Moscow suburbs, an untidy jumble grown up in an empty lot, as in an oven, hemmed in by three walls.

HE IS A glutton. He eats dinner out. Yesterday evening he came home hungry, decided to have a snack. There was nothing in the sideboard. He went out (there's a store on the corner) and returned loaded down with food: half a pound of ham, a can of sprats and another of mackerel, a large French loaf, a good half moon of Dutch cheese, four apples, a dozen eggs, and "Persian Pea" candy. He ordered fried eggs and tea (the kitchen in the house is communal, two cooks take turns).

"Dig in, Kavalerov." He beckoned to me and got down to it himself. He ate the eggs straight from the pan, chipping off bits of egg white as if scraping paint. His eyes became bloodshot. He kept putting on and taking off his pince-nez. He smacked his lips, snorted. His ears moved.

I spend my time observing things. Have you ever noticed that salt falls off the edge of a knife without leaving a trace—the knife shines as though nothing had been put on it; that a pince-nez sits on the bridge of a nose like a bicycle; that a human being is surrounded by tiny letters, like a scattered army of ants: on forks, spoons, plates, on a pince-nez frame, on buttons, on pencils? No one notices them, but they are engaged in a struggle for existence. They evolve from one type to another, until they become the huge lettering on posters! They rise—one species against another. The letters on street signs are at war with those on posters.

He ate himself full. He reached for an apple. But when he had lopped off its yellow cheek with his knife, he put it down.

ONCE A PEOPLE'S Commissar praised him highly in one of his speeches: "Andrei Babichev is one of our country's most outstanding citizens."

He, Andrei Petrovich Babichev, is the director of the Food Industry Trust. He is a great salami man, a great pastry man, a great caterer.

And I, Nikolai Kavalerov, am his jester.

Seven

. . .

ANGER

"Sing, O goddess, of the anger of Achilles, the son of Peleus . . ."

—*Homer,* The Iliad

"Never go to bed mad. Stay up and fight."

—*Phyllis Diller*

O f all the vices we have discussed in this book, the last, anger, can be the most valuable on a day-to-day basis—and the easiest to defend.

Anger is the emotion we experience in the face of an outrageous, intolerable situation—such as when we discover that our spouse has run off to Rio with a particularly well-toned member of the opposite sex. . . .

. . . or when we realize that, after a lifetime of paying exorbitant insurance premiums, our insurance company has decided to deny our claim. . . .

. . . or when we read about our elected leaders involved in the usual graft, corruption, and abject stupidity for which they are famous.

Such situations not only allow for anger: they cry out for it. Anger is the fire in the belly that forces us to take action, to right wrongs, to stand up against injustice and lousy service in restaurants. Not to be angry under such circumstances is a defect of character.

Yet, incredibly, many people today counsel against anger. They view it, as did the ancient Buddhists and Stoics, as an impediment to reason and the calm detachment that is enlightenment. Better to calm the fire of passion, these people say. Learn to relax. Practice meditation.

These critics point to the alleged consequences of anger: violence, urban decay, drug abuse.

But I would argue that these well-meaning people are mistaking the cause for the effect.

The problems that plague many modern cities, including violence and drug abuse, are not caused by too much anger but by too little. It is precisely because ordinary people are *not* angry, or at least not angry enough, that these problems exist. Most of us, when faced with an indignity—from marital infidelity to purse-snatching—merely shrug our shoulders and call our lawyer.

We're not angry. We're *numb*.

There is little doubt that the human capacity for anger, for righteous indignation, has declined dangerously in recent years.

No matter what outrage is now committed before us—no matter how rude a waiter is, no matter how long we are forced to wait in line at the post office, no matter how high banks set credit-card interest rates—people today just nod quietly and accept it without challenge or complaint.

In a more civilized age, if the politicians in a given country told more lies than usual and stole more than was believed fitting, the citizens, filled with fury, simply beheaded them!

Most of the great men and women of history had a temper of one sort or another. They knew when to be calm, and they knew when to be pissed off. Jesus Christ, after all, drove the money-changers out of the Temple with a whip!

Imagine how different the modern world would be if, when King George imposed his tea tax on the American colonists, they had shrugged their shoulders and, instead of dumping a few tons of tea into Boston Harbor, simply drank a few more glasses of ale.

In short, we could all use a giant dose of blood-boiling rage.

As loony as the Peter Finch character was in the 1976 film *Network,* he had it precisely right. Anger is the necessary first step to action. We all should go to our windows, stick our heads out, and scream at the top of our lungs, "I'm mad as hell and I'm not going to take it anymore!"

The selections in this chapter highlight anger in a wide variety of forms. From mere annoyance to mild outrage to full-blown sputtering fury, it is clear that anger can be, at least in some circumstances, an eloquent testament to the grandeur of the human spirit, a spirit which refuses to bear injustice with equanimity.

While some people may wince at the anger between the sexes highlighted in some of these pages—Cynthia Heimel trades barbs with the Roman writer Juvenal—I prefer to see such anger as a sign of the great conversation between men and women that has gone on since Eve offered Adam a bite of her apple. A little raw, perhaps, but real.

Remember: People who never get angry just don't give a damn.

You Gotta Play Hurt
Dan Jenkins

Dan Jenkins was a senior writer at Sports Illustrated *for more than twenty years and now writes hilarious comic novels about the fringes of professional sports. He is perhaps best known for his novel* Semi-Tough, *made into a movie with Burt Reynolds. In the selection below, the narrator of the novel* You Gotta Play Hurt, *who just happens to be a senior writer at a fictional rival of* Sports Illustrated, *vents a lifetime of pent-up rage at . . . editors.*

Here's how I want the phony little conniving, no-talent, preppiewad asshole of an editor to die: I lace his decaf with Seconal and strap him down in such a way that his head is fastened to my desk and I thump him at cheery intervals with the carriage on my Olympia standard. I'm a stubborn guy who still works on a geezer-codger manual anyhow, so I write a paragraph I admire, the kind he likes to dick around with, especially if it's my lead, then I sling the carriage at him, and whack—he gets it in the temple, sometimes in the ear. Yeah, it would be slow, but death by typewriter is what the fuckhead deserves.

I was daydreaming. I was sitting alone at a table under an umbrella on the veranda of the Regina, occasionally glancing up at the jaunty white duncecap of the Jungfrau, bonus Alp.

I had my Scotch and water, my Winstons, my pot of coffee on the side, my *Herald Trib.* Nice day. Sunny. Windbreaker weather. If you want the truth, I was doing three of my favorite things: smoking, drinking, not giving a shit.

Switzerland was where I was in that week that was the beginning of the rest of my life. I was there to watch a pack of ski tramps slide down a mountain so I could glorify them in the magazine that sent me over there to write a story about them, a story I would file to New York so an editor with no ear and no taste could take out a carving knife and flail at it like one of those chefs in a Japanese restaurant.

This was late February. I had already been sitting around for two weeks in the French Alps and Italian Alps. I was making my way, ski race by ski race, to the Winter Olympics in Austria. Always a thrill, the Winter Olympics. You get to watch waiters and babysitters figure skate. Americans fall down in the snow, and inhale the quaint odors of sweating Scandinavians who grow icicles in their noses and wear oversized flyswatters on their feet. Cross-country skiing's not a sport, it's how a fucking Swede goes to the 7-Eleven.

The managing editor or one of his lukewarm drones likes to cut that line. I put it in, the clean version, and they take it out, like they take out everything else they don't get.

Magazine journalism practices tyranny from the bottom. Editors become editors in the first place because they can't write. Then they jack around with stories that are written by the people who can write in order to justify their squalid existence.

It's an eternal truth in magazine journalism that an editor exists in large part to kick a writer where and when it hurts the worst. In all my years, I had known very few editors who could take a so-so story and improve it with their pencil, but they were absolute masters at fucking up good ones.

That was my view, anyhow. Some people said it was too harsh, but I'd never known a writer who disagreed with it.

It was a curious thing, I was thinking to myself at the Regina. I used to go to sleep dreaming about pussy. Now I went to sleep dreaming about killing people.

Notes from Underground

Fyodor Dostoyevsky

The great Russian novelist Dostoyevsky (c. 1821–1881), author of such masterpieces as Crime and Punishment *and* The Brothers Karamazov, *is noted for his penetrating psychological narratives. The selection below was printed in 1864 in Dos-*

toyevsky's and his brother's magazine, Epokha (Epoch), *and it
reflected, at least to some degree, the author's own bile.*

I am a sick man . . . I am an angry man. I am an unattractive
man. I think there is something wrong with my liver. But I don't
understand the least thing about my illness, and I don't know
for certain what part of me is affected. I am not having any treatment for it, and never have had, although I have a great respect
for medicine and for doctors. I am besides extremely superstitious, if only in having such respect for medicine. (I am well
educated enough not to be superstitious, but superstitious I
am.) No, I refuse treatment out of spite. That is something you
will probably not understand. Well, I understand it. I can't of
course explain who my spite is directed against in this matter; I
know perfectly well that I can't scare off the doctors in any way
by not consulting them; I know better than anybody that I am
harming nobody but myself. All the same, if I don't have treatment, it is out of spite. Is my liver out of order?—let it get
worse!

I have been living like this for a long time now—about
twenty years. I am forty. I once used to work in the government
service but I don't now. I was a bad civil servant. I was rude, and
I enjoyed being rude. After all, I didn't take bribes, so I had to
have some compensation. (A poor witticism; but I won't cross it
out. When I wrote it down, I thought it would seem very
pointed: now, when I see that I was simply trying to be clever
and cynical, I shall leave it in on purpose.) When people used to
come to the desk where I sat, asking for information, I snarled at
them, and was hugely delighted when I succeeded in hurting
somebody's feelings. I almost always did succeed. They were
mostly timid people—you know what people looking for fa-
vours are like. But among the swaggerers there was one officer I

simply couldn't stand. He absolutely refused to be intimidated, and he made a disgusting clatter with his sword. I carried on a campaign against him for eighteen months over that sword. I won in the end. He stopped making a clatter with it. This, however, was when I was still young. But do you know what was the real point of my bad temper? The main point, and the supreme nastiness, lay in the fact that even at my moments of greatest spleen, I was constantly and shamefully aware that not only was I not seething with fury, I was not even angry; I was simply scaring sparrows for my own amusement. I might be foaming at the mouth, but bring me some sort of toy to play with, or a nice sweet cup of tea, and I would calm down and even be stirred to the depths, although I would probably turn on myself afterwards, and suffer from insomnia for months. That was always my way.

I was lying when I said just now that I was a bad civil servant. I was lying out of spite. I was simply playing a game with the officer and my other callers; in reality I never could make myself malevolent. I was always conscious of many elements showing the directly opposite tendency. I felt them positively swarming inside me, these elements. I knew they had swarmed there all my life, asking to be let out, but I wouldn't let them out, I wouldn't, I wouldn't. They tormented me shamefully; they drove me into convulsions and—in the end they bored me, oh, how they bored me! You think that now I'm making some sort of confession to you, asking your forgiveness, don't you? . . . I'm sure you do . . . But I assure you it's all the same to me if you do think so.

Not only couldn't I make myself malevolent, I couldn't make myself anything: neither good nor bad, neither a scoundrel nor an honest man, neither a hero nor an insect. Now I go on living in my corner and irritating myself with the spiteful and worthless consolation that a wise man can't seriously make himself anything, only a fool makes himself anything. Yes, a man of the nineteenth century ought, indeed is morally bound, to be essentially without character; a man of character, a man who acts, is essentially limited. Such is my forty-year-old conviction. I am forty now, and forty years is a lifetime; it is extreme old age. To go on living after forty is unseemly, disgusting, immoral! Who goes on living after forty? Give me a sincere and honest answer! I'll tell you: fools and rogues. I'll tell all the old men that to their faces, all those venerable elders, those silver-haired, fragrant old men. I'll tell the whole world! I have the right to talk like this, because I'm going to live to be sixty! Seventy! Eighty! . . . Stop, let me get my breath back. . . . !

You probably think I'm trying to amuse you. You're wrong there too. I'm not such a cheerful fellow as you think, or as you perhaps think; if, however, annoyed by all this chatter (and I can feel you are annoyed), you ask me positively who I am—I answer, I am a Collegiate Assessor. I joined the civil service in order to earn my bread (and for no other reason), and when last year a distant relative left me six thousand roubles in his will, I retired immediately and settled down in my little corner. I lived in this same corner even before that, but now I've settled down in it. My room is mean and shabby, on the outskirts of the town. My servant is a peasant woman, old, crabbed, and stupid, and what's more, she always smells bad. I am told that the climate of St. Petersburg is bad for me, and that, with my insignificant means, it costs too much to live here. I know all that, a lot better than all my extremely wise and experienced advisers and head-shakers. But I shall stay here; I will not leave St. Petersburg! I won't go away because . . . Oh, after all, it doesn't matter in the least whether I go away or I don't.

However: what can a decent, respectable man talk about with the greatest pleasure?

Answer: himself.

Well, so I too will talk about myself.

Tom Jones

Henry Fielding

*For an epic chronicle of all human vices, you'd have a hard time
finding a novel more up to the task than* Tom Jones, *written in
1749 and one of the funniest and most touching human dramas
ever penned. The author, Henry Fielding (c. 1707–1754), was
a prodigious writer and dramatist with a wicked sense of
humor. In the scene below, the lusty Molly Seagrim, a poor girl
and lover of Tom Jones, wears a new dress to church to hide her
pregnancy. The dress or "sack" causes an uproar among the
other women of the parish, who are furious that a poor wench
like Molly would dare dress herself up in fine clothes. An epic
battle ensues.*

Mr. Western had an estate in this parish, and as his house
stood at a little greater distance from this church than from his
own, he very often came to divine service here; and both he and
the charming Sophia happened to be present at this time.

Sophia was much pleased with the beauty of the girl, whom
she pitied for her simplicity, in having dressed herself in that
manner, as she saw the envy which it had occasioned among her
equals. She no sooner came home than she sent for the game-
keeper and ordered him to bring his daughter to her, saying she
would provide for her in the family, and might possibly place
the girl about her own person when her own maid, who was
now going away, had left her.

Poor Seagrim was thunderstruck at this; for he was no stranger to the fault in the shape of his daughter. He answered in a stammering voice that he was afraid Molly would be too awkward to wait on her ladyship, as she had never been at service. "No matter for that," says Sophia. "She will soon improve. I am pleased with the girl and am resolved to try her."

Black George now repaired to his wife, on whose prudent council he depended to extricate him out of this dilemma, but when he came thither he found his house in some confusion. So great envy had this sack occasioned that when Mr. Allworthy and the other gentry were gone from church, the rage, which had hitherto been confined, burst into an uproar and, having vented itself at first in opprobrious words, laughs, hisses, and gestures, betook itself at last to certain missile weapons, which, though from their plastic nature they threatened neither the loss of life or of limb, were however sufficiently dreadful to a well-dressed lady. Molly had too much spirit to bear this treatment tamely. Having therefore—but hold, as we are diffident of our own abilities, let us here invite a superior power to our assistance.

Ye Muses, then, whoever ye are, who love to sing battles, and principally thou, who whilom didst recount the slaughter in those fields where Hudibras and Trulla fought, if thou were not starved with thy friend Butler, assist me on this great occasion. All things are not in the power of all.

As a vast herd of cows in a rich farmer's yard if while they are milked they hear their calves at a distance, lamenting the robbery which is then committing, roar and bellow, so roared forth the Somersetshire mob an hallaloo, made up of almost as many squawls, screams, and other different sounds as there were persons, or indeed passions, among them; some were inspired by rage, others alarmed by fear, and others had nothing in their heads but the love of fun; but chiefly Envy, the sister of Satan and his constant companion, rushed among the crowd and blew up the fury of the women, who no sooner came up to Molly than they pelted her with dirt and rubbish.

Molly, having endeavoured in vain to make a handsome retreat, faced about, and laying hold of ragged Bess, who advanced in the front of the enemy, she at one blow felled her to the ground. The whole army of the enemy (though near a hundred in number), seeing the fate of their general, gave back many paces and retired behind a new-dug grave; for the church-yard was the field of battle where there was to be a funeral that very evening. Molly pursued her victory and, catching up a skull which lay on the side of the grave, discharged it with such fury that, having hit a tailor on the head, the two skulls sent equally forth a hollow sound at their meeting, and the tailor took presently measure of his length on the ground, where the skulls lay side by side, and it was doubtful which was the most valuable of the two. Molly then taking a thigh-bone in her hand fell in among the flying ranks, and dealing her blows with great liberality on either side, overthrew the carcass of many a mighty hero and heroine.

Recount, O Muse, the names of those who fell on this fatal day. First, Jemmy Tweedle felt on his hinder head the direful bone. Him the pleasant banks of sweetly winding Stour had nourished, where he first learnt the vocal art with which, wandering up and down at wakes and fairs, he cheered the rural nymphs and swains, when upon the green they interweave the sprightly dance, while he himself stood fiddling and jumping to his own music. How little now avails his fiddle? He thumps the verdant floor with his carcass. Next, old Echepole, the sow-gelder, received a blow in his forehead from our Amazonian heroine, and immediately fell to the ground. He was a swinging fat fellow, and fell with almost as much noise as a horse. His tobacco-box dropped at the same time from his pocket, which Molly took up as lawful spoils. Then Kate of the Mill tumbled unfortunately over a tombstone, which, catching hold of her un-gartered stocking, inverted the order of nature and gave her heels the superiority to her head. Betty Pippin, with young Roger, her lover, fell both to the ground, where, O perverse fate, she salutes the earth and he the sky. Tom Freckle, the smith's son, was the next victim to her rage. He was an ingenious work-man and made excellent pattens; nay, the very patten with which he was knocked down was his own workmanship. Had he been at that time singing psalms in the church, he would have avoided a broken head. Miss Crow, the daughter of a farmer; John Giddish, himself a farmer; Nan Slouch, Esther Codling, Will Spray, Tom Bennet; the three Misses Potter, whose father keeps the sign of the Red Lion; Betty Chambermaid, Jack Ost-ler, and many others of inferior note lay rolling among the graves.

Not that the strenuous arm of Molly reached all these, for many of them in their flight overthrew each other.

But now Fortune, fearing she had acted out of character and had inclined too long to the same side, especially as it was the right side, hastily turned about: for now Goody Brown, whom Zekiel Brown caresses in his arms; nor he alone, but half the parish besides, so famous was she in the fields of Venus; nor indeed less in those of Mars. The trophies of both these her hus-band always bore about on his head and face; for if ever human head did by its horns display the amorous glories of a wife, Zekiel's did; nor did his well-scratched face less denote her tal-ents (or rather talons) of a different kind.

No longer bore this Amazon the shameful flight of her party. She stopped short and, calling aloud to all who fled, spoke as

*A*nger

follows: "Ye Somersetshire men, or rather ye Somersetshire women, are ye not ashamed thus to fly from a single woman? But if no other will oppose her, I myself and Joan Top, here, will have the honour of victory." Having thus said, she flew at Molly Seagrim and easily wrenched the thigh-bone from her hand, at the same time clawing off her cap from her head. Then, laying hold of the hair of Molly with her left hand, she attacked her so furiously in the face with the right that the blood soon began to trickle from her nose. Molly was not idle this while. She soon removed the clout from the head of Goody Brown, and then, fastening on her hair with one hand, with the other she caused the same bloody stream to issue forth from the nostrils of the enemy.

When each of the combatants had borne off sufficient spoils of hair from the head of the antagonist, the next rage was against their garments. In this attack they exerted so much violence that in a very few minutes they were both naked to the middle.

It is lucky for the women that the seat of fisticuff-war is not the same with them as among men; but though they may seem a little to deviate from their sex when they go forth to battle, yet I have observed they never so far forget it as to assail the bosoms of each other, where a few blows would be fatal to most of them. This, I know, some derive from their being of a more bloody inclination than the males. On which account they apply to the nose as to the part whence blood may most easily be drawn; but this seems a far-fetched as well as ill-natured supposition.

Goody Brown had great advantage of Molly in this particular; for the former had indeed no breasts, her bosom (if it may be so called) as well in colour as in many other properties exactly resembling an ancient piece of parchment, upon which any one might have drummed a considerable while without doing her any great damage.

Molly, beside her present unhappy condition, was differently formed in those parts, and might, perhaps, have tempted the envy of Brown to give her a fatal blow had not the lucky arrival of Tom Jones at this instant put an immediate end to the bloody scene.

This accident was luckily owing to Mr. Square; for he, Master Blifil, and Jones had mounted their horses after church to take the air, and had ridden about a quarter of a mile when Square, changing his mind (not idly, but for a reason which we shall unfold as soon as we have leisure), desired the young gentlemen to ride with him another way than they had at first proposed. This motion being complied with brought them of necessity back again to the churchyard.

Master Blifil, who rode first, seeing such a mob assembled and two women in the posture in which we left the combatants, stopped his horse to inquire what was the matter. A country fellow, scratching his head, answered him, "I don't know, measter, un't I; an't please your honour, here hath been a vight, I think, between Goody Brown and Moll Seagrim." "Who, who?" cries Tom, but without waiting for an answer, having discovered the features of his Molly through all the discomposure in which they now were, he hastily alighted, turned his horse loose, and, leaping over the wall, ran to her. She now, first bursting into tears, told him how barbarously she had been treated. Upon which, forgetting the sex of Goody Brown, or perhaps not knowing it in his rage (for in reality she had no feminine appearance but a petticoat, which he might not observe), he gave her a lash or two with his horsewhip; and then flying at the mob, who were all accused by Molly, he dealt his blows so profusely on all sides that unless I would invoke the Muse (which the good-natured reader may think a little too hard upon her, as she hath so lately

been violently sweated), it would be impossible for me to recount the horsewhipping of that day.

Having scoured the whole coast of the enemy as well as any
of Homer's heroes ever did, or as Don Quixote or any knight-
errant in the world could have done, he returned to Molly,
whom he found in a condition which must give both me and my
reader pain was it to be described here. Tom raved like a madman, beat his breast, tore his hair, stamped on the ground, and
vowed the utmost vengeance on all who had been concerned.
He then pulled off his coat and buttoned it round her, put his
hat upon her head, wiped the blood from her face as well as he
could with his handkerchief, and called out to the servant to
ride as fast as possible for a sidesaddle, or a pillion, that he
might carry her safe home.

Master Blifil objected to the sending away the servant, as they
had only one with them; but as Square seconded the order of
Jones, he was obliged to comply.

The servant returned in a very short time with the pillion; and
Molly, having collected her rags as well as she could, was placed
behind him, in which manner she was carried home, Square,
Blifil, and Jones attending.

Here, Jones, having received his coat, given her a sly kiss, and
whispered her that he would return in the evening, quitted his
Molly and rode on after his companions.

We're Gonna Get You, Suckers

Cynthia Heimel

*Even though Cynthia Heimel suffers from the usual monoma-
nia of her vastly overrated generation—the tendency to believe
itself superior, not only to all generations that came before it
but to all generations in the future as well—she has more self-
awareness than most babyboomers. A regular contributor to
both* Playboy *magazine and* The Village Voice, *Heimel's work
is collected in volumes such as* If You Can't Live Without Me,
Why Aren't You Dead Yet?, *from which the selection below
is taken. Men will never look at long red nails the same again!*

I thought I'd get my nails done, so I went to one of those nail
salons. I figured that since a Nails R Us or a Nails for Days has
opened on every street corner of metropolitan U.S.A., there
might be something to it. Not that I hold with manicures, I find
them pointlessly evanescent. But my neighbor, Mrs. Fishbein,
who *does* have beautiful nails and a doting husband, constantly
encouraged me to try it. And you fellas like to be a fly on the wall
when we gals are getting all pink and cozy and pretty and chatty.
And I needed a column.

So I duly walked into Nailward Ho! on my corner. "Hello," I
said to the pretty, scantily clad Korean receptionist.

"About fucking time," she snarled. I stood perplexed. Then
she shook herself and beamed. "What can I do for you today?"

"Well," I exhaled, "you know those, I think they're called
'French' manicures, where they paint white on the tip of the nail
and . . ."

She pointed to a manicure table where sat a gum-chewing

blond bombshell whose nails were, I swear, two inches long. "Oh, just sit the cocksuck down," she snapped.

Well. I sat the cocksuck down. "I think I'd like a French manicure," I said to the bombshell.

She leaned forward, exposing cleavage. "Call me Shirl," she said. "Don't you think manicures are pointlessly evanescent?" I gaped, speechless.

"Listen, doll, just follow me, now you're finally here," she said. "I got something with your name on it." She took my hand and went to a corner of the salon, reached over to a bottle of Persian Melon polish and twisted it. The wall fell away; we were in an elevator.

We descended quickly, silently, into the earth. The doors opened. There was deafening noise, smoke. The smoke cleared, revealing a target range. Two dozen women in camouflage fatigues and headphones were aiming automatics at paper replicas of men. *Bang! Bang!* The groin area of every replica was blown away.

"Very nice, girls," I heard a familiar voice say. I turned and almost fell over.

"Mrs. Fishbein! What are you doing here? God, what is all this?"

"Hello, Tottela, so you finally made it to our little hen party. Shirl, get this young lady a chair and some Sara Lee or she's gonna pass out.

"It's simple, honey," she continued as I tottered to a seat. "The men are right. We hate them. We are going to subjugate or kill them and take over the world. And we're ready to give it to those bums. Put your head between your knees."

"Wait, so this isn't a nail salon?"

"What, are you crazy? You think the demand for manicures is such that we need a shop on every corner? You want a mani-

cure, go to a hairdresser. You want to overthrow masculine op-
pression, come here. Each nail salon is one cell of our vast, all-
powerful conspiracy. We are organized. We are deadly."

"Mrs. Fishbein, you're a housewife. You cook flanken every
Tuesday night. You're devoted to your husband."

"Harold? That pisher who farts in his sleep? Oh, darling, you
know all women are diesel dykes. Aren't we Shirl?" She play-
fully tweaked the bombshell's nipple.

Shirl giggled and she handed me something. Something
black, and hard, and cold. Something with my name on it. "A
Beretta P92SB," she said. "Ain't it cute? Holds fifteen rounds,
shoots jacketed hollow-points. This week we tell them they're
not in touch with their feelings, next week we blow their fucking
heads off. More coffee cake?"

A frail Korean teenager carrying a load of schoolbooks came
running up.

"Mistress Medusa! Has the How Not to Have an Orgasm
workshop started yet?"

"Ten minutes, Kali," said Mrs. Fishbein. She looked at me
sheepishly. "They want to call me Mistress Medusa, I don't
mind. Who ever heard of a revolutionary named Estelle?"

"How not to have an orgasm?"

"Of course," said Kali, "psychological warfare at its utmost.
We close our eyes and think of old jockstraps, thus ensuring no
sexual excitement. Then we *pretend* to have orgasm."

"Drives them to suicide," said Shirl. "They know we're faking it, we know we're faking it. But what can they do? Sue? No.
They kill themselves."

"No American woman has had an orgasm since February
1953," said Mrs. Fishbein.

"At least not penis-induced," said Kali. "That's such a very
pretty blouse. Where did you get it?"

"I don't know," I said. "So what about all the women in the world who talk about how they love men, how they're feminists but *humanistic* feminists, how they want husbands and children? How about all the women who cry when he doesn't call? Who are desperate about the male shortage?"

"Oh, come off it," said Shirl.

"Don't be a dweeb," said Mistress Medusa.

"Clever propaganda while we work our destruction," said Kali. "Ninety-six percent of American womanhood is now organized and ready."

"Why am I the last to know about this?" I wondered.

"Feminists got no grooming, your cuticles are a mess, you never drop by," said Shirl.

The receptionist appeared. "The Asa Baber Study Group has to be canceled for lack of interest again," she said.

"Pitty," said M.M., "I suspect that pseudo-sensitive wuss may be the only one who's on to us. Come the revolution, he's the first to go."

"Wait!" I cried, suddenly horrified. "What about Mel Gibson?"

"You can keep him as a pet if you like," said Kali. "Oh, Mistress Medusa, five women have become inchers today."

"Capital," said M.M., "a mitzvah."

"I don't understand," I said.

"Nails, of course," said the receptionist. "The longer your nails, the more are your destructive skills. When you can reduce five men to gibbering morons in under an hour, you earn your inch. Two-inches can lay waste to an even dozen. Of course, a woman with a rhinestone imbedded in her nail is licensed to kill. You didn't think it was cosmetic?"

"Consider," said Kali. "All these salons are run by Koreans. It was at the Olympics in Seoul where we unveiled our Supreme Sister, with nails like stilettos and the legs of ten gazelles."

Flo-Jo!

And here I thought you men were just being paranoid.

Hate Thy Neighbor
Calvin Trillin

Okay, so I think Trillin is pretty funny. He grows on you. Here's one of his comic essays taken from his book If You Can't Say Something Nice.

April 6, 1986

My wife keeps telling me that I don't really hate the neighbor of ours who talks a lot about the importance of trim and gutter maintenance. I've had this problem with my wife before.

She is the person who insisted that I was only joking when I said several years ago that people who sell macrame ought to be dyed a natural color and hung out to dry. She is the person who tried to shush me when I told a man who pushed ahead of me in an airport line that only certified wonks wear designer blue jeans.

I haven't done any trim and gutter maintenance in so long that I'm no longer quite certain what there is about them that needs to be maintained. I also feel that way about the points and plugs on the car. I know they're important, but I can't quite remember why. The same neighbor—he can be called Elwood here, although around the house I always refer to him as Old Glittering Gutters—cannot see my car without patting it on the hood as if it were an exceedingly large Airedale and saying, "When was the last time you had a good look at the points and plugs?"

"I'd rather not say," I always reply.

It's none of his business. His points and plugs are, I'm sure, sharply pointed and firmly plugged in, or whatever they're supposed to be. His trim and gutters are, it goes without saying, carefully maintained. You could probably eat out of Elwood's gutters if that's the kind of person you were. I hate him.

"You don't really hate him," my wife said. "You may think he's a little too well organized for your tastes, and you may not want him over for dinner all the time. But you don't hate him."

Wrong. Elwood has a list of what's in his basement. He says the list is invaluable. He wonders why I don't have a list of what's in my basement. He doesn't seem to understand that if I made such a list, it would have to be a list of what might be in my basement, and it would have to include the possibility of crocodiles. Elwood's list is cross-indexed. A man who has a cross-indexed list of what's in his basement is not a little well organized, he's hateful.

The other day Elwood asked me what sort of system I use to label my circuit breakers. I tried to remain calm. I made every effort to analyze his question in a manner detached enough to prevent physical violence. I tried to think of reasons why Elwood would assume that someone who had already confessed ignorance as to the whereabouts of his 1984 gasoline credit card receipts ("There might be some stuffed in the glove compartment there with the spare points and plugs, Elwood, but I hate to open that thing unless it's a real emergency") would have his circuit breakers labeled at all, let alone have them labeled according to some system.

I calculated, as precisely as I could, what chance there was that a jury, learning of the question that preceded the crime, would bring in a verdict of not guilty on the grounds that the strangling of Elwood had clearly been a crime of passion.

"The system I'm using now," I finally said, "is to label them Sleepy, Grumpy, Sneezy, Happy, Dopey, Doc, and Bashful. However, I've given a lot of thought to switching to a system under which I would label them Dasher, Dancer, Prancer, Vixen, Comet, Cupid, Donder, and Bruce. I'm holding up my final decision until a friend of mine who has access to a large computer runs some probability studies."

"Probability of what?" Elwood said. I noticed that as he asked the question he retreated a step or two toward his own house.

"Just probability," I said.

When I got back inside my house, I told my wife about the conversation and about the possibility that Elwood now believed me to be not simply slovenly in the extreme but completely bonkers.

"Poor man," she said. "He probably thinks you're dangerous."

"He may be right," I said.

"You have to try to think of Elwood as a human being," my wife said. "Someone with feelings, and a wife and children who love him."

"I suspect his children sell macrame in public," I said. "Or maybe they're in a troupe of those street-corner mimes who've somehow got it in their heads that passersby are longing to see people with white paint on their faces pretend to walk slowly against the wind."

"Also," she said, "it really wouldn't be such a bad idea to label the circuit breakers."

I looked at her for a while. "You're right, of course," I finally

said. I got a felt-tipped pen, went to the circuit breaker box, and
stared right in: "Sleepy, Grumpy, Sneezy . . ."

To Novatus on Anger

Seneca

*Lucius Annaeus Seneca (c. 4 B.C.–A.D.65) was a Latin writer
who strongly influenced the development of Stoicism, a philosophical movement that looked askance at all strong emotions,
anger included. Seneca's practical advice on living, expressed in
his essays and sermons, seems quite sane, however. He was
quite successful in business and retired a millionaire.*

You have importuned me, Novatus, to write on the subject of
how anger may be allayed, and it seems to me that you had good
reason to fear in an especial degree this, the most hideous and
frenzied of all the emotions. For the other emotions have in
them some element of peace and calm, while this one is wholly
violent and has its being in an onrush of resentment, raging with
a most inhuman lust for weapons, blood, and punishment, giving no thought to itself if only it can hurt another, hurling itself
upon the very point of the dagger, and eager for revenge though
it may drag down the avenger along with it. Certain wise men,
therefore, have claimed that anger is temporary madness. For it
is equally devoid of self-control, forgetful of decency, unmind-
ful of ties, persistent and diligent in whatever it begins, closed to
reason and counsel, excited by trifling causes, unfit to discern
the right and true—the very counterpart of a ruin that is shattered in pieces where it overwhelms. But you have only to be-

hold the aspect of those possessed by anger to know that they are insane. For as the marks of a madman are unmistakable—a bold and threatening mien, a gloomy brow, a fierce expression, a hurried step, restless hands, an altered colour, a quick and more violent breathing—so likewise are the marks of the angry man; his eyes blaze and sparkle, his whole face is crimson with the blood that surges from the lowest depths of the heart, his lips quiver, his teeth are clenched, his hair bristles and stands on end, his breathing is forced and harsh, his joints crack from writhing, he groans and bellows, bursts out into speech with scarcely intelligible words, strikes his hands together continually, and stamps the ground with his feet; his whole body is excited and "performs great angry threats"; it is an ugly and horrible picture of distorted and swollen frenzy—you cannot tell whether this vice is more execrable or more hideous. Other vices may be concealed and cherished in secret; anger shows itself openly and appears in the countenance, and the greater it is, the more visibly it boils forth.

The Learned Ladies

Jean-Baptiste Molière

The master of the French comedy, Molière (c. 1622–1673), has something to say about almost everything, including female anger. This is a translation of Molière's play, Les Femmes savantes, *first produced in 1672.*

ARMANDE What, Sister! Are you truly of a mind
   To leave your precious maidenhead behind,

 And give yourself in marriage to a man?
  Can you be harboring such a vulgar plan?
HENRIETTE Yes, Sister.
ARMANDE Yes, you say! When have I heard
  So odious and sickening a word?
HENRIETTE Why does the thought of marriage so repel you?
ARMANDE Fie, fir! For shame!
HENRIETTE But what—
ARMANDE For shame, I tell you!
  Can you deny what sordid scenes are brought
  To the mind's eye by that distasteful thought,
  What coarse, degrading images arise,
  What shocking things it makes one visualize?
  Do you not shudder, Sister, and grow pale
  At what this thought you're thinking would entail?
HENRIETTE It would entail, as I conceive it, one
  Husband, some children, and a house to run;
  In all of which, it may as well be said,
  I find no cause for loathing or for dread.
ARMANDE Alas! Such bondage truly appeals to you?
HENRIETTE At my young age, what better could I do
  Than join myself in wedded harmony
  To one I love, and who in turn loves me,
  And through the deepening bond of man and wife
  Enjoy a blameless and contented life?
  Does such a union offer no attractions?
ARMANDE Oh dear, you crave such squalid satisfactions!
  How can you choose to play a pretty role,
  Dull and domestic, and content your soul
  With joys no loftier than keeping house
  And raising brats, and pampering a spouse?
  Let common natures, vulgarly inclined,

Concern themselves with trifles of that kind.
Aspire to nobler objects, seek to attain
To keener joys upon a higher plane,
And, scorning gross material things as naught,
Devote yourself, as we have done, to thought.
We have a mother to whom all pay honor
For erudition; model yourself upon her;
Yes, prove yourself her daughter, as I have done,
Join in the quest for truth that she's begun,
And learn how love of study can impart
A sweet enlargement to the mind and heart.
Why marry, and be the slave of him you wed?
Be married to philosophy instead,
Which lifts us up above mankind, and gives
All power to reason's pure imperatives,
Thus rendering our bestial natures tame
And mastering those lusts which lead to shame.
A love of reason, a passion for the truth,
Should quite suffice one's heart in age or youth,
And I am moved to pity when I note
On what low objects certain women dote.

Against Women

Juvenal

If Molière's learned ladies scorn men and the enslavement of marriage, earlier writers returned the compliment. The Roman writer Decimus Junius Juvenalis (c. A.D.60–130) is perhaps most famous for his biting criticism of women.

Chastity lingered on earth, I believe, in the reign of King
    Saturn.
She was seen then, for a while, a long time ago, when
    cold caves
Offered men tiny homes, and enclosed, in their common
    shadow,
Fire and the household god, the herd and the owner
    together.
Those were the days when a mountain wife had a
    mattress to lie on,
Made out of leaves or straw or the hides of the native
    creatures.
There were no city girls like Cynthia, known to
    Propertius,
None like the one who wept, red-eyed at the death of her
    sparrow.
No: these women had breasts for big fat babies to tug at.
Often they looked as rough as their acorn-belching
    husbands.
Men were different then, when the world and the skies
    were younger,
Sons of the riven oak, or scions of clay, unfathered.
Under Jove, it might be, you could still distinguish the
    footprints
Chastity might have left, but that was when Jove was a
    stripling,
Not yet the time when the Greeks swore oaths (and
    broke them); when no one
Feared the thief in his cabbage or fruits, when his garden
    was open.
Justice, by slow degrees, deserted earth for the heavens,
Chastity at her side, and so the sisters departed.

Postumus, it's an old custom, hallowed by ancient
    tradition,
To bounce another man's bed, put horns on the brow of
    its genius
Every other crime came in the Era of Iron,
But the Silver Age, earlier still, saw the rise of these
    cheaters.
Yet, in a time like ours, here you are, preparing for
    marriage,
Contracts, and pledges, and banns, and your hair getting
    combed by a barber
Un vrai maître de coiffure, and perhaps you have bought
    her the ring.
Surely you used to be sane. Postumus, are you taking a
    wife?
Tell me what Fury, what snakes, have driven you on to
    this madness?
Can you be under her thumb, while ropes are so cheap
    and so many,
When there are windows wide open and high enough to
    jump down from,
While the Aemilian bridge is practically in your back
    yard?
Or if no such way out appeals to you, isn't it better
To get some young boy in your bed to sleep with you in
    the night-time
Without threatening suits or insisting on costlier
    presents,
Uncomplaining if you refuse to breathe hard at his
    bidding?

But the Julian law suits you fine. So you want a sweet
    little youngster,

Heir to your vast estate, though you'll have to do without
    squab,
Filet of catfish, and all the nice legacy-bait of the market.
Postumus, what can't be done, if a woman takes you for
    a husband?
You, most notorious rake of all the tail-chasers of Rome,
You, who have hidden in closets, or under the bed of
    some cuckold,
You still your silly head in the marital noose? You go
    seeking
A virtuous old-fashioned wife? It's time to summon the
    doctors.
What a real sweetheart you are! If a decent and modest
    woman
Falls to your lot, flop prone on your face at the Tarpeian
    altar,
Bow and adore, and slay a golden heifer to Juno.
Not many women are worthy to touch the fillets of
    Ceres,
Many the ones whose kisses even their fathers recoil
    from.
So hang wreaths at your door, adorn the lintel with ivy!
Will she be satisfied with one man, this piece of
    perfection?
Sooner, I think, with one eye!

Among the Euro-Weenies

P. J. O'Rourke

Any American who has ever spent any time in a European bar can appreciate the selection below, from O'Rourke's book Holidays in Hell. *I still laugh out loud whenever I read it.*

The day before I left Berlin, I ran into a dozen young Arab men on the street. They were trotting along, taking up the whole sidewalk, accosting busty girls and generally making a nuisance of themselves. One was beating on a snareless drum, and the others were letting loose with intermittent snatches of song and aggressive shouts. They descended on me and loudly demanded cigarettes in German.

"I don't speak German," I said.

"Are you American?" said one, suddenly polite.

"Yes."

"Please, my friend, if you don't mind, do you have a cigarette you could spare?"

I gave them a pack. "Where are you from?" I asked.

"West Beirut," said the drum beater.

"I've been there," I said.

"It is wonderful, no?"

Compared to Berlin, it is. "Sure," I said. They began reminiscing volubly. "What are you doing here?" I asked.

"Our families sent us because of the war. We want to go back to Beirut but we cannot."

I told them I guessed I couldn't go back either, what with the kidnapping and all. They laughed. One of them stuck out his middle finger and said, "This place sucks."

$\mathcal{A}$nger
· · · · ·

"You should go to America," I said.

"There is only one bad thing about America," said the drum beater. "They won't let us in."

Back in London, I was having dinner in the Groucho Club—this week's in-spot for what's left of Britain's lit glitz and *nouveau* rock *riche*—when one more person started in on the Stars and Stripes. Eventually he got, as the Europeans always do, to the part about "Your country's never been invaded." (This fellow had been two during the Blitz, you see.) "You don't know the horror, the suffering. You think war is . . ."

I snapped.

"A John Wayne movie," I said. "That's what you were going to say, wasn't it? We think war is a John Wayne movie. We think *life* is a John Wayne movie—with good guys and bad guys, as simple as that. Well, you know something, Mister Limey Poofter? You're right. And let me tell you who those bad guys are. They're *us*. WE BE BAD.

"We're the baddest-assed sons of bitches that ever jogged in Reeboks. We're three-quarters grizzly bear and two-thirds car wreck and descended from a stock market crash on our mother's side. You take your Germany, France and Spain, roll them all together and it wouldn't give us room to park our cars. We're the big boys, Jack, the original giant, economy-sized, new and improved butt kickers of all time. When we snort coke in Houston, people lose their hats in Cap d'Antibes. And we've got an American Express card credit limit higher than your piss-ant metric numbers go.

"You say our country's never been invaded? You're right, little buddy. Because I'd like to see the needle-dicked foreigners who'd have the guts to try. We drink napalm to get our hearts started in the morning. A rape and a mugging is our way of saying 'Cheerio.' Hell can't hold our sock-hops. We walk taller,

273

talk louder, spit further, fuck longer and buy more things than you know the names of. I'd rather be a junkie in a New York City jail than king, queen and jack of all you Europeans. We eat little countries like this for breakfast and shit them out before lunch."

Of course, the guy should have punched me. But this was Europe. He just smiled his shabby, superior European smile. (God, don't these people have *dentists?*)

Acknowledgments

. . .

For permission to reprint copyrighted material, grateful acknowledgment is made to the following publishers, authors, literary estates, and agents:

The Golden Ass by Apuleius, translated by Jack Lindsay. Copyright © 1960 by Jack Lindsay. Used by permission of Indiana University Press.

"may i feel said he" is reprinted from *Complete Poems, 1904–1962* by e.e. cummings, edited by George J. Firmage, by permission of Liveright Publishing Corporation. Copyright © 1935, 1963, 1991 by the Trustees for the e.e. cummings Trust. Copyright © 1978 by George James Firmage.

Fear of Flying by Erica Mann Jong. Copyright © 1973 by Erica Mann Jong. Reprinted by permission of Henry Holt and Co., Inc.

The Satires of Juvenal translated by Rolfe Humphries. Copyright © 1958. Used by permission of Indiana University Press.

"Fatigue," from *Complete Verse* by Hilaire Belloc. Reprinted by permission of the Peters Fraser & Dunlop Group Ltd.

Excerpt from "A Leader of the People," from *The Bonfire of the Vanities* by Tom Wolfe. Copyright © 1987 by Tom Wolfe. Reprinted by permission of Farrar, Straus & Giroux, Inc.

Reprinted from *Liar's Poker, Rising Through the Wreckage on Wall Street* by Michael Lewis, by permission of W. W. Norton & Company, Inc. Copyright © 1989 by Michael Lewis.

From *Molly Ivins Can't Say That, Can She?* by Molly Ivins. Copyright © 1989 by Molly Ivins. Reprinted by permission of Random House, Inc.

"Lines Indited with All the Depravity of Poverty" and "Pretty Halcyon Days," from *Verses from 1929 On* by Ogden Nash. Copyright © 1931, 1934 by Ogden Nash. First appeared in *The New York American.* By permission of Little, Brown and Company.

The Inferno, reprinted from the John Ciardi translation of *The Divine Comedy,* Dante Alighieri, by permission of W. W. Norton & Company, Inc. Copyright © 1954, 1957, 1959, 1960, 1965, 1967, 1970 by the Ciardi Family Publishing Trust.

From *Rabbit Is Rich* by John Updike. Copyright © 1981 by John Updike. Reprinted by permission of Alfred A. Knopf, Inc.

From *The Histories of Gargantua and Pantagruel* by François Rabelais, translated by J. M. Cohen (Penguin Classics, 1955) copyright © 1955 by J. M. Cohen.

From *A Confederacy of Dunces* by John Kennedy Toole. Copyright © 1980 by

Acknowledgments
• • • • •

Thelma Toole, published by Louisiana State University Press. Used with permission.

From *Social Studies* by Fran Lebowitz. Copyright © 1981 by Fran Lebowitz. Reprinted by permission of Random House, Inc.

From *Kinflicks* by Lisa Alther. Copyright © 1975 by Lisa Alther. Reprinted by permission of Alfred A. Knopf, Inc.

From *Seven Pillars of Wisdom* by T. E. Lawrence. Copyright © 1926, 1935 by Doubleday, a division of Bantam Doubleday Dell Publishing Group, Inc. Used by permission of Doubleday, a division of Bantam Doubleday Dell Publishing Group, Inc.

"Breakfast with Gerard Manley Hopkins," by Anthony Brode. Reproduced by permission of *Punch*.

"Notes from the Overfed," from *Getting Even* by Woody Allen. Copyright © 1966, 1967, 1968, 1969, 1970, 1971 by Woody Allen. Reprinted by permission of Random House, Inc.

"A Song of Gluttony," by E. O. Parrott, published in *Punch,* November 30, 1960, as one of four runners-up in Toby Competition No. 139 ("Sin Song"). Reprinted by permission of *Punch*.

"The Jolly Glutton," by Margaret Cresswell, published in *Punch,* November 30, 1960, as one of four runners-up in Toby Competition No. 139 ("Sin Song"). Reprinted by permission of *Punch*.

"Steak and Chips," from *Mythologies* by Roland Barthes and translated by Annette Lavers. Translation copyright © 1972 by Jonathan Cape, Ltd. Reprinted by permission of Hill and Wang, a division of Farrar, Straus & Giroux, Inc.

Act 1, lines 1–75 from "Miles Gloriosus," from *Three Comedies: Pseudolus, Miles Gloriosus, Rudens* by Plautus, translated by Peter L. Smith. Used by permission of publisher, Cornell University Press.

"Act Three, Scene Five," from *The Misanthrope* by Molière, copyright © 1955 and renewed 1983 by Richard Wilbur, reprinted by permission of Harcourt, Brace & Company.

From *Muscle* by Samuel Wilson Fussell. Copyright © 1991 by Samuel Wilson Fussell. Reprinted by permission of Simon & Schuster, Inc.

Satires, Epistles and Ars Poetica by Horace, translated by H. Rushton Fairclough. Reprinted by permission of the publishers and the Loeb Classical Library from Horace, *Satires, Epistles and Ars Poetica,* Volume 2, Loeb Vol. 194, translated by H. Rushton Fairclough, Cambridge, Mass.: Harvard University Press, 1926.

"Penis Envy," from *New Introductory Lectures on Psycho-Analysis* by Sigmund Freud, translated by James Strachey, with permission of W. W. Norton & Company, Inc. Copyright © 1933 by Sigmund Freud, renewed © 1961 by W. J. H. Sprott. Copyright © 1965, 1964 by James Strachey, renewed 1993, 1992 by Alix Strachey.

From *Envy* by Yuri Olesha, translated by Andrew R. MacAndrew. From *Envy* by Andrew R. MacAndrew. Copyright © 1967 by Andrew R. MacAndrew. Used by permission of Doubleday, a division of Bantam Doubleday Bell Publishing Group, Inc.

From *You Gotta Play Hurt* by Dan Jenkins. Copyright © 1991 by D & J Ventures, Inc. Reprinted by permission of Simon & Schuster, Inc.

$\mathcal{A}$cknowledgments
• • • • •

From *Notes from Underground,* pages 15–17, by Fyodor Dostoyevsky, translated by Jessie Coulson (Penguin Classics, 1972), copyright © 1972 by Jessie Coulson. Reproduced by permission of Penguin Books, Ltd.

From *If You Can't Live Without Me, Why Aren't You Dead Yet?* by Cynthia Heimel. Copyright © 1991 by Cynthia Heimel. Used by permission of Grove/Atlantic, Inc.

"Hate Thy Neighbor," copyright © 1986 by Calvin Trillin. From *If You Can't Say Something Nice,* published by Ticknor & Fields. Reprinted by permission.

Excerpt from "Act One, Scene One" of *The Learned Ladies* by Jean Baptiste Poquelin de Molière, copyright © 1978, 1977 by Richard Wilbur, copyright © 1978 by Harcourt, Brace & Company. Reprinted by permission of the publisher.

"Among the Euro-Weenies," from *Holidays in Hell* by P. J. O'Rourke. Copyright © 1988 by P. J. O'Rourke. Used by permission of Grove/Atlantic, Inc.

From *After Henry* by Joan Didion. Copyright © 1992 by Joan Didion. Reprinted by permission of the author.

"Reflections at Dawn," from *Times Three* by Phyllis McGinley. Copyright © 1932–1960 by Phyllis McGinley; Copyright 1938–1942, 1944, 1945, 1958, 1959 by The Curtis Publishing Co. Used by permission of Viking Penguin, a division of Penguin Books USA Inc.

Some selections of fewer than 200 words have been reprinted under the doctrine of fair use. Reasonable care has been taken to trace ownership and, when necessary, to obtain permission for each selection included.

Index

•••

278

Index
. . . . .

Index
•••••